Katherine Debona studied History at Oxford University before working in investment banking. She lives in Kent with her husband and two children.

Also by Katherine Debona

The Girl in the Shadows

Love Me, Love Me Not

KATHERINE DEBONA

ONE PLACE. MANY STORIES

This novel is entirely a work of fiction. The names, characters
and incidents portrayed in it are the work of the author's
imagination. Any resemblance to actual persons, living or
dead, events or localities is entirely coincidental.

HQ
An imprint of HarperCollinsPublishers Ltd
1 London Bridge Street
London SE1 9GF

This paperback edition 2018

5
First published in Great Britain by
HQ, an imprint of HarperCollinsPublishers Ltd 2018

Copyright © Katherine Debona 2018

ISBN: 9780008310028

MIX
Paper from
responsible sources
FSC™ C007454

This book is produced from independently certified FSC™ paper
to ensure responsible forest management.

For more information visit: www.harpercollins.co.uk/green

Typeset by Palimpsest Book Production Ltd, Falkirk, Stirlingshire

Printed by CPI Group (UK) Ltd, Croydon CR0 4YY

For Dylan and Scarlett – who made me understand how many different types of love one person can hold in their heart.

'There are all types of love in this world
but never the same love twice.'

—F. Scott Fitzgerald

NOW

CHAPTER ONE

Stargazer Lily: Ambition, encouragement when facing a difficult challenge

Surrey, England, present day

Today isn't the first time I've thought about killing my best friend, but it is the first time I've done something about it.

I didn't mean to; at least, it must have been a subliminal thought because I never intended to pick up the wrong bottle from the back of the fridge. Honest mistake, given I was preoccupied with the sight of her at the edge of the lawn, arm outstretched as she leant over to pick one of my Passiflora before holding it up to her dainty little nose.

It was all I could do not to smack my hand against the windowpane and shout at her to leave it alone, to get her hands off that which didn't belong to her.

Instead I offered up a shaky wave as she caught me watching, a guilty smile tugging at the corners of her mouth.

She's sitting on the other side of the garden table now, bare legs tucked up underneath her skirt, palms wrapped around the mug of chamomile tea I made to help with her nerves. I sit down opposite, stirring a teaspoon of honey into my single caffeinated drink of the day.

'Are you allowed honey?' She sips her tea and fixes me with a doe-eyed stare. The innocence doesn't penetrate the way it would with someone who didn't know her as intimately as I do.

'You're getting confused with babies,' I say, handing over a plate of scones, my mother's homemade strawberry jam oozing from their middles. Her hand hesitates, as if deciding which one to choose, but I know it's more about the ever-tightening waistband; a waistband that used to hang on hipbones but now strains against the result of comfort eating. 'Besides, it's as organic as it's ever going to get. The hive's in next door's garden.'

'Of course.' Her eyes close as she bites down on the crumbling patisserie, the sweet fruit intermingling with thick, Cornish cream.

I know her weaknesses. I know everything about Elle.

A sigh, a stroke of hair as she wipes a crumb from her lips and gazes across the lawn.

'What's the matter?' I ask, not needing to follow her line of sight to see the picture of my garden. At this time of year it is particularly resplendent; the wisteria has bloomed, the alliums are starting to show and there is a constant chatter of visiting birds and wildlife who come to feast on nature's wares.

I should be fumigating the greenhouse and planting out my tomatoes instead of placating a drama queen.

'I'm sorry for barging in on you like this,' she says, but I know the words are empty. Elle has never needed to apologise for anything in her life; there has never been a moment when she has had to understand how it feels to be contrite, to ache with regret over a decision made.

She always left that to me.

'Don't be silly,' I say, sliding the plateful of temptation a little closer. 'I'm glad you came.'

She pulls another scone in two, red leaking into white and

4

spoiling the perfect, clean lines. I feel my jaw clench and have to look away.

'So how are you feeling?' she says, an unexpected moment of concern, the only one offered since she arrived on my doorstep, cheeks wet with distress, and at the very moment I had finished wiping down the work surfaces.

'A little tired, but otherwise fine. What about you?'

Tears brim from between dark lashes and tumble down her face, faint blush marks only adding to her beauty.

I give her hand a gentle squeeze, not trusting my tongue to control itself. There's a hole at the cuff of her cardigan and the cashmere has begun to bobble. A crack in the otherwise polished veneer and I wonder how much of this has been noticed by Patrick, or whether he needs another prod.

'Is he still travelling a lot?' No harm in throwing another log on that fire.

Elle sniffs, patting underneath her eyes with a manicured hand. Her skin still holds the sun from a Caribbean break little more than a month ago. A last-minute attempt to fill the caverns of her womb with her husband's seed.

'It's because of the promotion,' she replies, ever ready to defend his absence. 'He says all the brown-nosing is necessary to make sure he's a frontrunner. Once he makes partner he'll have more time.'

'For what?'

'For us, of course. For the baby.'

'Still, it's a shame he's not coming to the scan.'

'It doesn't matter.' A twitch of shoulder, fingers turning diamonds round and round the bone. 'He'll be at the next one.'

'Of course.' I swallow my sweetened cup of Lady Grey tea, breathing in its comforting scent to try and forget the perfumed lilies Elle thrust upon me earlier.

I'd presumed she meant them as an apology for coming here so early, and unannounced at that, but really, lilies? I could have told her they were a funeral flower, gifted at a time of mourning, but instead I freed them from their plastic prison, snipping off the pollenated stems and placing them in an aquamarine vase that now sits on the console table in the hallway. They will act as a reminder of her every time I pass by over the coming days, watching their petals tumble to the floor, crumpled and beginning to rot.

'I thought I was meeting you at the hospital after your yoga class,' I say. That would make this the third class in a row she's skipped. Too many prying eyes and unwanted questions about her attempts to conceive from women whose own children fill the gym's crèche while they try to shed the excess weight. Because, clearly, the imprinted memory of a life that grew inside of them is a burden their bodies need to be rid of.

'I didn't know what to do with myself,' Elle says. 'The house feels so empty when he's not there.'

Elle doesn't do alone. She isn't used to filling the silence that comes with living by yourself. It was a silence I used to look forward to at the end of the working week, but is one she runs from, always needing someone to provide her with the reassurance she craves.

So here she is, in my house, all self-complacent and full of faux concern for the one person who has always been there for her, no matter what.

We all have our weaknesses and Elle is mine. She has this uncanny ability to make people do her bidding, albeit unconsciously. One of those creatures who just demands attention, even if all she's doing is standing at a bus stop or queuing up to pay for milk in the supermarket. It's as if she has this aura about her that is impossible for other humans to resist. Especially men. Especially Patrick.

Then there's me, Jane, as if my parents named me knowing I would always be dull. Dark, bulbous eyes set a little too far apart, pallid skin and hair too wily to tame. Like Snow White, but without the beauty. I am the shadow to Elle's glory and have followed her for nearly half of my life, desperately hoping some

6

of her shine would fall onto my skin and seep through my pores rather than rushing off like rainwater on plastic.

Except now I have something she does not. A baby. Her husband's baby no less. Patrick's baby. My baby, if the plan works.

I may only be the surrogate, but if Elle isn't around any longer then it's only logical that I take her place.

Murder. So absolute, so final. It's been a secret longing of mine, one I've wrapped around me in the night when I think of everything that could have been. But I never dared to make it anything more than an indulgent fantasy, accepting that my place in life would always be second to Elle.

Until I was able to give her what she wanted more than anything else in the world. The one thing she craved with every ounce of her being. The one thing she was unable to do for herself.

Every second of every day we make a choice. We have the ability to control so much more than we think. It is something I am adept at, noticing the opportunities, the moments when others are caught off-guard and I can choose which way to go.

Which is perhaps why my fingers sought out the second bottle on the left of the top shelf of the fridge instead of the third. It's the only reason I can think of that I didn't stop myself, despite registering the bitter scent that curled into my nose as I squeezed the dropper and released half a dozen globes into her tea. It was supposed to be an extra something to help her sleep.

Only belladonna might make it harder for her to wake up in the morning. Eventually. Because although this poison can kill, I have learnt, when administered in the right dosage, death isn't certain and, instead, all sorts of other, peculiar symptoms can occur. Symptoms that will not only make Elle suffer both physically and emotionally, but suggest to all those who adore her that she isn't so perfect after all.

Here's hoping.

'More tea?' I rise from my chair, resting a hand on the curve

7

of my stomach, watching as her eye follows, envy always so tricky to conceal.

I understand that knot in your throat, the taste that refuses to go away. It burrows deep within you, gnawing away at everything else until it becomes like some yapping little dog that follows wherever you go.

I know what it is to want that which someone else has. I've known it from the very first second I encountered Eleanor Hart. Fifteen years ago, my first day at a new school, when the door of a 4x4 arced wide, gleaming metal reflecting sunlight onto my sallow skin. The silhouetted figure of a girl emerging from its leather interior accompanied by the animated barks of two choc-olate-brown Labradors held captive in the boot. She wore a fitted Barbour jacket, over-the-knee socks wrapped around gazelle-like legs, and the hem of her skirt was several inches higher than was stipulated in the school handbook.

A flick of hair, followed by the scent of rosewater and some-thing else, something I knew all too well by its absence in my own home. Money. It was unique and untouchable; barely notice-able yet a protective cloak to those that owned it. Even before she turned her head, even before I was presented with the sight of her exquisite face, I knew I was in love.

'Do you remember Miss Patterson?' I place a fresh mug of tea in Elle's outstretched hand.

'Frizzy hair and a permanent smell of fish?' Elle's nose wrinkles at the memory. 'She hated me almost as much as she loved you. Did everything she could to fail me that first year of GCSEs, do you remember?'

I remember. The way the corridors throbbed with incessant conversation, the squeak of new shoes and the musky scent of hormones. Designer backpacks jostling for position with over-sized watches and sunglasses perched on hair slick with gel.

I felt the full weight of each glance, the passage of eyes up and down my skinny frame as they took stock of my financial status, and I was easy prey with my cheap glasses and second-hand blazer. Just one look placed me in the camp of nerd, my position firmly fixed on the bottom rung of the ladder before I'd even stepped across the threshold.

'Do you ever wonder what would have happened?' Elle looks over at me with more than just this question behind her eyes.

'If you hadn't sat next to me in maths?' Of course I do. It's what changed everything. I've always wondered if the two of us were paired up on purpose, the more able children sat beside those whose parents had lined the headmaster's pockets in order to get their offspring past the first hurdle. For everyone has their price, even the leader of an esteemed private school in the middle of the Surrey countryside.

Or was it simply a twist of fate? I may have been a shrew sat next to a peacock, but to me it was the only thing I needed. Every great journey starts with the first step, and I was given an opportunity I knew not to squander.

'I loved the fact you were so different.' She's staring across the lawn now to where a squirrel is busy burying its winter wares.

'By different you mean poor.' I take a sip of my tea and resist the urge to throw something at the vermin. Hopefully it will get snared in the trap I have set so I can drown its rancid body in the river once Elle has gone.

'No make-up, hair scraped back and the most enormous, incredible eyes. I loved how you didn't care what anyone thought of you.'

'I was the freak, the outsider, Elle. The only reason anyone ever talked to me was because of you.'

Every school has a system, a hierarchy of sorts, and the trick was to choose your position within it with care. For once you're in, once your camp has been chosen, it is nigh on impossible to break ranks.

At my previous school I had gratefully accepted the camp of geek. Not only did it keep me away from the glue-sniffers, the vagabonds, the dregs that linger at the outskirts of social decency, but I also managed to set up a side business in what I liked to

9

refer to as 'homework assistance'. Which basically meant that for the right price I was willing to do the work for you.

But I had arrived that fateful morning at an altogether different kind of establishment. Too much gloss, the air thick with boasts about where Tobias and Grace and Elijah had spent their summers. A constant battle of one-upmanship as teenagers compared the size of their parents' bank balance. The only reason I was there was because of a scholarship my mother took great pleasure in reminding me could be rescinded if I weren't able to live up to my potential.

I knew I had potential. Just not the kind she was hoping for.

'They were jealous of us,' Elle says as her lips begin to tremble. 'Of how close we were.'

I wonder which part of our history is making her react in this way.

'They thought I was in love with you.'

She nods her agreement. 'Until France.'

Until the summer we spent in a house overlooking the Côte d'Azur. The summer when Elle was getting over a breakup by wrapping her legs around a local boy called Jean-Pierre who rode a Lambretta and had skin as dark as a conker.

The summer she found someone willing to rid me of my virginity, my innocence camouflaged by red wine and teenage lust. A diminishing experience that took place in an iron-framed bed with white cotton sheets, the complaint of springs drifting down to where Elle sat smoking in the garden below. A night she embellished when we returned to school, thereby putting to rest the rumours about my sexuality, but never quite erasing the sting that came with being poor.

Years were spent acquiring Elle's friendship, her trust. Each and every time I stepped aside, edging her ever closer to the light, it was done for my benefit as much as hers.

Until she took something that belonged to me, something I now want back.

10

'You've always been there, no matter what.'

The 'what' being my first love. My one and only. The man I thought I was going to marry, spend the rest of my life with. But she knew even this wouldn't be enough to break the love I had for her. She knew that I, along with everyone else, would always, always put her first.

It's a privilege reserved for the impossibly beautiful, the ones who are so used to adoration, to the heads that turn whenever they enter a room. I wouldn't even call it an assumption, because if something has always been there, if you have forever been placed on a higher rung of the ladder, does it not simply become part of you?

'It's what best friends are for,' I say, and she looks at me with such a pathetic look of gratitude on her face I have to stop myself from picking up the vase of flowers and hurling it at her irritatingly perfect features.

'But now I'm not so sure,' she says. 'Perhaps it's too much. Perhaps we've asked too much of you, especially when…' She hesitates, uncertainty no doubt a novel experience for her.

'What is it?'

Sitting forward on my chair, I bite back the temptation to push her answer. Could this be it? Have I done enough to make her question that which she holds most true?

'I think Patrick's having an affair.' She avoids my eyes, the bottom half of her face obscured by the grinning picture of a Cheshire cat on her mug as she continues to drink. I picture the warm liquid travelling down her throat and into her stomach. Little by little the poison administered will unfurl into her bloodstream. But as with everything else already set in motion, such an outcome will take time.

I allow myself a moment to inhale the words she has finally spoken, to let them settle inside of me in the shape of a smile. Patience is a virtue, my mother always said, and I have it in droves.

So it begins.

THEN

CHAPTER TWO

Narcissus: Rebirth and renewal, but also self-obsession

Oxford, nine years ago

I saw him first.

Sat in the corner of the library with thick-rimmed glasses reminiscent of a certain schoolboy wizard. The sleeves of his jumper pushed up and the bones of his wrist tensed as pen scratched paper.

But he didn't see me. Not then. Nor as I followed him down the cobbled alleyway that led to the pub. Not as he supped his pint and swapped ideas, hopes and dreams with his chosen friends. He didn't notice the way I lingered at the bar, my arm a breath from his own as he passed over a crumpled note to the student serving pints.

He didn't see me at the back of the lecture hall, watching the curl of hair at his neck, the twitch of leg as he listened. He didn't realise that I overheard his comment about Professor MacGillis's tutor group. About his joy and fear at having been chosen. A

15

group I knew I was good enough for. A group that would change everything, if only I could find the golden key that would allow me to enter.

'So all I need to do is keep the water topped up and it will flower, even in December?' Professor MacGillis peered at the Narcissus's sculptural tangle of creamy tendrils, moving too slowly for the eye to see. A small gesture of my appreciation, a thank you of sorts for allowing me to join a study group usually reserved for grad students. He made an exception in my case, based both on a recommendation from my own college professor and the fact I had scored the highest results in the university for my first- and second-year exams. Having me as one of his students made him look good; he knew I was worth more to him than the other way round.

'Plants are like numbers, they follow the rules as long as you know what they are.' I turned the vase full circle, just to check all was okay. Because I always looked. I always noticed if a root had grown... If a root had grown, a leaf unfurled, a petal's hue lightened by the sun.

'And you don't mind me keeping it?'

'Not at all. I can always grow more.'

'It would seem your talents aren't just limited to numbers, young lady.' A pat on the hand that lasted a moment longer than was acceptable. A lowering of lids that failed to hide his intention.

There was a letter opener on his desk and I allowed myself to imagine what it would be like if I were to thrust it between his carpal bones, snapping the tendons between his lusty fingers. To register the surprise on his face as it transformed to pain. For him to understand I was not someone he could manipulate into a cliché. I didn't need his help, nor his desire.

University was a new world, much the same as before but filled with subtle intricacies that allowed me to simply be. I was no longer the geek, the nerd, the girl with all the answers. Instead my ability was praised, revered and I was not alone in my brilliance. But in two years I hadn't made any real friends. Hadn't found anyone to fill the hole I thought could only ever be filled by Elle.

'Professor…' I began. But then the door to his study opened and the room shifted, air pushed aside as my real reason for being there entered and I scuttled back to my seat. The breath in my lungs started to spasm but I didn't dare let it go, to turn, to move until I was sure it was him.

A space opposite, a seat not yet taken. Tucked into the corner, half-hidden by a bookcase, I waited as he greeted his classmates in turn, their peaty scent coiling over that of dusty books, stale beer and the Christmas chill that lingered in clothes.

I glanced at my notebook, the lines of my sketch making their way over questions already answered. Then my hand froze above the page as he kept moving around the room, stopping only at the seat next to mine.

'Is that a cornflower?' He unwound a bright-red scarf, each circle of his neck covering me with tiny particles of tobacco laced with eucalyptus. I pictured him rolling a cigarette, tongue running along the paper's edge to keep it in place.

'You shouldn't smoke if you have a cold.'

The words escaped before I was ready and I cursed myself for not thinking first. But he surprised me, then as always. He understood me in an instant and, instead of finding me repellent, was accepting and kind.

'True, but we all have our vices.' His teeth were crooked and, when he smiled, a dimple sat in each cheek.

I knew all about vices, only mine weren't the sort you admitted to. Would he like me still if he knew every part of me? I longed for it, for someone to recognise the depths that murmured underneath, willing themselves free. For someone not to care because in a way they understood them too.

The snow in his hair was melting. Droplets of water like miniature globes reflecting back an upside-down version of the world.

I wanted to touch them, to taste whatever part of him still clung to the liquid.

'I'm Patrick.'

'I'm Jane.'

'Pleased to meet you, Jane,' he said, holding out his hand and waiting for me to slip my fingers into his palm.

That was when I became undone. A shifting inside of me at the nearness of him, something that before was missing but now made perfect sense. It came with a hunger, a painful longing that was a world away from the pull I had towards Elle. It was altogether more basal, which made it true.

'A group of us usually head to The Turf after MacGillis has finished talking about himself. You're more than welcome to join us.'

I couldn't reply. All my senses were compounded into the pressure of his skin against my own. All my capabilities, the words I had accumulated over the years, disappeared, because when I looked at him I saw a future never before imagined. A future I had believed wasn't for someone like me.

He had a mole on the edge of his jaw and I wondered what it would be like to kiss it. His hands, stained with ink, and nails, bitten down to the cuticles, were ones I longed to have trace over every inch of my skin. I watched the way he scratched at the tip of his nose with his pen when he was trying to figure out a problem. I wanted to know each and every one of his mannerisms, tuck them away to be remembered in years to come.

That night, I walked home looking ahead of me instead of down at the cobbled streets. I allowed myself to contemplate what it would be like to have a friend here. A real friend who understood and accepted me with all my flaws and imperfections.

What surprised me more than anything was that when I pictured his face it made me smile. When I slipped beneath the starchy sheets of my bed that night, looking out to watch clouds skate past the moon, I remember hoping that tomorrow, and all the tomorrows after that, wouldn't let me down.

We started out as friends, as oft the story goes. Sharing a love of equations, of mathematical probabilities and how far each concept could be stretched and explored. But being a mathematician, a rationaliser, didn't stop me from appreciating beauty. It made me look at a flower and see its inherent structure, allowed me to imagine it on a cellular level. It meant I saw how it was designed to make itself attractive to insects, how nature has a way of getting what it needs. Add to that the lessons I had learnt from Elle and it meant I understood the world in a way others could not.

So I gave him the time he needed to realise I was different. Because life is nothing more than a series of interconnected moments. Just the passage of time that we anoint with purpose and meaning, only distinguished by what we do with our intentions.

It was the night of the summer ball. The end of the beginning, or perhaps the other way around. I was dressed in midnight satin, my hair caught up in filigree hair slides, lips stained the same colour as a robin's breast. Patrick and I were sitting at the edge of the river under a heaving silver sky, as music from the main quad spun over the walls along with the drunken mating calls of our peers.

'It seems strange to think our time here is nearly over.'

'In what way?' I looked over at him, at the thin line of red on his chin. No doubt the result of a shaving accident, his hands somewhat out of practice after weeks when time was reserved for poring over textbooks. Weeks fuelled by strong coffee and a somewhat narcissistic desire to be the best, the scholar, the one everyone else aspired to beat.

'I make sense here,' he said, gently bumping against my shoulder as I leant in to his touch. 'So do you.'

He was talking about my move to London. About pursuing a career at a prestigious investment bank. A career he thought I was worth more than and, to a certain extent, I had to agree.

'I want a different kind of life.'

He shifted his weight beside me. 'Meaning money.'

He didn't understand why I would choose money over intellectual prestige. Why I had no desire to build upon my existing knowledge of plants. To apply for a second degree in botany, stay here and use my brain for something altogether more worthwhile than making rich people richer.

Curling my bare toes into the grass, I watched as an ant climbed aboard my little toe. 'You say that like it's a dirty word.'

'That's because it is. You know as well as I do that money causes nothing but fear and loathing.'

Patrick came from money. Old money, handed down over generations, which meant he could afford not to care about it, or at least pretend not to. But I understood in a way he never could how intrinsic money is because of what happens when it is absent. What happens when your mother has to choose between putting food on the table or paying the electricity bill.

'Money makes things easier.'

I could feel him watching me, could picture the slant of his brow as he decided what to say next, but I didn't trust myself to look. Didn't trust myself to do something that would ruin what I could sense was about to transpire.

'Don't you want to do something more with your life than filling a pot with gold? Don't you want to be remembered for something: an idea, a concept future generations will read about and learn from?'

That was when I turned my face, looked up at him from under lashes laden with mascara and arched my back in the exact same way I had seen Elle do over and over again. He needed someone who would let him shine and not try to take away from his brilliance. He needed someone who was just as capable, who understood his ambitions, but had no desire to challenge him. We would make an incredible team because I would let him take centre stage. I'd had years of practice, of letting someone else bask in all the glory, but now it was time to claim my reward.

'I never really thought about my future before I met you.'

He blinked. Once, then twice more. Lips parted and became heavy with intent before he sprang to his feet and threw his empty glass into the river where it promptly collided with the side of a punt. None of its inhabitants seemed to take any notice; too busy were they in grappling with one another and I remember hoping that at least one of them would topple into the water and drown.

'Look at them,' he said, flinging his arm in the punt's direction. 'So unaware of the privilege they're experiencing just by being here. Such a waste.'

I loved him because he saw how unfair the world could be. That there were too many people who succeeded simply because of what they were born into. That it wasn't just the ignorant who sucked the life from this planet, but the ones who assumed they were better than everyone else because they were rich.

I loved him because he too had a darker side. One I didn't want him to lock away, because when I was around him the voices inside my own head seemed to still and I was slowly becoming open to the possibility of allowing myself to be happy.

For as long as I could remember I had wanted to do harm, both to myself and others. My stomach was littered with tiny silver scars that were testament to all the nights when I would sit in the shadows and ask the voices to leave me alone. To all the nights when my only release had been to feel the cut of skin, the slow slither of blood as my very essence seeped into the floorboards on which I lay. Because without it I knew my hands couldn't be trusted not to carry out the twisted imaginings of my mind. Without that release, the voices would not stop.

'*Walk with the wise and become wise. For a companion of fools suffers harm.*' Standing at the edge of the river, Patrick watched

21

the punt make its precarious journey towards the horizon as I sat and stared at his silhouetted profile.

'Is that a poem?' I asked.

'Proverb,' he said as he came back to me. 'Seems my Sunday mornings weren't a total waste of time.'

'What is it you're trying to tell me, Patrick?'

'You're the only woman I've ever met who really gets me.' He placed his hands either side of my neck, the weight of him against my frantic pulse. 'You understand that people like us have a duty to give back to the world. To do something with the gifts we've been given rather than squandering away our time.'

'Did you know that the probability of our relationship succeeding is about the same as being struck by lightning?' I could feel my entire body shaking, certain that if he were to let me go my spine would betray me and I would slip into the river, be taken into its depths and drift out to sea.

'There's always an exception to every rule.'

His mouth came down to mine, smothering my nerves, and I decided to give him everything because I thought it was what I wanted.

CHAPTER THREE

Peanut: To dream of eating a peanut is a sign of trying to uncover a hidden truth

Surrey, eight years ago

Finals were over, the hours poring over textbooks were behind us and the cellars of every student bar had been emptied during weeks of potent celebration. I was due to start work in just over a week and, despite my best attempts to dissuade her, Elle had convinced her parents to give me a proper sendoff at their home. They agreed, both because they knew my mother never would, and also, I suspect, as a thank you of sorts for my supposed good influence on their child. A child who always got what she wanted and loved any excuse to dress up and flaunt her wares at all and sundry.

'So what's he like?' Elle leant towards the mirror that filled an entire wall of her bedroom as she painted a line around her lips.

'Who?' I asked, taking a long sip of my drink. Homemade elderflower gin with a squeeze of fresh lime. Distilled by my own hand, ever since Nana first showed me how. The familiarity soothed my troubled mind, if only for a moment.

'Patrick.'

My insides constricted, an internal warning of what was to come. I should have trusted them.

In less time than it takes a seedling to sprout, we had mapped out and agreed every step of our future together. A two-bed flat within spitting distance of Covent Garden. Owned by his parents but perfect for his desired placement at the London School of Economics where he could continue his research. In return I'd agreed to pay the majority of the bills and we even drew up a rota to avoid any arguments over chores. We had the conversation about our futures, our ambitions, the understanding being we both favoured career over family. We had ironed out all the wrinkles, all the concerns we thought might arise from moving in together. The only anomaly I hadn't properly accounted for was my best friend.

'Why do you ask?'

She tilted her head from side to side. 'I've got this picture in my mind of what he's going to be like.'

'And?'

'You.' A wicked grin. 'Only male.'

The insult was clear. But I couldn't find the words to tell her how wrong she was.

'I can't believe you have a boyfriend I've never even met.'

There was a reason for that, but not one I could share. It was why I'd been so against him coming to the party, protesting the need for him to move into the flat and set up his study just the way he wanted. That he would hate being surrounded by people who didn't understand him.

That I was terrified of what would happen if he met Elle.

'Do you like him?'

'Of course I do. What sort of a question is that?'

Her eyes found mine in the mirror and I had to look away, to try and conceal the truth behind my guilty words.

'No, I mean like him, like him.'

The flush on my face was as if she had slapped me and I

hurried from the room. She followed me in silence, but it was a silence alive with noise, with unspoken, treacherous things.

I pushed my way through the crowd of well-wishers, people who had filled my life without any kind of meaning, but seemed to think they knew me. I wasn't interested in their congratulations, I just wanted to find him, to shelter him from this cosseted world.

There he was. Shirt untucked and hair curling around the arm of his glasses. He was nodding at something Elle's brother was saying, fingers used to nursing a pint now gripping the stem of a champagne flute.

She waltzed past me, pushing the air aside and announcing her arrival so that, as his head turned in my direction, he was overcome by the sight of her instead of me.

'You must be Patrick,' she said, going in for the kill with a kiss either side of his mouth, one hand resting on his shoulder to keep the gap between them small.

His face was too open, his thoughts and desires laid at her feet, but she was so used to such adoration she didn't recognise its perfection. I couldn't look at him; he looked like I felt.

'He's not at all what I expected.' She was sat on the edge of the swimming pool, long limbs stirring the water. I imagined it to be like the tornado that ripped Dorothy from her home, wondered what would await Elle if she were plunged into another world.

'What did you expect?' I handed her one of the platefuls of food I'd busied myself collecting from the buffet. Anything to avoid watching him watching her.

'Not sure. He's rather sweet.'

Sweet. That was all she could come up with to describe the most enigmatic, talented and breathtaking person I had ever met? The only human in existence who could rival her? But then Patrick's appeal was not so transparent, not something everyone would be able to understand.

Maybe I didn't have anything to worry about after all.

'So, have the two of you ever…?' She picked up a smoked

salmon blini and popped it into her mouth, along with a long sip of champagne.

'No.'

'What, not even after a drunken night out?'

I glared at her, annoyed by her assumption that Patrick would only ever be interested in me sexually if he were inebriated.

'He understands I want to wait until we're living together rather than simply doing it in a bed that contains the sexual residue of a thousand past students.' He said it didn't bother him, but I had seen the way he looked at her, at the longing that stretched over every part of his skin, and realised it meant he wasn't bothered because it was me. That while I made sense on paper, Elle appealed to a different kind of reasoning.

'Huh.' Another morsel passed her lips.

'Why do you sound so surprised?'

'I assumed he was either ugly or gay. Why else would he stay in a relationship where he wasn't getting any?'

Because, when it comes down to it, what else is there between a man and a woman other than sex? Why bother to have a relationship with someone who stimulates your mind as well as your body?

'You wouldn't understand, even if I did try and explain it to you.'

She smiled to herself and I wanted to ask what she was thinking. 'You just seem so... the same.'

'In what way?'

'A bit awkward, a bit unsure of who you are. But then, when you start talking about something, it's as if you're the only person in the world who really gets it.'

I thought I could see her point, even if it was tumbled up in nonsensical English.

'Sounds like he was talking about bats,' I reply. Ever since Patrick read *Dracula* as a kid he had been obsessed with the folklore behind vampire bats; how not all cultures believed them to be signs of evil, with some viewing them as symbols of rebirth or long life. I liked to think of them as portals for change, as an opportunity to become something more.

'Yes. But I didn't have a clue what he was going on about.'

'*Suspicions amongst thoughts are like bats among birds, they ever fly by twilight.*'

She drained her glass, then pointed it at me. 'That's exactly what he said. But I can't remember who it's by.'

Francis Bacon. Not that it would have meant anything to her because Elle's literary abilities had never stretched beyond the love triangle between a girl, a vampire and a werewolf.

'Don't worry, he does it to everyone, especially when he's nervous.' It was his failsafe, his way of trying to interact with people with whom he had nothing in common. We used to joke about the way people responded to his theories, would laugh at their ignorance of the world around them.

'I asked him whether he had a Batman costume at home.'

Okay, I was definitely safe.

'He laughed and asked me if I had a Catwoman one.'

She did. Skintight latex that was worn to every Halloween party with a fluffy tail she used to entrap that year's victim. No doubt she showed him a photograph, asked him whether she made a convincing cat. Not so safe after all.

I looked down at the plates of food between us. At the miniature chocolate cupcakes I knew she loved. Four in total. Two with icing slightly darker than the others.

'You know, I think he likes me.'

But he wasn't hers. He was mine and I wasn't about to allow her to steal him from me, to assume she could have anything she set her sights upon. Not him. Anyone but him.

'I wouldn't have thought he was your type.'

'Exactly. Perhaps it's time to go for the geek instead of the jock. Up my standards. Isn't that what you're always telling me?'

I looked back down at our plates. Wondered whether I should switch or let fate intervene.

'He's my boyfriend, Elle.'

'Of course. But it can't be that serious if you haven't even done the deed. I mean, aren't you worried he'll find someone else to scratch that itch if you won't?'

I hadn't been. Not until she planted the doubt in my mind. Watered it with the imaginings that were creeping around inside of me.

I had never wanted to hurt her before that moment, but one glance from her and it was unravelling so fast I had no idea how to try and put it back the way it was supposed to be. One glance from her and all of my darkness came spinning back to the surface. All of the whispers, the insecurities, the desire to cause harm that had dissipated whenever I was around him, came flying back into my consciousness and I was overcome with the urge to make her scream.

'So where is he now?' I picked up my own cupcake, waited for her to see me do so, then watched as she wrapped her lips around one, head dropping backwards as sweetness slid down her throat.

'I think he's talking to your mum,' she said in between mouthfuls.

Good. There was time.

Have another.

'So have you decided what you're going to do?' I had to keep her talking. Keep her eating.

'No idea. Dad says I can take my time, help out with the business, but can you imagine how dull that would be?'

Yes, I can. But no worse than online shopping and days at the spa, which is how Elle had spent her summer thus far.

'You could always teach.' Because those that can't, can.

'Funny you should say that.'

'Funny ha, ha, or funny, that's so ridiculous I can't quite believe what you're suggesting?'

'Don't be a bitch. Just because I'm not as clever as you doesn't mean I can't do something worthwhile with my life.' Her hand reached out for the second cake, then stilled, eyes stretching wide before the same hand scratched at her neck.

'What is it?' I offered her a drink and she swiped it away, the glass shattering on the tiled surround of the pool. 'What's the matter?' I knew what the matter was, but folded confusion into my face just the same.

She pointed at her throat, tongue slowly filling the space created by her fish-like mouth. Fingers seized my arm, pressing down hard on skin that would show the outlines of her fear in days to come.

'The cake.' My hands came up to my mouth in a caricature of shock. 'But you had one too, so it can't be.' But it can. All too easy to pretend I didn't know which cupcakes had toffee and which had peanut icing. Silly mistake to make. Silly old me.

The hand of fate had decided, held me back from switching the plates. Made me choose him over her. A defining moment, you could call it; the first time I realised the full extent of my feelings, understood he had taken her place in my heart.

Still clutching at my arm, Elle's lips began to swell. I imagined the sensation of her ballooning from the inside out. Flesh pressing against her skull, skin stretching tight in preparation to split wide, her beauty destroyed by one tiny nut.

'Jane, what's going on?' Patrick asked. Where the fuck did he come from? Only a second ago it was just her and me, then suddenly he popped up behind us like some veritable boy scout.

Four words from him and everything was annulled.

'She's in anaphylactic shock.' I leapt up, her nails leaving behind accusatory lines. 'Lie her down, find something to prop up her head.'

'Is she going to be all right?'

I turned away, couldn't risk him seeing the guilt leaking from my pores. Didn't want to witness his concern for her. There was a cabinet on the wall behind the bar, a cabinet I'd been shown by Elle's mother the first time I was invited round for a swim.

'*Just in case*,' she had told me. '*I need you to know what to do.*'

Just in case her child was dying, she thought someone would be there to save her.

People choose what they want to see, what they want to believe.

Jackie wanted to believe I wasn't capable of hurting her child. That I didn't hesitate before stabbing Elle in the thigh with an EpiPen as she ran screaming across the lawn. She blamed the caterers for not labelling the food correctly, despite their protestations of innocence. Because if she'd known I had even considered the possibility of hurting Elle, she would have had to ask herself not only why, but how it was that she'd invited me into their lives in the first place.

The only person who noticed the danger, the only one who stood at the edge of the crowd, with arms crossed and eyes silent, was my mother.

*   *   *

I kept my promise to Elle's mother after that fateful day; to always be her friend, to protect her no matter what, but I came to hate the weight of it. By swearing allegiance to her family, by accepting her mother's terms, I was tied to them, my conscience forever torn between what I wanted and what I had promised to be.

Elle wouldn't have done the same. She would have waited for me to leave this world behind, made sure there was no one who could change the course of her own fate with the man she loved. In a way, this was exactly what she did the moment my back was turned, and I was a fool to ever believe otherwise.

Sometimes I think my own darkness might devour me. But I wanted to do it, to watch her choke out her last breaths, wondering why I wasn't saving her. I still do, don't I? It was him that stopped me, him that forever stops me from becoming what I fear. I have to be good, on the outside at least, because inside is a turmoil I battle against every day.

But I know that, however much I ignore it, it's always there. My desire, my pain, sits coiled and tight; desperate to escape, to run free.

CHAPTER FOUR

Yellow Rose: Joy, protection against envious lovers

London, seven years ago

'Where are you?'

Patrick sounded annoyed. Furious even, and it took me a moment to figure out why.

'I'm on my way.'

'Are you? You know what, never mind.' And he hung up. Didn't wait for an explanation as to why I was still at work instead of by his side at the fundraising dinner he had asked me to attend only the previous week.

I checked my watch. Looked over to where my boss was still at his computer screen, decided it was worth the risk. Patrick was worth the risk, because we were turning into strangers and I needed to make things right.

Fifteen minutes later and I was beginning to regret my choice of dress. And shoes. And of not remembering to wash my hair that morning when I left before Patrick woke. Before

31

he could accuse me once more of putting the job first.

But it was exhilarating, being in that environment. Surrounded by people who were just as ruthless, just as ambitious as I. Always competing for first place, for the nod from your superior that said you were the one they wanted with them when they presented the idea to their client. People who worked harder than they played, because there was always, always, someone willing to take their place.

And I was bloody good at it.

At first Patrick had understood, so immersed was he in his own new adventure. We would swap stories about our colleagues over bottles of wine and Chinese takeaway, wrap our limbs around one another as an apology for never having enough time. At first it had been exciting and new and wonderfully selfish, doing what it was we both loved and finally, finally sharing our bodies as well as our minds. But there was always this doubt in my mind about whether it could last. Always the fear he was becoming jealous in some way of what I had achieved, that he knew the awe I had for him was slowly fading.

So I did what any dutiful girlfriend would. I slipped into a gown made of midnight satin, painted my face into a smile and walked into a room screaming with money.

Hedge funders. Even more ostentatious than investment bankers, with an extra layer of gloss on everything. My boss may have had a house in Chelsea and an extra one in the country just for weekends, but this was a world of private jets and Swiss bank accounts. They were like the cool kids at school. Sleek, polished and completely untouchable. It was what I wanted, what I was aiming towards, but it was Patrick they had invited, not me.

I found him at the bar, deep in conversation with one of the fund's managing partners.

'Hello,' I said, placing a kiss at the edge of Patrick's mouth. 'So sorry I'm late. I'm Jane.' I turned to his companion, offered him my hand in greeting, and he lifted it to his lips, held on to it a moment longer, then let me go.

'There's two of them?' He was looking at me with amusement from behind a pair of frameless glasses.

'Two of who?' I asked, taking a glass of champagne from the tray of a passing waiter.

And that's when I saw her. Wrapped up tight in scarlet sequins that glittered with every tiny movement. I saw her head thrown back to expose the line of her throat as she laughed at what someone next to her was saying. I saw how everyone around her was unable to look away, unable to focus on anything else in the room.

Including him. Including Patrick.

'What's she doing here?' I held tight to my glass, tried to use it to stop my hands from shaking.

'Apparently she's screwing my business partner. But better keep quiet as his wife's here somewhere.' The fund manager was watching her too, a predator stalking its prey. One more prize for him to collect. One more sign that he was better than everyone else and it made my insides curl. She wasn't some trophy men could compete for. She wasn't some symbol of their success.

'Patrick, give some thought to what we discussed, but I'll need an answer before the end of the week. Pleasure to meet you, Jane.' Then he was gone. Gathered up by someone else who wanted a piece of his fortune.

'He offered you a job?' I attempted to sound nothing more than surprised, but we both knew my words were laced with jealousy.

'He did.' Patrick tapped his signet ring against the stem of his own glass. 'Apparently he read my paper on the role of information in debt crises and thought it was masterful.'

A paper I helped him write, but that little detail seemed to have escaped my boyfriend's attention. Everything but her. Even then, even when he was supposed to be sharing his news with me, he couldn't help but let his eyes drift back to her.

'You can't work for him.'

'Why not?'

'Since when have you wanted to do anything other than prove to the world how incredibly clever you are?' Since when was he willing to sacrifice his whole moral code, become the very person he claimed to despise?

'I thought you'd be pleased for me.'

'I am, it's just...'

'Just what, Jane? We're turning into some kind of ridiculous Fifties' sitcom, except I'm the housewife sitting at home, waiting for her husband to come back and enjoy the dinner she's made.' He didn't even bother to hide the contempt in his voice. Didn't bother to conceal the bitterness behind his words. Bitterness aimed at me, at the way I had made him feel.

'It won't be for much longer. Everyone knows the first year is a killer, but once I've closed this deal, once I've proved myself...' I laid my hand on his shoulder, but he stepped aside.

'Because you always have to prove yourself, don't you? Prove how much better than the rest of us you are.'

He drained his glass, slammed it down on the nearest table and walked away. As he manoeuvred his way through the crowd she noticed him, raised her hand to beckon him over, and he changed direction, went instead to her. She stepped back to let him into her circle, stepped back to find me watching.

The time-space continuum crap everyone goes on about. That we all begin and end at a certain point. And here was my defining moment in all its fucking glory. The second I realised it was pointless even to try and compete with her because, really, why bother when all the odds are so stacked against you? Mathematical probability at its finest. But understanding something doesn't make it any easier to accept.

So I left. Went back to the office in my beautiful gown. The same one Elle had gifted me for a school leavers' ball. The same one I had worn the night I first kissed Patrick.

34

'Are you okay?' I lifted my head from my desk to see one of my fellow graduate trainees standing over me.

Carter. A man with eyes as dark as his intentions and hands that looked as if they could keep me up all night.

'I was about to make some tea,' he said, and I imagined him trailing those hands along the length of my spine. 'Can I tempt you with yet more caffeine?'

I sat back in my chair. Crossed and uncrossed my legs, watched him watching the movement. 'Did you know the Chinese often offer tea as an apology.'

'Are you saying I've done something wrong?' He perched on the edge of my desk, close enough for me to taste him in the air between us.

'I'm saying that maybe I want you to.'

His eyes narrowed, but there was a wrinkle of lips that told me what I needed to know.

'So what's really going on? Why are you sitting here looking ever so delicious in that dress instead of being appreciated by whoever you put it on for?'

I stared at him. Tried to concentrate on the scar above his top lip. Tried to imagine what it would be like to wake up next to someone other than Patrick.

'What if the Universe showed you the one thing you'd always wanted, the one thing that would make you happy, then refused to let you have it?' I swallowed my tears, didn't trust them ever to stop if I let even one of them go. 'Just dangled it in front of you like some fucking carrot but never let you get close. Kept it there in your peripheral vision. The very epitome of look but don't touch.'

'I bet no matter where you were, you still wouldn't feel like you fitted in. But who wants to, really?' He reached out, traced a finger along the back of my arm as he bent down to kiss me just behind my ear. 'We're all alone, but some of us deal with it a whole lot better.'

I liked him. No pretence, no bullshit, no trying to impress. He was comfortable with who he was yet had no desire to flaunt it. And he wanted me.

Two hours later I walked into the place I was supposed to call home with the stench of Carter between my legs. Patrick was waiting for me, holding on to a bunch of yellow roses already beginning to wilt in the fetid atmosphere. A kind of symbol, as it were, of how rotten our relationship had become, because I chose to leave instead of staying, instead of laying claim to what was mine.

'I slept with someone,' I said as his eyes slid over mine.

'Well,' he replied, his face slackening. 'I guess that changes things somewhat.'

CHAPTER FIVE

Ivy: Eternity, fidelity and strong affection

New Forest, six and a half years ago

The lines on my arm were darkening, day by day, and I was spending more and more time alone. A haphazard picture of my grief, a reminder that, no matter how hard I tried, I would always be a little strange, a little out of place.

My time had been spent hibernating, either at work or in the rancid pit that was my new abode. A soulless studio at the end of a corridor where all the doors looked the same. Two rooms within a steel structure where only a handful of lights were ever turned on at night because no one really lived there. They were investment properties owned by people with more money than they knew what to do with. If I opened the bathroom window wide and leant right out I could just about see the Thames, boat lights winking in the distance.

The first time I cut myself was by accident. I was trying to recreate one of my father's terrariums and dropped the glass dome, shattering it against the workbench in his shed. At first the pain didn't register and I watched my sliced flesh as it slowly pooled with red. Then the sharp sting of recognition as air hit the inside of my arm, cold on warm making me draw in breath, then sink to the earthy floor.

The second time was deliberate. A way to control my feelings. To decide when and where the pain would occur. Not when someone pushed me over in the playground or took my bag and dropped it into an icy puddle. This was my pain to bear. My blood to spill.

It was a coping mechanism, a way to block out all the hurt and anger, to channel it into a single, sharp point that I would run over my skin, creating patterns with red. Replacing the voices in my mind that told me I wasn't worthy, letting them out of my veins, spilling them to the ground below.

Over the years I have read all sorts of theories about self-harm. A mixture of benign and idiotic for the most part, but one study nearly came close to giving me the answer I craved.

In 2013, a doctor named Franklin carried out an experiment that showed most people felt better after experiencing pain and how, over time, self-harm could become addictive because of the association of relief with pain. The high after the low. It fascinated me, not because of any kind of revelation about my scars; it was more that any one of us could learn to enjoy pain. Anyone at all.

After Patrick told me to leave I had no way of lessening the ache inside that would not leave me be. No matter the hours I worked, the bottles of gin I emptied or the amount of times I opened my skin. Until I became nothing more than a pretence. A memory of the person I wanted to be, thought I could become. Someone with a life, a love, a purpose.

For it felt as if each and every person who found it in their hearts to love me was slowly slipping away and I could not escape the voice that told me it was all my own doing. It felt as if every time I got close to someone, my demons would snatch them back, and now they had set their sights on my beloved grandfather. The man who'd helped raise me, who'd taught me how to ignore the darkness when it cried out in my mind.

I looked back towards the bed where Gramps was sleeping. My substitute father, the only man who truly knew me and loved me just the same, was sick.

Dark splotches of bruise on one side of his restful face. There was a sling holding a broken collarbone in place and bandages wrapped around a sprained wrist. But the doctor had told me the real damage was hidden beneath his skull. That there was an illness lurking within the synapses of his brain which we hadn't been able to see. Or was it that we didn't want to see? Had we allowed his stubborn refusal to ask for help to blind us to his illness?

Had I been too caught up in my own distress to realise he was in need as well?

A hand on my arm made me stop the pacing I was unaware of. A hand I knew was now more accustomed to touching someone else.

'What are you doing here, Elle?' I couldn't bring myself to look at her, didn't want to see the happiness that should have been mine.

'The care home still have Patrick's number on file. When they couldn't reach you…'

'Of course.' So many things left unfinished. So many things I ran from, had been hiding from, until fate intervened and threw us back together once more.

'I'm so sorry. I know how much Gramps means to you.'

'Do you?' At this I spun round with every intention of striking out, of making her feel some semblance of the pain she had caused me. Of smashing her head against the wall, plunging my hand into her chest and ripping out her still-beating heart. Of making her understand what it was that she had done to me, and how she had taken away my belief that I too deserved to be happy.

Instead all I could do was stare at her, at the sorrow on her incredible face, and curse myself for wondering what the matter was.

'I never meant to hurt you,' she said, taking a step closer, then another, watching to see how I would respond. When I didn't move she pulled me into a hug I didn't know I wanted until it happened. Let me wet her with my tears, my remorse, my absolute bewilderment at the power she had over me. 'You're my best friend, the sister I never had, and I miss you.'

Some people seem to be blessed, others cursed, by an invisible hand I didn't know how to understand or appease. For why shouldn't I have a share of life's elusive wonders? Why did she get to have it all?

'I want to help,' she said as she released me, searching my eyes for an inch of forgiveness. 'What does Gramps need? What do you need?'

I didn't know. I didn't know what to do with all the new information. With Gramps being debilitated by an illness no one paid any attention to. With my mother nowhere in sight, choosing as always to bury the problem under a mountain of ignorance. With Elle standing so close I could feel the warmth of her skin. With her offer of help, of returning to my life, catapulting any resolve I'd had to stay away far beyond my reach.

She was always so impossible to resist and I hated myself because of it.

'I'm still mad at you,' I said, walking away as a smile formed on her lips.

Going out into the hospital courtyard I sat on a bench next to a whitewashed wall covered with ivy, the twisting tendrils reaching ever outward, seeking new places to stretch and grow. It made me think of the story about Tristan and Isolde. How King Mark buried them in separate graves so that even in death they couldn't be together. Except ivy vines grew from their graves to meet and entwine. Proof that nothing can break true love's bond.

'Why didn't you return my calls?' Elle sat beside me and I noticed her looking at the scratches on my arms. Marks I could have easily explained away as a gardening accident, except I hadn't been anywhere near a garden for months. No, those marks were my way of feeling something, anything, other than wretched. Wretched because he left. Wretched because I led him straight to her. Wretched because I thought they both loved me the most.

'Why do you think?'

Elle took out a packet of cigarettes. Lit one then crossed her legs as she blew smoke into the sky. The scent of tobacco mixed with a sweet perfume that once upon a time I had inhaled every day. So many years, so much time spent with one person, all tossed aside in favour of another.

'Nothing happened between us that night, Jane. Nothing happened until after you had broken up.'

'I know.' I knew because Patrick told me. In a letter no less, left by the side of the bed for me to find when I woke next morning. Telling me too much had changed, that the life we were living wasn't the one he wanted. That he didn't think he could forgive me for what I had done. That he would give me until the end of the week to move out.

As if he was completely innocent. Because there was no denying the inevitable. The irresistibility of something, someone, so precious.

The first year of university I had missed her with such ferocity it terrified me. I would lie awake, listening to other students revelling in their freedom, wishing I could go back to the home I had spent the past decade trying to escape. I wrote her letters that I never sent, afraid she would laugh at my neediness, my immaturity, my intrinsic desire to have her in my life.

'Are you okay?' She was looking again at my arms. No doubt trying to recall when I had last decorated myself with such skinny lacerations.

'I'm fine.' Except I wasn't fine. The voices wouldn't leave me be. Voices that had taken hold during my second year at university. Telling me I wasn't worthy, following me around the cobbled streets, into lectures and libraries and everywhere I went. That woke me in the night to remind me that anyone I loved would eventually leave, that no matter what I did it would never be enough. Voices that laughed when I stood on a bridge, looking down at another river, wondering how long it would be before someone realised I was gone.

It was only when I met Patrick in my final year that the desolation began to melt and I felt there was a purpose for me after all.

'I never intended for it to happen. You have to believe that?'

'Still doesn't make it right.'

Who was the one to make the first move? I couldn't imagine Patrick diving in for a kiss, or perhaps he had. All teeth and awkwardness, like a teenager whose balls are so swollen they take over from any rational thought.

My brother, Robin, had called a week, perhaps two, after I left. Telling me how he'd bumped into them both at a party. At how they had sat, huddled under a rug on the rooftop while Patrick pointed out the constellations. About how he was unable to look at anyone else.

My little brother thought he was doing me a favour. Telling me not to waste my life on people who didn't feel the same way. But he didn't see me lying on the bathroom floor, night after night, wetting the tiles with tears.

'I'm not asking for your forgiveness, Jane, because I didn't do anything wrong.'

'He was my boyfriend, Elle.'

'And you slept with someone else.'

'Because of you.'

'You slept with Carter because of me?'

It sounded ludicrous. I knew this, but it was her fault as much as mine. If she hadn't been at that fundraiser then maybe we would have stood a chance. If she'd never met him. If I'd never met him. Who knows? Maybe things could have been different.

Or maybe it was the wake-up call I needed.

'It doesn't matter anymore,' I said.

'Which part?'

She meant us. Her and me. Best friends forever, wasn't that the way it was supposed to be? Because you can't stop a heart that's made up its mind. But how does it choose? How does it know? How can we stop it from breaking?

'Do you love him?' I looked at her and found her eyes already locked on mine. Staring. Searching. It made me want to gouge them out, stop her from ever looking upon anyone ever again. Stop her from invading my every thought.

'Love is a little word that people throw around too much without thinking about what it actually means.'

So that was a no. Or at least she hadn't quite decided yet if he was worth anything more to her than a part-time distraction.

'Does he love you?'

I have no idea why I asked this. No idea why I invited her to add more weight to the feelings of inadequacy multiplying like some kind of swarm inside me. The feelings of rage and frustration that, no matter what I did, I would never be good enough. For I had tried and tried to be someone more, someone other than me. To have for myself what so many others took for granted.

She looked away, gave a half-hearted shrug as she tossed her cigarette to the ground, grinding out the embers with her shoe. 'You know how he is. Outward expressions of emotion don't exactly come easily to him.'

He'd never actually said the words to me, but I thought he didn't need to. I thought his agreement to be part of my life, to bind himself to me, was proof enough that he was mine.

Stupid to think I was worthy, even more so to hope he wouldn't be drawn to her. He was blindsided by her beauty, but I was confident she held little other appeal. He was so far removed from her world, too intellectual, too well-read, too disinterested in the fabric of society and all the show of wealth Elle held dear.

But it was his very otherness that made her want him.

'Are you still seeing Carter?'

'He's moved to Hong Kong.'

'Was it serious between you?'

As serious as casual sex ever could be. Sex that had become more aggressive, more urgent, every time I turned up at his flat in the middle of the night, with gin on my breath and demons in my mind. Sex he wanted to turn into something more, but I knew my heart wasn't ready for that.

Carter claimed to be leaving for the sake of his career. But part of me admitted I had pushed him away. One more person incapable of loving me.

'How's your placement going?' I asked and her face reassembled itself into a genuine smile.

'It's incredible. To see them every day. To know I'm part of their developmental journey, that I'm making a difference in their lives, it's just so special.'

So it would seem one of us at least had found their calling, their raison d'être, their place in this world. Who would have thought the prom queen would end up teaching five-year-olds their ABCs?

As I sat there, letting her words fall over me, watching the true delight on her face as she spoke about her pupils and all their little foibles, the beginnings of an idea seeped into my mind. Slowly at first, then with greater presence, as if unsure of its weight, its significance.

Elle loved children. Despite the battles with her own mother about how to live her life, Elle had never made any secret of the fact she wanted babies. Lots of them. But Patrick didn't. He and I had both agreed they were an unwelcome distraction, the very antithesis of what was needed in order to be successful. That there was no guarantee which part of your gene pool would make its way into the bodies of your offspring, so why take the risk of having a mediocre one?

There was still time to win him back. To change the hands of fate. To show him that while Elle might fulfil all his basal male fantasies, she wouldn't make sense in the long term. I would forgive him for straying. Allow him his moment of weakness. A reflex reaction to learning I had slept in another man's bed.

Every moment of every day gives us a choice.

44

CHAPTER SIX

Anemone: When Aphrodite wept over Adonis' grave her tears grew into anemone flowers

Five years ago

'I can't go in there.' I shook my head back and forth, bare feet tucked up underneath me and my stilettos tossed into the far corner of the bathroom.

'You have to.' My mother rolled her eyes, swivelling her wrist round to linger on her watch, a deliberate reminder that we didn't have time to dwell on my little emotional outburst. Always the same. Always doing something she didn't approve of. Always making her clean up my mess.

'Why?' Couldn't I just stay in here a moment longer? Wrap myself up into oblivion and pretend none of this was even happening?

'Because you chose this for yourself.'

She turned her back to me, showing me the zip along the length of her dress, the clasp of her necklace jiggling as she started to wash her hands. Slow, repetitive movements as she sluiced water between her fingers. There was no need for her to clean her skin. It was simply a way of keeping those hands from reaching out to me.

'How can you say that?' Would she ever offer me anything resembling a normal reaction? Simply support me, placate me because I was her daughter? Why the constant need to remind me I wasn't what she expected?

'You chose her as your friend. I warned you against it for this very reason.'

'Of course, Mum.' I picked at a loose thread on the hem of my dress. 'You had a crystal ball that predicted this precise outcome the very moment Elle and I became friends.'

'And here you are, sitting in a pool of self-pity and proving me right.'

'Thanks for the support.' The thread stretched out and I wrapped it around my little finger, tighter and tighter until the tip of my finger turned white.

A long, drawn-out sigh, as if my mere existence exhausted her. 'Oh, Jane, why can't you see that all I've ever done is support you?'

'Meaning the version of me you thought was best.'

She didn't reply as she turned off the tap and shook away the excess droplets of water. One landed on my cheek, mixing with the tears that had been flowing ever since I'd locked myself away from the sight of Elle in her wedding dress.

'Get up,' she said as she hauled me to my feet. 'Prove that you're so much better, that you're who I raised you to be, and don't ever let them see you cry.'

Dark eyes skimmed over mine and I wanted to ask her how she'd dried up all her own torment. How she'd managed to lock it away and never let it escape.

'Be the better person.' She touched one hand to my cheek and I couldn't help it, I flinched. A nod, a tiny movement of understanding before leaving me alone with nothing more than a crumpled heart, all its hope long since drifted away.

Everyone was waiting for me. The maid of honour. The one who had helped Elle plan every detail of the perfect wedding, right down to the choice of flowers for her bouquet. White roses for purity along with dusky pink peonies to bless the newlyweds with prosperity and luck. I'd convinced her to add in some hydrangeas for vanity, although she liked them simply because of the way they complimented her dress.

My own bouquet had a smattering of anemones. A symbol of my unfading love for Patrick as well as protection against the evils of this world. Much like the way the flowers closed their petals when rain was approaching, I found myself curling inward, fighting against all the pain that awaited me on the other side of the bathroom door.

It was too late. For months I'd told myself that at some point one of them would realise the mistake they were making, that this was not how the fairy tale was supposed to play out. But the only thing staring back at me from the mirror was the answer to a question I never needed to ask.

He chose her.

* * *

'If anyone has any objections, speak now or forever hold your peace.'

The vicar's voice washed over me as I stood, mute, while he went through the necessary proceedings to promise a woman to a man. All it would take was a few more words and then they would be linked to one another in the eye of God.

I could feel my mother watching me from a few rows back. As if her fingers were stretching through air to burrow beneath my skin, pulling the invisible strings that bound us, making sure I didn't do anything untoward. Anything to bring attention to us.

My own fingers scratched at my wrists, hidden behind my wilting bouquet. Scritch, scratch, scritch, scratch they went. Not stopping until I felt my flesh give way, I slowly brought my hand up to my mouth, licked away the blood from underneath my manicured nails.

Nobody loves you.

Did I speak the words aloud? For Elle's head turned to me, a line between her brows as she asked a silent question, one I was unable to understand. One I did not want to hear because I was no longer capable of feeling. No longer capable of putting myself through the torment of giving but never receiving.

Nobody wants you.

All of me was numb, apart from the fresh line of red that itched to be made more. One more step along the world we go. Words that filtered through to my subconscious as the congregation sang its final hymn. Something banal about always moving onwards, something as ludicrously ill-conceived as everything else about that loathsome wedding. A wedding I helped create. A wedding I did nothing to prevent, assuming the Universe would fold and settle in the way it was supposed to. I'd been stupid enough to think there was nothing I needed to do and suddenly it was too late.

One more step into the chasm of forever as my body did what was required of it and stood dutifully outside the church, posing for photographs I never wanted to see. My treacherous mouth formed itself into a smile, pretending all was as it should be. A mouth that never spoke the words screaming inside my mind. It was supposed to be me. All of it should have been mine, not hers.

The guests formed a semicircle around the happy couple. Took their own photographs as evidence they had been there. Commented on how perfect and special the two of them were. How well-suited. How gorgeous and wonderful and incredible their offspring would be.

'Isn't she simply exquisite?'

'Stunning.'

'Never seen her look so beautiful.'

I pushed through the throng as all their words echoed inside my head. Headed for the manor house that was only a hop, skip and jump from the picture-perfect chapel that had sat in the grounds for centuries, bearing witness to so many holy unions before that day.

Scritch, scratch, scritch, scratch went my fingers, for otherwise I didn't know what they might do.

Walking through the main reception, there were people every way I turned. Idiotic guests adorned with more sparkle than a ballroom-dancing competition, along with fake tan and layers of cologne to match. Waiters navigated the crowd, offering up glass after glass of vintage champagne along with morsels of food too delectable to turn down.

At the bottom of the staircase a woman sat astride a harp lilting notes of Mozart that weaved through the reverie, a symphony that no one was paying any attention to, but which no doubt would be commented on when the wedding was relived in days to come.

'Such a beautiful service, don't you think?' Katya, one of the other bridesmaids, stood by an antique mirror, watching me in its reflection as she adjusted the scoop of her dress, two bulbous breasts jostling for the attention she'd craved ever since school.

'Depends what your interpretation of beautiful is, I suppose.'

'Careful, Jane,' she replied. 'That mask of yours is in danger of slipping.'

She walked away before I could reply, followed the procession of people out and into the marquee where the celebrations would continue.

The house had been chosen not just for its looks, but also for its links to aristocracy, because of what it said about the family who were paying for such a grand show. There was croquet set up on the lawn, a rose garden, a lake and even a fucking peacock that paraded about the place, snapping at anyone who got too close.

I liked that bird. Could identify with it. Because I had done what my mother told me, gone back out to help Elle finish getting ready and just about managed to hold my shit together until she presented me with a little blue box containing a thank you gift for all I had done. A golden hair clasp made up of interweaving vines that matched the beaded collar of my dress. A clasp she wanted me to wear on her special day. A clasp that made me think of the night I'd given myself to the man she was about to marry.

I was supposed to be in the middle of it all, celebrating the union of my two nearest and dearest, but instead I stood in the gardens, looking across to the lake and wondering what lay beneath, in that pool of darkest blue, and whether it was safer down there than up where all my fears were coming true.

I edged away, past the kitchen where the final touches were being put to the veritable feast that was about to be served. Roasted pig fought with the honeyed perfume of hundreds upon hundreds of oranges, but the air I breathed was bitter on my tongue. Despite all the beauty, everything tasted wrong.

'Jane?' My brother. As faithful and attentive as any pet. By my side with a look full of understanding as he went to offer me a drink and saw I wasn't willing to show my hands.

'You shouldn't be here,' he said. Eyes searching behind the bouquet I was still clutching.

Robin knew. He was the one who'd found me wrapped around an empty bottle of homemade gin after the engagement had been announced in *The Times*. Curled up next to my own vomit with a gash along one hip where I'd tried to climb the stairs and stumbled over my grief. He was the one who'd washed my face and tucked me into bed, brought me painkillers and coffee the next morning.

'Well, I could hardly not show up, could I?'

'It's like some kind of sick joke, the way they treat you.'

He was the one who listened as I poured my soul into his ears, navigating his way around my wretched heart. Never once did he tell anyone else what I told him. Never once did he question my twisted allegiances, my need to always forgive and forget, to let bygones be bygones and all that crap.

'I'm leaving.'

'What, now?'

'Tonight. I've taken the job in Hong Kong.'

'But you can't, Jane. Please, you said you wouldn't.'

'If I stay here, I'll kill her.'

My mother was heading in our direction, eyes fixed on mine as she navigated her way across the sweeping lawn in heels she wasn't accustomed to wearing. Each faulty step revealed to me her agitation.

'You don't mean that.'

'Don't I? I'm not a good person, Robin, and I'm terrified of what I'll do if I don't go.'

She was pointing in the direction of the marquee. Where all the other guests had congregated, awaiting the arrival of the bride and groom. She was mouthing something about where the hell had I been, thinking I was doing her a disservice by hiding away instead of spouting some shit to anyone who would listen about how glorious this day was. Except they were all far safer with me lurking in the bushes, staying out of reach, away from all that was tempting me to do wrong.

'At least take some time to think about it.'

'It's all I ever think about. Don't you see? I can't live, I can't breathe because of them. Everything I ever do or think or say is because of them and it's consuming me. It's breaking me apart, day by day, so that soon there'll be nothing left. I'm supposed to have a life too. Where's my happily ever after? It sure as hell isn't here.'

She was getting closer, jaw clenched and eyes alive with rage because I wasn't doing as I was told, and I saw there was no other choice. What will be will be and all that crap.

'What about me?'

'Robin, I love you, but I can't do this anymore. Please. You have to let me go.'

I dropped the flowers to the ground and snatched from him one of the golden flutes, pouring its bubbly contents down my throat as I strode past my mother and into the marquee where all heads turned at my arrival. Seconds later a trumpet sounded and in the happy couple came, accompanied by cheers, whistles and rapturous applause. So beautiful. So touching. So fucking blah.

But still I looked. Still I watched as she glided through it all, like Jesus parting the waves. An ephemeral being so beloved by all. So utterly unaware of the damage she had done.

The crowd stilled as the bride and groom took their places at the top table, perched high above, where they could look upon their minions. Then murmurs of conversation floated between the tables as attention was pulled back to the free drinks.

'Before the food arrives, I just wanted to say a few words.' Elle remained standing, her voice laced with emotion I didn't want to listen to. 'I know it's unconventional, but I need to say it now or else I'll lose my nerve.'

It wasn't part of the plan. Elle had never said anything to me about making a speech and I wondered what it was she didn't want me to know in advance?

'As some of you may know, my favourite song is "Ironic" by Alanis Morissette. Of course, words aren't exactly my strong point, so I didn't really understand what she was going on about until someone pointed out to me that it wasn't sweet and romantic after all.' A few polite laughs as she looked across at me.

'But there's one part of the song that has always meant so much to me, especially now. Especially today. "*Life has a funny way of helping you out when you think everything's gone wrong and everything blows up in your face.*"'

She was still looking at me. They all thought she was talking about Patrick, were even ooh-ing and aah-ing in mock appreciation. But I saw her looking over at me with tears that threatened to fall and I allowed myself a moment to enjoy her attention once more. To remember what it was like when all she seemed to care about was me, only me and no one else.

'I wouldn't be standing here today if it weren't for you, Jane.'

All eyes on me.

'I'll never forget that day at school when you ran through the showers naked, not caring what anyone thought. Teaching me not to be afraid to be yourself because that's when love means the most.'

The last of her words were lost among a sea of mirth, of lewd comments and knowing looks from the women who had revelled in my humiliation that day. Who'd stared at me when I didn't cover my breasts. Who called me a lesbian, pointed out the hair between my legs as if I were the unnatural one for not waxing it all away.

I lifted my glass to my lips, drank long and full, my own eyes never leaving hers over the top of its polished rim.

'Because sometimes it's the people you never expect anything of who end up defying all your expectations.'

She thought the memory was hers, that somehow it could be used to define her relationship with Patrick. That my torment, my utter humiliation, belonged to her. That she could embarrass me all over again because it was her right to lay claim to absolutely everything about me, past, present and future.

'My world is a better place because of you.' At this she turned to Patrick, shone her traitorous light onto his upturned face. Leant down to bestow upon him a lover's kiss as the crowd called out in glee.

The stem of my glass split in two and I was left holding a jagged stick, like a fencer's foil that jittered in anticipation.

Told you so.

I saw it all laid out in front of me. No one would question

53

why I rose from my chair and made my way over to my best friend in all the world. No one would stop to think why I was bending forward to whisper something in her ear. No one would believe it possible that I could slit open her throat, covering the wedding feast in crimson waves. No one would understand what had happened until it was too late.

'Jane.' My brother's voice slipped inside my fantasy, broke it apart before I could carry out my desire.

'I have to go,' I replied, releasing my weapon and pushing back my chair. He made no effort to stop me. He didn't ask me to stay.

CHAPTER SEVEN

Edelweiss: Deep love and devotion

Hong Kong, one year ago

I wasn't going to come. Tried to ignore first the email then the message on my phone announcing his arrival in Hong Kong. Wondering whether I would be free to have dinner with him. He'd heard wonderful things about the Tin Lung Heen restaurant and knew it overlooked the harbour.

His voice. Winding through from thousands of miles away, as clear as if he were standing right beside me, the effect on my resolve the same. And so I replied. Of course I would meet him. It would be so lovely to catch up over dim sum and extortionately priced wine. Why not? We could even share opinions on the state of the economy and chuck in a few memories along the way.

Four years and counting. Four years since I'd scurried away from their celebrations and cried myself to sleep on the plane before arriving in a city built on water, fishermen living alongside corporate bankers, tourists and thieves. Each of us drawn to the ocean in our own way. From the balcony of my high-rise

55

apartment I could see both sides of the city – jutting shards of brick that rose from the ground like stalagmites, the stretch of ocean that cut through its centre. I would sit and watch the passage of ships, windows open to the sky and breathing in the night. Wondering what they were up to. If they, too, looked upon the stars and the moon and thought of me.

It had taken me so long to allow myself to simply be. Not to compete, not to worry about fitting in. It took so long to be forgiven by my brother for running away, to justify that it was what I needed both personally and professionally. It took me so long to start spending all the money I was making, to start creating a life for myself that didn't include them.

And it worked. The darkness that used to consume me every night slowly subsided. The cuts on my skin healed because I chose to forgive myself for what had happened. Because I had pursued him. I had been the one to bring Patrick into our lives and it all would have been so much better if I had never met him.

For the first time in so many years I would wake in the morning and not wonder where he was. If he was happy. If Elle had replaced me too. For the first time I allowed myself to believe my father would be proud of who I had become.

We are our own worst enemies. Looking back, looking forward, brings nothing but sorrow and regret. I had learnt to live in the here and now, but one phone call from him and it was like an earthquake had gone off in my soul.

I arrived at the restaurant early. Sat with flushed cheeks and jittery limbs as I gazed across the harbour. There was so much opulence, so much money to be won and lost. But despite my capabilities, I didn't quite fit. Single, rich and attractive, but not looking for a husband. The native women were as mistrustful as the ex-pats, sheltering their own conquests from me, drawing rank, keeping me at the very periphery of the circle.

So I took a lover. Then some more. Hiding my loneliness in the arms of faceless men, none of whom ever brought me either comfort or peace. All of whom disappointed when my eyes opened to discover they were not who I still dreamt of night after night when exhaustion finally won.

I found Patrick in the periphery of my vision, watched as he strode past the maître d' to lift me from my chair and into an embrace I had tried to recreate with strangers. He was there. Real. Bone and flesh. So why did I taste remorse instead of joy?

'You look really well. Life out here is clearly suiting you.'

'So do you, Patrick.' He didn't – he looked like a well-trodden doormat, all sallow skin and melancholy eyes. I accepted the plate of scallops the waiter put in front of me, the sweet aroma of ginger and lemongrass reaching my taste buds.

'I hear you've been climbing the ladder faster than they can carve the rungs,' he said, and I watched as he dipped his head to inspect his own meal, revealing the curl of hair against his collar. 'You made a great decision coming out here.'

'It was a fantastic opportunity.' Which was true. Hong Kong had provided me with a job I never would have secured in London. It's amazing what you can achieve when you're desperately hiding from your past. No distractions, no ties, just mathematical formulae I was able to translate into bucketloads of cash.

Money makes the world go round, and while Elle was trying to fill her womb with chubby offspring, I'd been adding zeroes to my bank balance.

'Why didn't you tell us you were leaving?'

'Fear can do that to a person.' I wanted it to be more. So much more. But the voice inside my head, telling me I wasn't like her, that I wouldn't be chosen, forbade me from taking that risk.

'I didn't think you were afraid of anything.'

He was so far from right it was almost laughable. But fear wasn't my only torment, not anymore. It was like I could feel the devil on my shoulder, trying to claw his way back in. Part of me had missed his taunts, his malevolent ways. Part of me understood I could no more resist him than I could stop my heart constricting whenever Patrick looked at me. Part of me knew that to ignore my darkness only gave it strength.

'How's Elle?'

'She can't get pregnant. We've tried everything and, as much as I want to support her, it's becoming a definite issue.'

There was more to this visit, this meeting of minds, than first suggested. But was he simply the messenger, the go-between, or something more?

'You're having problems?' She hadn't mentioned anything in her emails. It was all sunshine, hearts and flowers as far as she was concerned. Or at least that was what I was supposed to think, even though I could see through her carefully constructed comments all too easily. The observations about how many of her friends were now mothers, how her social circle seemed obsessed with the benefits of co-sleeping versus controlled crying. How dull their evenings out were now, as everyone was worried about pumping and dumping or the increasing cost of childcare.

How she tried not to think about creeping ever closer to thirty and wondering at the way her life had turned out. As if thirty were some kind of barometer by which we should set our goals in life.

But I forbade myself from ever asking, because all it took was one slither of doubt, a single step back towards being her support system, and my escape would have been for nothing.

'There's still time, surely?'

'If only it were that simple.'

'I'm assuming you've had the tests?'

He took a long sip of his drink, refilled his glass before the waiter could do so for him. 'I don't think there's a single test I haven't been subjected to.' He said this without meeting my eye and I could only imagine the horror he must have felt at being interrogated about his personal habits. About having to fill a cup with his seed and hand it over to a nurse for examination.

'And?'

'They can't find anything wrong with either of us.'

'What about IVF?'

'Two rounds already. Costs an absolute fortune, but Elle says it's not about the money.'

Easy to say when there was no limit to how much she would be willing to spend in order to get the picture-perfect family. It would have been killing her, the inability to do what came so naturally to others. To watch as, all around her, people were delighting the world with yet another screaming child. It should have given me nothing but pleasure to learn she was being denied something she craved with every part of her soul.

So why couldn't I help but feel sorry for her? Wonder why didn't she confide in me?

'What about alternative therapies? Chinese medicine has been used for centuries to treat all sorts of issues. I'm sure I could find out about local clinics if you had time during your stay?' I wanted to help. I wanted to be the one to provide the solution to their little problem. I wanted to be the one who could do more.

But I could tell by the look on his face that she had already tried it all. Anything and everything to prove that she too could be a mother.

'Like I said. She can't get pregnant and Elle isn't used to things not working out as she expects.'

Surely we all have our limits? Surely we all reach a point when we wake up and realise we're no longer the person we aspired to be when we were young enough to still have dreams?

'You do know children are a dealbreaker for her?' I said it even though he already knew, already understood that without the requisite heir to the family fortune, Elle would never be content.

He changed the subject then. Something about an expedition to Guatemala where a new species of bat had been discovered in the Lanquin caves. His face relaxed back into itself as he spoke, the excitement fizzing away, the promise of carrying out his own wishes for once instead of following the routine of baby-making.

It was a trip Elle would never want to join and I only half heard him when he invited me to go instead.

'I can.' I said the words before they even registered in my mind. Before I even decided what it was I was offering.

'You'll come with me?'

I would run to the ends of time for him, but unfortunately that wasn't the idea that chose to announce itself when I should have been thinking about nights camped out under the Milky Way with nothing but a campfire and whisky to keep us warm. How treacherous and shrewd my mind could be, almost as if it chose to punish me for something I wasn't aware of having done.

'I can get pregnant.' It was something I could do that she could not. Something that set me apart, that made me indisputably better than her.

'I really don't see what this has to do…'

'I can get pregnant.' I became manic, overly excited, pawing at him like a woman possessed. 'For you. For both of you.'

'Well, that's awfully kind, but I couldn't possibly…'

Except he could. The hesitation before he spoke was enough for me to see the workings of his magnificent brain. The triumphant return, making him once more the hero in her eyes. The sacrificial lamb resuming her duties and giving the queen what her heart most desired.

'Would you at least consider it? I mean, if she really does want a baby, then surely this wouldn't be such a ridiculous idea?'

A small shake of his head as he scratched the tip of his nose. 'Why would you do that, for us?'

'Because it doesn't make sense without you.'

I held my breath. Waited for him to reply. For him to understand what it was I was trying to tell him. Trying to apologise for my mistake all that time ago. Trying to see if this might be my opportunity to turn everything around, steer the path my way.

I don't know if in that moment I ever truly meant to keep my promise, to see my ridiculous plan all the way to its rather bitter end. But then he did something so subtle, yet so unspeakably clever, that it took me forever to understand the weight of one sentence.

'She feels the same. She misses you more than you could possibly know.'

She doesn't miss you. She betrayed you.

There it was. My own private Lucifer, risen from the depths. Giving me the push I needed to throw myself in, all of me. My entire existence pulled back to her.

'Then I should come home. Talk to her. Tell her I want to help.'

'What about your life here?'

'It was never going to be forever. I always knew on some level where it is I really belong.' The idea that had started out as nothing more than a throwaway comment, a desperate bid for attention, began to germinate and bloom. Just like the life that would feed from me, that would be nurtured by my womb, so too would the plan to take back even more than I'd ever thought possible.

Because if Elle was no longer around, who would take care of my beloved? Who would take care of the baby?

CHAPTER EIGHT

Mistletoe: Celtic Druids believed mistletoe had the power to bestow life and fertility

England, six months ago

'Here you go.' Patrick slid my glass across the battered wooden table, a snail-like trail of foam left between us. The silver cufflinks at his wrists winked their taunt at me, the tick of his oversized watch laughing its reminder that he wore her gifts like a badge that screamed at me to stay away, not to touch. His fingers held the scent of expensive aftershave, nails displaying clipped cuticles that used to be stained with ink but now moved over a keyboard instead of paper.

I rubbed my thumb from the bottom of the glass to the top, catching the spillage before licking my skin clean.

'Don't tell Elle,' I said as I took a sip, watching him as he did the same.

'Need to know basis.' He attempted a smile but it didn't quite work.

'It's only half a pint, but she would worry.'

'To the point of paranoia.'

I nodded my agreement.

'Besides,' he said in between gulps. Most of his drink was already gone. 'My great aunt drank a pint of Guinness a day and she lived…'

'…To be ninety-four,' I finished for him. I knew all his stories. Replayed them over and over in my mind just to try and remember the exact intonation of his voice.

'You could argue it's good for the baby.'

'But we won't tell Elle.' I could imagine her face if she knew what I was up to. She would accuse me of putting my own selfish needs before those of the baby. Which, of course, I was.

'Probably best not to,' he said, as if it was for his wife's own good.

So many untruths, so many lies we pretend aren't there because the words have never been said. We tell ourselves it doesn't matter, that sometimes it's necessary to filter out the truth, that what we do is for the benefit of others. To protect them from harm, when in fact the one we want to protect is ourselves.

Poor Elle. Poor, ignorant Elle. She has been protected her entire life, only ever shown the version of a world that is as close to perfect as it's possible to be. But she has chosen to believe. To ignore anything that threatens to pollute her glossy existence and everything in it. The house, the car, the five-star holidays. The cleaner, the gardener, designer clothes and the three-carat diamond that catches the light as she moves. I almost feel sorry for her. Almost.

She styled their existence to its very limit, but none of it is real. Take away the money and all that's left is two people hiding from one another because they're so afraid to reveal the true versions of themselves.

'I'll be back in a minute.' Patrick's chair complained as he stood. A cigarette sat behind his ear, a lighter concealed in his fist. One more thing Elle chose not to see. A habit he's supposed to have broken long ago, just like her, for the sake of their unborn child, but part of him still clings to it. A small rebellion against everything she has changed.

'Those things will kill you.'

'I'm tougher than I look.'

Except he's not. We're all just flesh that can so easily be cut, blood spewing from the wound as our hearts, the very organ that feels, that gives us meaning, pumps life from our withering bodies. For death is as certain as the setting of the sun. But we do our best to ignore it. One more lie.

Patrick rubbed at his eye, pink around the edges of contacts he has worn ever since his wife told him not to hide behind those awful plastic frames.

'Back in a sec.'

I watched him navigate his way through the crowds of people drinking their way through whatever it was they were trying to forget. Shoulders heavy as he passed underneath an exposed beam still clinging to a few strands of Christmas mistletoe.

He was doing it for her. He never wanted kids. Not really. Then again, he never wanted the lifestyle to which Elle had become so accustomed.

Taking hold of his glass I pressed my lips to the rim, an absent kiss that activated a memory I hold most dear. At the same time my hand retrieved a tiny glass vial, hidden in the bottom of my bag, and as the glass found its spot on the table once more I emptied the contents of the vial into Patrick's drink. My whole body was slightly off kilter, stood ready, waiting, fear and excitement tangled up together.

There was still time to undo what I had been turning around in my mind for several weeks. Still time to reconsider what I was about to do. Still time to make another choice, to accept what I had agreed over lunch in Hong Kong.

She knew how much you loved him, yet she took him anyway.

'How did we get here?' He returned with the smoky cloak of

a familiar friend, the taste of which would linger in his mouth, on his lips.

'What do you mean?' I stuffed my hands under my legs to stop them from snatching back the poisoned chalice. Fate had nothing on me because I always, always planned ahead. I had double-checked the required amount, made sure there was no possibility of harming his splendid self, but there was a part of me, a voice that couldn't be stilled, which cried out for me to stop. To find another way. Not to risk doing harm. Not to risk the pain I knew was still to come.

'Here. Now. This life.' He scratched the back of his neck as he looked at me, willing me to understand so he didn't have to spit out the words.

'I always imagined you holed up in a college somewhere, with books as pets and students instead of children.' I drained my glass then refilled it. 'I never had you down as a suit, a maker of money.' That was always my ambition.

'Nor I, but we do what we must.' He didn't need to sigh for me to hear his remorse. 'Don't get me wrong. I love Elle.'

Don't we all, in our own, twisted way, changing ourselves in order to fit her exacting requirements. My transformation came first, way back in school, when I realised, if I was going to survive, I needed to fit in, to slip inside a different persona. I did what was required. I cut my hair, I changed my glasses, I discovered how to create the perfect smoky eye. I squeezed my limbs into too-tight jeans and learnt everything else I needed to know from MTV. I practised and I practised and I practised, all so I would be good enough, one day, for someone like him.

For it is entirely possible to be anybody, anybody at all, as long as you're willing to work at it.

But Patrick didn't need to change. He was already perfect. For me. But not for her. It was subtle, to the untrained eye, but his osmosis had a helping hand that brushed hair from his forehead, bought gifts of Burberry overcoats and custom-made shirts to replace the battered leather jacket and M&S jumpers. Took him on weekend retreats in Tuscany where he learnt to appreciate the difference between Barolo and Sassicaia. Hosted dinners and attended corporate events, mingling with wives and partners, swapping stories about ski weekends in St Moritz and New Year in the Maldives. Keeping up with the Jones's at its best.

Because we all have something that we want. And Elle wanted to escape the stain of her father's working-class roots. She wanted a different kind of life, a different kind of money that was both accepted and envied. A world that Patrick's pedigree and intelligence could provide.

Of course he never saw it, never suspected, due to his utter disbelief that she had chosen him. Was that my fault too? Did I fail to protect him? To protect his true self from her intoxicating spell? The fact he'd chosen her wasn't what surprised me, more that I'd never believed her capable of such blatant manipulation, of taking away my happiness for the sake of her own.

'I'm not sure I can do this.' He clutched his glass and looked at me.

'What is it?' Go on, go on, go on.

'Nothing. I have nothing to complain about.' He rested his hands on the table, fingers splayed, my traitorous eye as ever finding the platinum band on his third finger.

'Everyone has something to complain about.'

'Even you?' A mocking eyebrow stretched high.

'Even me. For example…' I tilted my glass in his direction. '… This will shortly be forbidden.'

'I'm surprised Elle hasn't put you on some kind of pre-pregnancy detox.'

'She has tried, believe me, but I refuse to spend my last days of freedom either juicing or partaking in sunrise yoga.'

He raised his pint. 'I'll drink to that.'

She never had asked what he intended to do that weekend. How he would pass the time while she stretched and starved her body on a yoga retreat in Ibiza. Happy instead to bathe in the ensuing compliments about the healthy glow that would result from the consumption of nothing but plant water for three days.

'Jane?'

'Sorry, what?' I raised my eyes to his.

'I said she's like a woman possessed. I thought that once, you know…' Another nod to my belly. '…She would calm down a bit, but if anything, she's worse.'

'You're talking about the charts.'

'She won't give up on the possibility of it happening naturally.'

Of course she wouldn't. She'd never had to play second fiddle to anyone, least of all me. The incongruity of having to accept help from the ugly duckling, all because her womb was rejecting him. I loved that on some level he knew she wasn't right for him. His body somehow understood that the most basic of animal instincts, the need to reproduce, was impossible with his wife.

According to the doctors there was no medical reason why, with the right medication, Elle and Patrick couldn't conceive a child of their own, but there are forces in this world far greater than us and there's nothing you can do if Mother Nature is determined not to let you grow a child inside of you.

Then again, Mother Nature picked a strong opponent in Elle. She had tried everything, and I mean everything, to get what she wanted. The conventional drugs, going teetotal (something Patrick tried his best to resist), the diets, acupuncture, even musical therapy. Anything, no matter how far-reaching, anything at all in order to conceive. And taped to the glass cabinet in their en-suite bathroom was her ovulation chart, dutifully compiled using a similar sort of stick to the kind you pee on in the vain hope that you are pregnant.

I helped her. Of course I did. For I had to be just as well informed, if not more so, than the competition. I read every book, researched every article and logged my own menstrual cycle right up until the moment the surrogacy procedure began.

Which was why I knew I was ovulating that night. Why I slipped a vial containing the concentrated essence of marijuana into Patrick's drink when he popped outside for a smoke. Why I bundled him into a taxi as the tincture took hold, directed the driver back to my house, and even asked him to help Patrick upstairs and into bed.

I will never forget how he felt inside of me. The taste of his skin on my lips, the touch of his mouth against mine. I will never forget squeezing him tight as I rode on top, his arousal wonderfully responsive even though he was delirious. Marijuana is pretty potent stuff when administered in a strong enough dose. I learnt that the hard way.

I tried to make it last, to delay his response as well as my own. But it was too much, too powerful to contain, and I thrust my body against him over and over, crying out as I felt his seed enter me.

I watched him sleep, counted every freckle dusted on his shoulders, examined every single inch of him, for I knew it would be another eternity until we could be together again.

When he began to stir I curled up beside him and closed my eyes.

'What the…?' A befuddled question as he realised it wasn't his wife beside him. 'What the fuck happened last night?' Voice high-pitched and wrinkled as he discovered his lack of clothes. I imagined him trying to make sense of the scene in front of him, to remember anything other than sharing a couple of drinks in the pub with one of his closest friends.

Plants are such incredible things. Marijuana has a number of side effects, some of which are considered detrimental, but the short-term memory loss was of particular benefit that night. I wanted him to question what had happened. To wonder whether the images that flashed in his mind were real. To question if the body he had so enjoyed belonged to me or his wife.

'Hmm?' I feigned sleep, turned over while wiping fingers across my face, then scrabbled backwards to stand before him in nothing more than a silk negligee.

'Shit. Do you think we…?' He flicked a hand towards me, unable not to dare a look along the length of my body and back up again. He seemed unabashed by his own nudity, as if it were the most natural thing in the world to be in the bedroom of your wife's best friend, naked as the day you were born.

I picked up his clothes from my side of the bed and threw them at him. 'Stop panicking. You were so drunk I thought it was safer to bring you back here, make sure you didn't choke on your own vomit.'

'So how come I'm naked?'

I looked away. 'I started to help you undress, but…'

'But?'

A small chuckle. 'You thought I was Elle.'

'I thought you were…?' His tongue darted from one side of his mouth to the other, a familiar gesture that always told of his nerves. If only I could see the thoughts running through his mind. How much did he remember? How much would he choose to believe? It was perfect, for even if he did recall the exact way his body felt as it moved inside of me, I'd done enough to make sure he wouldn't dare ask.

'Elle must never find out.'

'Of course not.' I pretended to agree. Yet another secret to keep.

But one day I will tell her that the baby growing within me may not be her own. One day I will tell her how I went along with the plan, pretended to take the estrogen supplements, to wipe progesterone cream into my private parts. I will confess that I didn't inject myself with Lupron, so that, when I bled, it was real, and my own fertility remained on track. She will discover that the day after her own eggs were harvested and she fled to a Mediterranean island, I took advantage of her husband; and when she accompanied me to the hospital, watching as I spread my legs wide and allowed the doctor to inseminate me with two of her fertilized eggs, I knew there was a chance Patrick had impregnated me only days before.

The life, the new beginning, the perfect family belongs to me. She hasn't been the one to crave it, to miss having two parents waiting for her at home. To wonder if she would have been someone different, someone better, if her father hadn't disappeared.

Patrick was supposed to be my promise of a better future. A future I had been working towards long before she laid eyes on him.

It was always supposed to be him and me, Elle was never part of the plan.

I saw him first.

NOW

CHAPTER NINE

Daisy: New beginnings, childhood and maternal love

'You'll never guess who called me.' Elle holds up a pale-pink babygro with poor imitations of daisies stitched around the collar.

'Who?' That was quick. Less than twenty-four hours since I let him buy me coffee, having serendipitously bumped into him after all this time. Except there's no such thing as fate as far as I'm concerned, just carefully executed plans. Made far easier by the fact he gets his morning coffee from the same café every day. One of those independent establishments that has a separate menu for the vitamin 'shots' you can put in your organic smoothie and has a barista instead of a waiter.

A person's choice of breakfast tells you all you need to know. For example, the person in question has a single-shot soy macchiato and gluten-free blueberry muffin. My father had porridge in the winter and muesli in the summer, but every Friday, without fail, it would be a bacon sandwich with brown sauce. Elle has a glass of hot water with lemon, because she read somewhere that's what all the top Hollywood actresses do.

'Go on, guess.' She puts the babygro back and moves along to a row of dresses trimmed with lace. Completely impractical for a newborn, even more so when I see the price.

I roll my eyes, but play along just the same. 'Gandhi? Winston Churchill? Jamie Dornan?' I doubt she is aware that only one of my guesses is still alive, but you never know.

She smiles, the effect it has on me after all these years never failing to surprise and annoy in equal measure.

'None of the above, but I wouldn't say no to a slice of Mr Grey.'

I wait, assured in the knowledge that she will divulge his name. The titbit too tasty not to share. She always shares, always passes on her good fortune, for it multiplies the more people she tells. It will be interesting to see how generous she is if things progress as I intend.

'Harry White.'

'Wow, that's…' Brilliant. I knew he wouldn't be able to resist.

'I know, right? After what happened I wasn't sure I'd ever hear from him again.'

What happened was that she broke his heart, but not before he broke mine.

'What's he up to these days?' I know exactly what he's up to, having followed his path ever since school. I keep tabs on them all, every single one who has a debt they owe. I look and I see. I really see. All the little details no one ever truly manages to conceal. Details that can be used to my advantage whenever I see the need.

'He's a film producer.'

'I always thought he'd end up in the music industry.' Which was perfectly reasonable given the number of nights we'd spent in moist rooms, swaying to an amateur attempt at music saved only by his voice. A voice that reached deep inside and ripped out emotions you didn't even know were hidden. 'What did he want?'

Her. He always wanted her. Even though at first he said he wanted me.

'Just to catch up.'

Which roughly translates as wanting to know whether she's willing to swap bodily fluids. For old times' sake. After all, I guess she could argue it's not cheating if it's an ex. Not really.

You see, I realised long ago that there's a moment in every day that tips the balance one way or the other, that determines whether it's a day to be remembered or forgotten. I will remember what happened that night for all the wrong reasons, but I am also grateful, for it taught me not to trust anyone, even my so-called best friend.

A party. A gathering of wayward souls in a house unguarded by adults. A boy. The chosen one as far as Elle was concerned. Except he came instead to me. Offered me a beer from a bucket filled with ice as he took a long sip from his own drink; grey, feline eyes that watched me with curious intent as he climbed atop a low garden wall to reveal battered Doc Martens. It was all I could do not to click the heels of my own oxblood pair together.

A group was huddled around a wooden table, their location given away by circles of orange light that grew brighter whenever they drew on a cancer stick, as my mother insisted on calling them. Minuscule particles of ash danced through the damp air, one of which found its way past the clunky frame of my glasses.

He told me I looked better without them and I did everything I could not to reply. Not to give in to the temptation, because I knew he belonged to Elle.

Then he held up something very much not a cigarette, putting the thinner end between his lips and igniting the other, a halo forming around his face that cast all else into shadow.

Stop staring, I told myself, unable to look away as he inhaled, the joint's tip lit up like a mini volcano.

Stop staring, I repeated as he moved closer, lips pursed and eyes squinting. The blush inched over my jawline and every pore on my face seemed to be radiating heat as two hands reached out to cup my face, the burning embers of the joint singeing the end of one of my hairs. But I couldn't move, didn't dare to, for I wanted to remember the exact pressure of his skin on mine, the fullness of his pupils, the sensation of all else falling away as he blew smoke into my mouth.

'So what do you think?' Elle asks, pulling me back to the here and now.

I look at the crib she's fingering, complete with hand-stitched blanket. 'I don't see the point in buying all this stuff if you don't want to find out whether it's a boy or a girl.'

It's a boy. I knew even without having to see the pictures from the last scan. Of course, I looked when the nurse told us not to if we wanted it to be a surprise. I needed to know, to be certain after weeks of guessing, of talking to him and telling him how incredible he is. Weeks of picturing his face, eyes the colour of emeralds, just like his dad.

'I meant, do you think I should meet him?'

'Who?'

'Harry.'

Harry had turned out to be no better than any of my other classmates. Someone saw us. Someone told. Someone betrayed me to Elle because they wanted to take my place by her side. Whispers passed between them, lies and counter-lies that grew with each telling of the tale.

Underneath it all, Harry was just as afraid of being cast out of the social circle. Which is why he said it was nothing. I meant nothing.

'I don't see why not.' I hand her a book on baby-led weaning. Let the little ones decide what's best for them nutritionally, because Mummy won't have a bloody clue.

'Exactly. I mean, what harm could it do?'

Hopefully a whole lot more than I've already done.

'Can I help you with anything?' A doughy excuse for a sales assistant sidles over, her smile not reaching the eyes that skate over us both, assessing. Coming to rest on the swell of my stomach, the arch of spine as my body learns to adjust to the new weight inside of me.

'No thanks, we're just looking.'

'When are you due?'

I hate this about being pregnant. The lingering glances, the questions, even the touching. I've never been great at sharing my personal space, but it would seem that as soon as you're pregnant it gives people free rein to stroke a hand over your stomach and simper up at you.

'A few more months.'

A step closer, invading my territory, and I lean against the stack of cuddly toys behind me.

'This is the best bit. Before you get so large you can't see your feet to tie your own shoes. Did you have any morning sickness?'

'A little, but mostly hungry.' I move around the display, pretending to show interest in a breast pump. An image of me cradling his warm body while he feeds, tiny fingers grasping at mine as Patrick stands in the doorway, watching.

'Carbs or sweets?'

'Cheese and ham sandwiches.' I'm oversharing. I never share.

'Must be a boy. My nan always told me it was carbs for boys and cakes for girls. Plus you've got that pregnancy glow. When I was pregnant with my Lucy I looked like a beached whale. Swollen ankles, acne and a backside as wide as I'm tall. Definitely a boy.'

'You're probably right.' Because there's always an old wives' tale to back up whatever crazy theory you have about the sex of some stranger's unborn child. And it's not as if there are a million possible options to choose from. Boy or girl. Pretty much a 50/50 chance every single time.

'So, where's Daddy?'

Why is she still talking to me?

'He couldn't make it,' Elle interjects, and I hear the strain behind her words. 'Busy with work.'

A golfing weekend she insisted he went on because it would

be good for his promotional prospects. Patrick hates golf almost as much as he hates social events, but Elle isn't someone you say no to.

'Oh.' The assumption made all the more obvious by her eyes falling to my left hand and taking in the lack of a wedding ring, then looking over at the rock adorning Elle's. 'Still, it's nice you've got each other, isn't it? Always lovely for two friends to experience pregnancy together.'

Elle stiffens beside me and her skin takes on an altogether more clammy, less radiant, look than usual. Nails dig into my palm as I quell the desire to smack the assistant round the head with the wooden, pull-along crocodile sitting on the shelf just within arm's reach. The wonderful sound it would make as it hit her skull, flinging what little brains she has over the perfect white surface of every last pair of booties in the shop.

'Actually, I told him not to bother turning up anymore. I mean, now he's done his bit there's not much need for a man, is there?' I drag Elle from the shop, leaving the sales assistant standing with mouth agape, the cogs in her fat head turning.

'You okay?'

She shrugs off my touch and pats the corner of her eye with one knuckle, checking it for traces of mascara. 'Why do you torment them so? She was only trying to be friendly.'

'I don't like touchy-feely. And she was about to offer to be my birthing guru, partner, whatever you call them.'

'Doula.' She steps aside as another pregnant woman walks past us into the shop, the longing on Elle's face all too apparent as the woman places a protective hand on her stomach.

I know what she's thinking. How wonderful it would be to have everyone ask you about your baby. For her to be the centre of attention instead of me. The baby carrier. The oven. The means to an end.

'It's so unfair.' She strides off down the street and I hurry to keep up. Even with my relatively small extra burden I'm not as nimble as I used to be and I find myself half-shuffling, half-skipping behind. I can hear her muttering to herself, agitated swipes of her hand through the air as people stare at her out of curiosity instead of the usual admiration. It's all rather amusing, the sight of this glorious creature acting like a lunatic.

A young couple pushing a stroller cross the road, a spaniel trotting at their side. As they step onto the pavement the child drops its teddy and his mother bends to retrieve it, revealing her swollen belly. She catches Elle watching.

'I swear he does it on purpose. A million times a day, drives me mad.'

Elle doesn't respond, instead staring at the child, at his dimpled cheeks, oversized eyes and rosebud lips that suck the teddy's ear. A sound akin to a guttural roar escapes her mouth and she tries to cover it with trembling fingers. I pull her away, doing my best to steer round the cacophony of prams and children that fill the pavement. It's as if they've spilled from every crevice, like flying ants on a summer's day.

We duck into a bar and take a seat near the back. A bearded young man approaches, handing a menu to Elle before me, because even in her most agitated, dilapidated state, she is still the axis towards which all men tilt.

'Large glass of white wine and a mineral water, please.' The barman looks at me as if he had forgotten I was there, then skulks away.

'Every day,' Elle mutters. 'Every fucking day I have to see, talk to, touch them. And not just at work.' She takes a packet of cigarettes out of her bag, turns it around and around on the tabletop. Interesting, especially as she's supposed to have given up. Patrick too, but clearly there are some things husband and wife choose not to share. Which helps me immensely.

'I have to listen to them moan about unsupportive husbands, about juggling a million things at once, being unappreciated, having no time to themselves, and it's all I can do to stop myself from slapping them, from yelling at them to stop moaning, you silly cow, be grateful for what you have.'

This is nothing new. I've heard it at least a thousand times over the past year. Best to let her just get on with it, give her hand a gentle squeeze and nod in understanding.

'I want to touch every newborn baby, feel its solid little body between my hands. I want to cuddle my pupils so tight, to smother them with kisses and tell them how wonderful and precious they are. Each time I see those children running out of the school gates and back to their mothers it's like my heart has been shredded. I want to collapse on the playground and sob until there are no more tears inside of me. I want this feeling to stop.'

'But it will stop.' I say the same thing every time, but I don't think she's interested in the words, more the fact that I pretend to listen and to care. Because who is she to complain? To the outside world she has everything, so how can she explain that it's not what she signed up for, how she imagined her life would be?

The barman returns and places our drinks on the table. Elle takes two large gulps, puts the glass down, then picks it up and drains its contents. This is good. This shows the beginnings of a pattern, one I will encourage and disapprove of in equal measure.

'I know I should be grateful. But it's like there's this snake inside of me, screaming at the injustice of it all.'

I sit a little straighter. This is new.

'Why can't I be pregnant? Why can't I be the one with morning sickness, swollen ankles and feel the baby move? Why do you get to have my baby growing inside your womb? Why can't it be me?'

'I thought this is what you wanted?'

She swipes the back of her hand across her leaking nose in a move so completely out of character I have to swallow a laugh. It's working. The seams are beginning to loosen enough for me to edge the demons inside.

'And of course Patrick doesn't understand. He says I chose this, that we agreed this was a better way.'

She means better than the anticipation each month, only for the traitorous drops of red to return.

'He says it was my decision not to adopt, but how could we when the doctors have said there's still a chance I could get pregnant?'

Ah, so there it is. Hope. So powerful and dangerous an emotion, one I understand far better than she.

'Patrick will never understand,' I say. 'He's just a man. All they do is plant their seed and be done with it.'

She manages half a chuckle, swiftly replaced with a frown.

'Here.' I push my drink towards her, along with another small glass bottle I collected from the fridge this morning. 'Drink this.'

'I'd rather have another glass of wine.' But she does as she's told, opening the bottle and using the built-in pipette to squeeze half a dozen drops of belladonna into the water. I wait for her to start drinking.

'Are you sure this stuff is safe?' She holds up the bottle, peering at its contents as if they hold the answers she so desperately seeks.

'I've been giving it to Mum for years and she's perfectly healthy.' If you ignore the fact that the tincture I make for her is derived from Laceflower, which, when taken in small doses, acts as a cardiac tonic for her angina. So if it were the same essence in that bottle, then yes, it would be completely safe for Elle to take, but what's one little lie among friends?

'You're the only person I know who simply accepts me for who I am, no questions asked. Even Patrick...'

'Even Patrick?' I know what she fears. That she's not good enough for him. Not intelligent enough, not from the right sort of background, not capable of producing an heir. She's right, but I can't let her know I agree, that she's never been good enough, never will be. That I make so much more sense as his wife.

She sits, her silence telling me more than the way she's picking at a hangnail on her thumb, the twitch of her mouth as a round globule of blood appears. We all possess a fear too great for any of us to give voice to. The irony is that we both share the same one, but which of us deserves him more? Which of us will he choose when it all unfolds?

'Harry told me you saw him, so you can stop pretending.'

And so we turn full circle. It's like a mosquito; you forget about it after the initial bite, then it begins to itch and you can't leave it alone. She's thinking about him, as I knew she would. Thinking about the two of them together, how he idolised her, complimented her, treated her like a goddess in a way Patrick never does.

'He asked how you were, that's all,' I say, pouring myself a glass of water.

'Why don't you go out with him?'

'Harry's not my type.'

'He used to be.'

'That was years ago.' Before I realised I'd been waiting for someone else all along.

'Maybe I will meet up with him. Just for a drink.'

Just a drink. Or two. Or maybe a whole bottle. Because all sorts of things can happen when we let go of the inhibitions that bind us.

She takes a cigarette out of the packet, then puts it back again. 'We need to talk about what happens when the baby's born.'

'I thought we'd been through all the logistics already?' I signal to the waiter to bring us another round, checking she's still drinking her infected water. The tincture alone isn't strong enough to kill her; no, that's not how I intend for this to end. But I need to monitor the dosage carefully, make sure the effects don't take hold too soon.

'I mean about what happens if you change your mind.'

Shit. Not what I was expecting.

'I've signed the contract, Elle.' Signed on the dotted line. Agreeing in the presence of a lawyer and a witness that I will carry this child to term and then hand it over to its rightful parents. Except I made sure to include the words *biological parents*. Just in case. 'It's your baby, Elle.'

'But in a way it's yours too. You're the one who's nurturing it, protecting it, feeling it grow and move inside of you. What if that means it loves you more than me?'

'Stop worrying about what may or may not happen.'

'Imagine if I got pregnant.' She stares past me, eyes focused inward, the image in her mind no doubt looking like something out of a Ralph Lauren catalogue.

'Then you'd end up with two newborns for the price of one.'

'Or we could raise them together.' Her eyes come back to me, both of us contemplating what it is she has just said. One each. Now wouldn't that be something.

'Think about it,' she continues, taking my hand and wrapping those fingers tight. 'It would be perfect. No men to distract us, to come between us. Take away all the hurt and confusion they always cause.'

Is she talking in general, or specifically about our sordid little threesome? Her index finger is scratching at the back of my hand as she looks away, down to the floor, back to me, then away again. Round and round in circles like my mind as I try to make sense of what she is saying.

Because it's all I've ever wanted. What I used to dream about when we were friends, way back when. A house with a wraparound porch on which we would sit as elderly spinsters. Grandchildren running through sprinklers and a catalogue of memories stored in our minds. Elle would be resplendent in violet silk with bright-red lips holding on to a homemade cigarette, sweet curls of dope-fuelled smoke helping to ease her arthritic limbs. I would be the one swearing like a sailor at the housekeeper and stroking the malevolent cat on my knee.

Before I have a chance to fully process the idea that perhaps she would let me keep this child, my boy, without any bloodshed, the waiter returns once more. He's hovering at the edge of the table, but Elle gives him nothing more than a cursory glance as she hands over her empty glass.

'You promise he hasn't said anything to you? Because maybe I pushed him too hard. Maybe he's found someone to give him what I can't.'

It's as if she's asking me to feel sorry for her. To tell her that, whatever Patrick does, it's not her fault.

'I've told you, he's not having an affair. Patrick wouldn't recognise a come-on if someone pushed his face into their bosom.'

This rewards me with something resembling an actual laugh and I hate myself for feeling grateful.

'It feels like too much. As if we're trapped inside a house, thinking we're safe, but a storm's coming and there's nothing we can do to escape.'

'It's a baby, Elle, not a Hitchcock film.'

'But it's not. It's so much more, don't you see? It's about you and me and Patrick and how it never works when one of us is missing. About how we're all so connected, how we rely on each other for everything, and I'm terrified of what will happen if it breaks. I don't want to lose you again.'

I have no idea how to respond for I can't yet decide what to feel about this admission. I find my hand reaching out to move away the glass tainted with poison as she stares across the table that divides us. No words, just a thousand unspoken thoughts that neither of us seems able to share. Then the sound of an old-fashioned ringtone cuts into the air, like a story from a lifetime ago. Elle reaches into her bag, frowning as she sees who is trying to take her attention from me.

'Shit, it's my mother.'

'Problem?'

'Not as such. But I promised to meet her. To go through the seating arrangements for Dad's party. I'd better go or she'll only keep on ringing.'

'Of course.'

'Call you later?' As if we were teenagers once again and had all the time in the world to decide what to do with our lives. No matter how close, no matter how much we claim to belong to another, there's always so much left unsaid. So much left unresolved.

Then she sweeps out of my day, leaving me with nothing but the scent of her perfume and the constant to and fro of my decision. The question of whether this convoluted plan was ever going to be worth the consequences I already feared.

Humans find violence inherently satisfying, but remove the satisfaction, the reaction to what it is you are doing, and the act of violence itself becomes obsolete. I wasn't doing this for any kind of recognition, so even if it satisfied me on some level to be rid of Elle, what then? What would I need to do next? That was what terrified me more than anything. That even with her gone I would still have the desire to do harm.

CHAPTER TEN

Snapdragon: Deception and graciousness, but sometimes used as a charm against falsehood

'Mum?'

'In here.'

The kitchen is hidden under a thin blanket of icing sugar. It makes me think of the way Nana would beat her hall carpet, hanging it over the washing line as dust mushroomed over the garden to settle on the plants until the rain came to wash all remnants of us away.

Mum is standing at the kitchen island, sleeves rolled up to the elbows and wrists deep inside a vast china bowl with a ring of blue elephants around the rim. There's a chip on the side I can't quite see, the scar on my index finger a permanent reminder of when I tried to be helpful by washing it up unaided, only to be reprimanded for being careless.

Back then Mum never baked and her cooking repertoire just about stretched to spaghetti Bolognese and a roast on Sundays. I learnt to cook through trial and error, hunger forcing me to rummage in the cupboards and concoct something halfway edible instead of waiting for Mum to get home from work and announce she hadn't had time to stop at the shops so cereal would have to do.

Back then she was focused on keeping a roof over our heads.

'Can you fetch me some more milk?' She rubs the back of her hand over a cheek, leaving a smear of cake mixture on her skin. I know better than to try and wipe it away.

The fridge is, as always, taken over by several large sponge cakes, along with a row of milk bottles in the door, enough butter to fill a bathtub and carton upon carton of eggs. Apart from a solitary wilted lettuce and half a block of cheese the space remains devoid of any other items of food.

'Mum, you need to eat.' I hand her a bottle of milk, watching as she pours the requisite amount into the bowl before the stirring resumes.

'I do eat.' Her focus never strays from the task at hand.

'I mean real food, not just whatever happens to still be edible. The doctor was very clear about your blood-sugar levels…'

'Oh, tosh. I'm as fit as I've ever been.'

And two stone heavier thanks to her new business venture, because my mother has never done anything by halves.

'*If a job's worth doing, it's worth doing properly,*' she would say while whirling around me in a state of frenzied activity.

I first witnessed this side to her personality after my father left. I came home from school to find the hallway stacked with cardboard boxes. The walls had several gaps, rectangular patches where the flowered wallpaper was darker, like a handprint of what once was. Every time I blinked I could see the photographs that used to hang in those spaces, could picture my father's face grinning back at me from various stages of his life.

One day was all she needed to eradicate him from our home and no amount of protestation from me had ever made her change her mind.

* * *

Twenty-five years ago

'Where's Daddy?'

'Daddy's gone.' My mother's voice spilled into the kitchen sink, her neck bent forward so she looked like a headless zombie.

'Gone where?'

The blades of her shoulders jutted out at me through her frayed cotton sundress.

'Just gone.'

I looked over at his work boots on the mat by the door out to the garden, squelchy mud on red leather. 'When will he be back?'

'He's not coming back.' The clatter of china and a tap turned on, my mother's hands busy with something I could not see.

I walked over to the back door, opened it and peered down the garden to Daddy's shed. I could just make out the handle to his spade, which always leant against the wooden slats.

'But he has to come back. He promised to finish my swing.'

My mother's head lolled back on its spine, accompanied by a low growl at the base of her throat. It was a noise she reserved for moments when I was being particularly bothersome.

I frowned. I thought I had left enough time between the faded notes of their argument and coming downstairs.

'He's gone to live with his whore,' she screamed as she turned to me with a face filled with rage and despair.

I ran into the garden, opening the door to his shed, half-hoping he would be crouched over the workbench, pipe held in the corner of his mouth and brow crinkled in concentration.

But it was empty.

My bare feet curled underneath themselves, cold on the wooden floor. I nudged a terracotta flowerpot with my big toe, watching as it toppled onto its side, puking out its earthy contents. I drew a circle in the soil, damp brown specks creeping under my nails. No doubt Mummy would tell me off when I got in the bath. Would make me scrub until my skin blushed deep, adding more hot water until she deemed me clean.

A line of seedlings stood to attention on the makeshift table. Snapdragons, chrysanthemums and sweet peas. I had been in charge of selecting which one was next, passing it over as Daddy eased it into its new home, covering its sides with fresh compost and gently pressing down around the edges.

We made sure to label them all, so that I could learn; so Daddy could teach me the same way his father had taught him. My shaky letters were written down in pencil, tongue grasped between teeth as I tried to remember which way to start an 'e'. Then we took the pots outside, ready for watering. But I remembered the swing and asked Daddy, please, pretty please, with a strawberry on top, to fix it first.

My heart squeezed as I found the ashtray on the windowsill. A box of matches sat between two different types of glass but his pipe was gone.

That's when I knew Mummy wasn't lying. He was gone. To live with his 'hor', although the word wasn't one I understood. The sound when I said it made me think of breathing through mittens on Bonfire Night.

I went outside and picked up a trowel, turning it around in my hand so the curved silver threw back a glimpse of my mottled face.

He made a promise. And he had broken it.

The first pot escaped my aim, one thin arm slicing through the sky as I stumbled. But as my arm flew back again, over and over the echoing ring of metal on fired clay wobbled around me, my skin turning into that of a Dalmatian as earth burst forth from pots, leaving the fledgling plants exposed and helpless on the lawn.

When the battle was won I stood back, pudgy hands on hips and heart scrabbling around inside of me. My mother was watching from the kitchen window, a peculiar expression on her face. She turned away when she found me watching back.

* * *

I have always wondered what she thought in that moment. Was it pride, sorrow, or fear? I expect it was a little of each.

We are not in control of ourselves when we enter this world. Everything about us is derived, in the first instance, from that which our parents give us. Thereafter it is dependent on both our experience and the people who raise us. But deep within, right at the very core of our bodies, there is a being, a creature, who wants to be heard. For most people this creature is largely ignored because they have nothing interesting to say. For others, it's all we can do to try and ignore its indignant screams.

I am more like my mother than my father. I have her fervour, her determination, her will to succeed. But I also have her darkness.

For the most part she has always been able to control her temper, to suppress the desire to strike out, and I suspect my very existence is responsible for this. But there have always been moments when I see her deciding which side of the line to fall; an internal battle of wills that made me understand from an early age there's no such thing as fate. We are what we choose to be.

* * *

Now

'Your brother called.' She lifts the bowl, a chocolate wave falling into a waiting tin.

Half-brother, conceived before our father left his first family for the second. I pick up the spoon, licking around its edge. 'Is there coconut in this?'

'He asked how you were, said you've been avoiding him.' Prising open the oven with one foot she slides the tin inside then closes the door with a thud.

Of course I have. I don't need to speak to him to know what he's going to say. 'And some cardamom? It's really good.'

She cleans her hands on her apron. This one has dozens of stick men parading over her bosom, like mountaineers trying to reach the peak.

'Just because you don't always see eye to eye doesn't mean you can't be accepting of his opinion.'

Now she sounds like one of those ridiculous self-help books she borrowed from the library, every week without fail, for the first year after he left. She devoured them, as if the answer to life itself lay within the tear-stained pages.

She didn't know I would creep out of my bed at night, sit with my back to the wall outside her bedroom, knees tucked under my chin, listening to her sorrow.

I didn't understand how she could rid the house of every last molecule belonging to him and then weep at the injustice of it all. My mistake was thinking she was crying for him, when it fact she was mourning the life she could have had.

My mother turned her soul inside out, forgave my father for what he had done and seized the opportunity to start over. To prove to herself that never again would she rely on someone else, a man, for money. For nearly twenty years she worked as an administrator in a law firm, climbing the ranks to become office manager and collecting friends along the way. Friends with deep pockets and nothing to spend it on.

When they offered her early retirement she spent the best part of a month pacing the length of the kitchen as she deliberated whether or not to take the very generous settlement on offer.

'I don't really see what the issue is,' I had said while observing my mother as she made her way from one side of the room to the other.

'But what will I do?'

'Do whatever you want.'

'That's exactly my point. I've never been able to do what I want; it's always been a case of doing what was necessary, for you.'

At this I had taken a long sip of my coffee, swallowing my answer before it created an argument.

'I mean, you've always had your gardening.'

I nodded, ignoring the bait about my father.

'But I never had any time for hobbies.'

No, because of the burden that is me. I have always been the noose around her neck, the shackles that bind her, although she's never gone so far as to say it. She at least has the fortitude to lay the blame solely at my father's feet.

'Why do you have to do anything? Why not travel the world, learn a new language, take up salsa dancing?'

'Now you're being trite.'

This was true. My mother would no more embark on a round-the-world trip than I would wear a kaftan or pierce my belly button.

And so my mother's kitchen was transformed from a stale, perfunctory room into the epicentre of a thriving business. She was completely self-taught, through the wonders of YouTube, and employed the services of her neighbour's sixteen-year-old son to set up and monitor both a website and Instagram account for her.

She managed to create a thriving business in less time than it will take me to welcome a baby into this twisted, tortured world. But as talented a baker as she is, understanding numbers has always been something of a bugbear for her. That particular talent of mine was inherited from elsewhere among the family tree.

As a result I come to her once a month to go over her books while we talk about anything and everything other than my life and the gaping absence of a significant other.

'Is this all of them?'

My mother nods her reply as I thumb through the stack of receipts, my eye falling on a familiar name. 'I didn't know you were doing a job for Elle's mum.'

'It's nothing really.' My mother's evasive response is enough to pique my curiosity because this so-called nothing is costing over £1,500.

Ever the overachiever, my mother wasn't content with Mary Berry rip offs, instead advertising her wares as 'architectural delicacies', a hybrid between design and taste. Which meant she could charge her clients a fortune, and of course this only made her services all the more desirable.

'What made you change your mind?'

'I don't know what you mean.' The sound of running water camouflages her innocence as she deposits her tools into the sink.

I nudge her aside and plunge my hands into the scalding bubbles. 'Of course not, Mum, my mistake. It's not as if you've made a point of telling me how much you disapprove of my friendship with Elle for... oh, I don't know... ever since we met.'

'I never said such a thing.' She snatches a whisk from my soapy hands, rubs at it with a tea towel and shoves it in the requisite drawer.

'You didn't need to.' Mum didn't like the hold Elle had over me, the way I would always put her first. She'd tried to get me to make new friends, friends with whom I had more in common. She meant more intelligent, less chavvy, but would never actually admit to her own inherent snobbery. The problem was I'd opened the box, peered inside and seen what it was like to be one of the popular kids, even by default. I wasn't going back then and I sure as hell won't do it now.

'Yes, well, that's all in the past and I thought, as we're all to be a family now, I should bury the hatchet, so to speak.' Two dots of colour on her cheeks and I hear the creature within her stir.

'We've been over this.' For someone with relatively little maternal instinct, my mother was adamant that what I was doing was a terrible idea. Part of me wants to tell her the truth, to share my secret with someone who might understand the motive behind my plan. But it's not a risk I'm willing to take.

'Oh, so it's someone else's womb that's carrying their child, is it? Without you there would be no baby.'

We stare at each other in the window's reflection. Eye contact has never been a strong point between us, but, then again, neither were hugs or bedtime stories. She was always too busy for that kind of thing and I was scared she'd squeeze out my tears.

'They're my best friends. Of course I'm going to help them.'

'What happens when it's born?'

I'm keeping him. He's mine.

'What do you mean?'

'It's not as simple as you think.' She looks down at her hands, up at me, then back again. 'I don't see how you can grow something, someone, inside of you, give birth to it, then hand it over and carry on as if nothing has happened.'

This is a rare show of emotion, one I have no idea what to do with. In any normal family I guess this would be the moment when I'd wrap my arms around her, or she me, and then we'd cry and declare our love for one another. But we're not normal.

'I do wish you would think about the consequences of what happens if you change your mind.'

All I do is think about the consequences of my actions. About what will happen after Elle has gone.

'I'm not going to change my mind.'

'No, I don't suppose you will. Always stood your ground, ever since you were tiny. Once you make your mind up about something…'

A talent I learnt from her. If only she knew how much talent I really have.

CHAPTER ELEVEN

Dahlia: Commitment to another person but also a warning against potential betrayal

The silver birches that line the drive have been wrapped in rainbow fabric, a troop of acrobats are tumbling around the side of the house, and the DB5 is being removed from its swaddling cloth and buffed to perfection. No doubt Mr Hart will be arriving to some kind of fanfare, his bulbous girth straining against whatever fancy dress his wife has bullied him into wearing this time.

Elle's parents, like the home she grew up in, are the very epitome of bad taste. So tomorrow's celebrations should be memorable.

'Remind me again why we're here?' Elle looks out of the car window as the front door opens and her mother clips out on stilettos, her Pomeranian dog, Binky, tucked under one arm. I swear the thing doesn't know how to walk; it's either shoved in a handbag or carried wherever it goes.

'Just think of the inheritance.' Easing my legs out of the passenger side, I grip either side of the door and pull myself up to standing. The imprint of my hand on the white paintwork slowly fades to nothing, as if I had never been there.

'Money isn't everything.' She glares at me across the roof then goes over to greet her mother with a pretend kiss on either side of her face.

Of course money is everything. It's the very force that hurls us ever onward. But I've discovered that people who have always had money seem to think it's dispensable. That it doesn't mean anything. That there is more to life than your net worth. I'd love to see Elle go a month without her cleaner. Get her hands dirty scrubbing the shit out of her own toilet rather than paying someone else to clean up her mess.

Mind you, her mother's no better.

'So lovely to see you, Jane,' she simpers at me, her face so frozen it's a wonder her lips can still move.

'You too, Jackie,' I reply. 'How was the cruise?'

'Wonderful. Just what we needed after all the recent stress.'

The stress she is referring to is having to explain to anyone who will listen exactly why her daughter is resorting to the use of my womb instead of her own in order to produce an heir to the Hart fortune. A fortune that was made from the sale of scrap metal rather than inherited over generations, but best not to mention that in Jackie's presence.

I follow them into the main reception hall, with its chequerboard floor and two staircases that curve round either side of an oversized crystal chandelier hanging from a double-height ceiling. I remember the first time I came here, standing in the doorway with my mouth hanging open. Now, as then, there are no unnecessary items left out on display, no dirty footprints on the floor, no speck of dust on the mahogany banisters.

'Didn't you bring a change of clothes?' Jackie's attention falls upon her daughter, along with a swift appraisal of the way Elle's dress is clinging to her curves. Curves Jackie herself used to possess before the Weight Watchers and a little help from a Harley Street doctor.

Elle pulls her stomach in and heads for the kitchen. 'I left straight after school, Mum, but don't worry – I'll make sure I change into something more appropriate before any of your guests arrive.' Jackie trots after her daughter, the head of her miniature dog bouncing as she goes.

The kitchen is my favourite room in the house, the only one that doesn't look as if it's been prepped for a feature in a glossy magazine. The American fridge is polished like a mirror, but to it are stuck photographs and drawings from when Elle and her brother were children, held in place by homemade magnets. In the corner are two battered cushions for Mr Hart's beloved Labradors, and the marble countertops are strewn with evidence of everyday life.

Bifolding doors cover the entire length of one wall, opening out onto a flagstone patio that leads the eye over to where an enormous marquee is being erected for tomorrow's celebrations. As ever, the house is alive with people, people working hard to ensure the Hart party will be talked about for months to come.

I open the fridge and take out a jug of chilled lemonade along with a bottle of champagne and wave them at Elle.

'Have you told them yet?' Jackie asks, sliding onto one of the zebra-print barstools at the kitchen island. She places the dog on the one next to her and adjusts its diamante collar.

'Told who what?' Elle takes the bottle of champagne from me, finds herself a glass and fills it.

'That you're leaving.' Jackie watches Elle take two long mouthfuls, pause, then take another. 'You'd better hurry up as they'll need time to find a replacement.'

'Replacement for what?'

Elle refills her glass and Jackie's eyes slide over to mine. She'll be thinking about the conversation we had a few days ago, when I called to ask if there was anything I could bring for the party and casually let slip that I was a little worried about how Elle was coping at the moment. I hadn't mentioned her drinking; best to let Jackie figure that one out for herself.

'Yes, for when the baby arrives.'

Elle's glass sings against the marble countertop, an expensive spillage hastily wiped away. 'Mum, I fully intend to return to work after the agreed maternity leave is up.'

'Why on earth would you do that? I just assumed...'

'Well, perhaps you shouldn't just assume.' She pulls at the hem of her skirt, runs shaky fingers through her hair. 'Try asking instead.'

'What do you think?' Jackie turns to me, a thousand questions behind her fake lashes.

'Me?'

What do I think? I think Mrs Hart has led a gilded existence, one so far removed from normal people that she's forgotten what it means to actually work for a living, rather than sponging off her husband while he funds all her little hobbies.

'Yes, after all, you're as much the baby's mother as Elle.'

Years of getting whatever the hell she wants means Jackie doesn't have a filter in her tiny brain. I watch as the veins on Elle's neck tighten.

'Mum, how can you say that?'

'It's true. All you've done so far is provide the egg.'

I step in before Elle hurls the glass at her mother. 'I wouldn't go so far as that, Jackie. Elle has been wonderfully supportive.' As much as I would love to see the two of them go a couple of rounds, the focus needs to be on Elle, on making her family aware of the apparent instability I have been hinting at.

'As well she should be. I still can't believe they're not paying you for your troubles.'

Troubles. Because children are an inconvenience to some people. Get in the way of the rest of their lives. But no matter, as everything can be improved with money, preferably insane amounts of it.

'I wouldn't dream of asking them for any money. Elle and Patrick are like family to me, you all are, and I love the idea of helping to bring everyone closer together.' And before long they will be united, both in grief for her and gratitude to me.

'You really are a wonderful woman. I don't know what Elle would have done without you.'

She never would have met him and none of this would be necessary.

Elle makes a sound halfway between a laugh and a cry. It's directed at her mother; I know this because of the other conversation we have had repeatedly over the years. About how her parents have mapped out her entire life for her since the moment she first appeared in the world.

Apparently she didn't cry when she was born, just gazed up at her parents adoringly before she was handed over to the first in a long line of nannies. Elle has never complained, and for the most part gone along with whatever her parents deem best, but her choosing to work has always been a particular irritant for her mother.

Why work when you can stay at home, let your husband take care of you? Why fill your days with snotty, irritable children and pushy parents who think their dimwitted offspring is in fact the next Stephen Hawking? Why do anything at all when you can pay someone else to do it for you?

Personally, I'm siding with Jackie for once, but only because I don't understand the point of going through the agony and supposed heartache if all you're going to do is palm the child off on a stranger at exorbitant cost. Not that I'd let such an indiscretion slip. I'm staying firmly out of this one. No extra stirring needed.

Jackie removes Elle's glass from the countertop and passes it to me. She watches as I take it over to the sink. I rinse it out then use it to water a rather decrepit-looking dahlia that sits on the window ledge. They're not particularly difficult to grow, but I've never tried, because they remind me of the cheap paper lanterns my mother used to buy as Christmas decorations.

'Just you wait and see how exhausting children really can be,' Jackie says. 'Especially girls. Let's just hope you have a boy and be done with it. Far easier are boys. Never had any trouble with your brother.'

'How is Eddie?' I can't resist asking.

Jackie's mouth stretches as wide as the surgery will allow. 'He's coming later this evening after he's finished off some investor meetings in London. He really is just like his father. Ever so good with people as well as numbers.'

He's not, he's an imbecile who can barely spell his own name, let alone balance the books of a multimillion-pound business. Which is why he came to me for help, as long as I promised not to tell his parents how utterly incompetent he really was.

'I don't know how the business would have survived if he hadn't stepped up and offered to help run things, you know, after Frank's little problem last year.'

Frank's little problem was a Brazilian housekeeper called Flavia who had been performing some extracurricular activities on him, resulting in a heart attack and subsequent fitting of a pacemaker. Jackie has been terribly understanding about the whole affair, saying she was grateful really, because her energies could be put to better use elsewhere. Namely the gardener, the yoga instructor and, rumour has it, even the ball boy at the tennis club.

Nothing like a good old cliché to liven up Christmas dinner.

So Eddie dutifully stepped forward and took over the family business. Elle wasn't given a look-in, because, as far as her parents were concerned, a woman's place was in the home. With her husband and children.

Of course, she thinks this is something to battle against rather than embrace. At least she had two parents who loved her, who gave her anything and everything she could ever dream of. At least she had parents who wanted to look after her, rather than constantly telling her never to rely on anyone apart from herself.

'I'm going to take a shower,' Elle announces.

We both watch her leave and I wait for Jackie to start the interrogation.

'How long has she been like this?' She's still watching the doorway and stroking Binky's fur.

'I didn't notice, not at first.' Of course I noticed. How could anyone not see the ashen skin, the lopsided gait to her walk, the way her tongue curled round the edge of her words? The side effects of belladonna are numerous and I couldn't be sure which of them Elle would be afflicted by, but so far, so good.

'And the drinking?'

There it is. The reason why my choice of poison will be so convincing, so easily missed. For nearly every single consequence of taking it can be mistaken for alcohol abuse.

'I'm not sure. But it reminds me of my father.' At this her face constricts. Jackie knows all about my father from the stories my mother tells whenever people asked whether she is married. About his addictive personality, his depression, his inability to remain loyal to his family, all of which were found at the bottom of a whisky bottle.

What I remember is the way he would make me laugh just by wiggling his finger in my direction. The stories he would read me when I was tucked up in bed at night, shining a torch against the wall and making shadow puppets with his hands. But I also remember the arguments. The banging of doors and the awkward silences over breakfast. The pink circles under my mother's eyes and the downward slant of my father's mouth as he kissed me goodbye on his way to work.

People are mainly soft. If you offer up something they think you may not want them to know, it shows both compassion and vulnerability. For this is what makes us human, but it also makes us weak. One quick comparison of my father to her daughter is all I need.

'I think I'll go check on her.' Jackie buries her face in the dog's fur. Like some kind of comforter a child would have, protection against all the monsters hiding under the bed.

'Good idea,' I say, leaving her to think and wonder and come to completely the wrong conclusion.

Guilt. One of those emotions that sneaks up on you when you're unprepared. Like a jack-in-the-box, you know it's there, waiting, but it still manages to shock when it finally explodes in all its glory.

Because on some level I am indebted to Elle and her family. For all the times they pretended not to notice my mother's absence. For the generous birthday gifts, the loan of dresses for social occasions and the sanctuary of their gilded walls whenever the loneliness became too much.

Jackie may be incessantly boring, but she has always been kind, especially to a teenage girl who had no one else to turn to when she first began to bleed. Who had no guidance as to what kind of underwear should be worn with a strapless dress, and didn't know which shade of lipstick turned you from goth to goddess.

Who let you stay with them while your mother was recovering in hospital after driving her car off the road.

Elle asked me if I thought she'd done it on purpose, her eyes never straying from the projector screen as one hand moved between the bucket of popcorn propped up next to us and her mouth.

Apparently my mother had fallen asleep at the wheel. Unaware of the car pulling to the right, so deeply asleep she didn't register the flash of headlights from an oncoming vehicle, the screech of brakes or blare of horn that warned her of what was about to happen.

That's when Elle found out about my mother working late. About how, more often than not, I was left to my own devices while she attended to the needs of men in bespoke suits and women whose handbags were worth more than our car. That's when Elle asked me if there was anything else going on. Anything she needed to worry about.

I couldn't stop the doubts in my mind that questioned whether my mother really had drifted off into oblivion, or whether she had simply had enough of this world, this life. I understand darkness all too well, but mine is of a different variety. My mother carries grief around like an unwanted cloak, the burden that is me, left behind by an absent father. My personal demon has a different agenda altogether.

Instead I told Elle how I wished I could talk to my dad as my hand snuck into hers. The implication clear enough. She was my family and I didn't ever want to let her go. But there was more. The knowledge of what would happen to me if ever things between us were to change. I needed her more than she did me and this understanding terrified me.

Even now, I'll sometimes catch sight of someone who looks like him, or looks like the memory of him, so that I find myself following a stranger, seeking out something in the way they walk, or the tone of their voice, that is similar to his. Hoping that, in fact, that it's him, in disguise, come back for me.

He had loved me. It was one of the few things I felt certain enough about not to question. Every time I closed my eyes and thought of him, of the stories he would tell and the adventures he would create in our own backyard, my heart would sing its belief that his love for me was real.

CHAPTER TWELVE

Lilac: Folkore warns against bringing it into a home as it will bring bad luck and possibly death to those who live there

A noise draws me out to the garden. My eyes search through the marquee, busy with people setting up trestle tables, carrying chattering glasses and bucketloads of flowers across the lawn. I see phlox, lilac and dozens of anemone twisting their heads to the light, towards him. Towards Patrick.

There he is, stripped to the waist and wielding a sledge-hammer in order to erect the poles from which dozens of lanterns will later hang. My skin lifts as though a breeze has disturbed the air.

He finds me, raises one arm in greeting, which tugs at my insides. Happiness and sadness mixed together, made from the sun and the moon and everything in between. It pulls me back and forth, high and low, yes and no. A constant merry-go-round of what could be. But what if he knew? What then? How many secrets to keep and how many to spill?

My gaze lingers at the line of downy hair that runs south from his belly button as he shrugs on a T-shirt and closes the space between us.

'I didn't know you were here.'

'Elle gave me a lift.' My breath snatches in my lungs as he bends to kiss me.

'Oh.' He looks towards the house then back at me. 'How was the journey? Can't have been very comfortable for you in that ridiculous car of hers.'

I bite the inside of my cheek to stop myself from grinning at his concern for me, for our child.

'Not too bad, we missed the worst of rush hour. Elle said you weren't coming until later?'

'Meeting was cancelled and Jackie was talking about chopping down one of the trees to make space for the stage, so I thought I'd better come and make sure Frank hadn't decided to do it himself.'

'There's going to be a stage?'

He gives me a look. 'Frank said something about a burlesque dancer and a giant glass.'

'I hope he's remembered to take his medication.'

I store away the chuckle that follows for another time, when I will turn it over and over in my mind.

'Hang on, which tree was she talking about?'

'The one to the left of the swimming pool.'

It's an *albizia julibrissin*, a Persian silk tree; only able to survive the English winter because of the air vent from the indoor heated swimming pool that provides it with a year-round blanket of warm air. The fan-like flowers that arrive at this time of year are spectacular, the honey produced from their nectar both delicate and sweet. I would buy this house purely for that tree.

'Don't worry, Frank convinced her not to.'

'Frank convinced her not to what?' Elle's father approaches in his usual bandy-legged manner, drink in hand and head gleaming with sweat. 'Hello, my love.' He wraps me in his arms then stands back, directing his gaze at my stomach. 'And how's my favourite grandson doing? Lots of kicking? Is he going to be good enough to play for Chelsea?'

'What if he prefers cricket?' Patrick asks, the idea of trying to play football written in despair all over his wonderful face. While he can remember the statistics, knows the transfer fees and scoring records for every player in the Premier League, he just can't bring himself to worship the game in the same way as his father-in-law.

'What if it's a girl?' I say with a too-bright smile, because no one knows apart from me. No one is supposed to know because that's what Elle decided.

'Yeah, yeah, whatever.' Frank waves away my comment. 'I'll love the little blighter just the same. Still, would be nice to have a boy first, wouldn't it? Keep up the family tradition and all that?'

Diplomacy isn't one of Frank's strong points. But he has never been anything other than kind to me, accepting me into the fold as one of his own. On some level I think he felt sorry for me, understood what it was like to come from a broken home. On another, I suspect he was hoping some of my intellect would rub off on his children so he could raise them to be more self-sufficient than his wife. As much as Jackie loves to spend her husband's money, Frank is forever trying to show his children that he wasn't handed his wealth on a silver platter.

'Frank…' I bring his attention back to me. 'Please tell me you're not going to lay even one finger on the Persian.'

'The what? Oh, the tree. Keep your knickers on, pet. I told Jackie what you told me, that it was bigger than the one in Kew Gardens, and so she's agreed to keep it.'

Of course she has. Because having the biggest, the best, of anything is what's important to her.

'While we're on the subject of plants and the like, I wanted to ask you about my joints.'

'Your joints?'

'Yeah, ever since I had that bleedin' heart attack I've had all sorts of troubles with my knees.'

'I'm not a doctor, Frank.'

'I know that, but if I go to the local quack he'll just give me another load of pills.'

Likes to do things the natural way, does Frank. Ever since his doctor told him the blue pills he had been taking in an attempt to keep up with his young mistress were a contributing factor to both his heart attack and ongoing irritable bowel. So now the East End lad, born and raised on pie, mash and gallons of tea, has developed an interest in homeopathy. As amusing as the concept is, when coupled with the fact that I am the one ultimately providing him with an heir, my position within Frank's inner circle is now pretty concrete.

'Try chilli.'

Frank grunts in response. 'Not supposed to have anything too spicy.'

'You don't have to eat it. Capsaicin is the compound in chilli that gives it heat, but most arthritic creams contain a derivative of it. Otherwise yams.'

'What the bleedin' heck is a yam?'

'It's a starchy tuber not too dissimilar to a sweet potato.' Patrick's answer earns him a look from Frank resembling that of a disgruntled walrus.

'*Bit of a know-it-all,*' is how Frank described Patrick after their first introduction, and their relationship has never really moved beyond tepid acceptance. Not that this is surprising given they have absolutely nothing in common, apart from Elle.

'Walking textbook, you are.' He pats at his forehead with a Union Jack handkerchief. 'I'm only glad some of it brushed off on my Elle. Would've been lost without you, that one.'

This is the thing. While Patrick and I both have IQs at the very top end of the spectrum, I have learnt to feign interest in action-adventure films and a round of darts at the local. Which is why Frank accepts me as one of his own. Try as I have over the years to teach Patrick how to play the game, he just doesn't have it in him to pretend to be anyone other than himself. Which is both inspiring and infuriating.

'But is it safe to ingest?' Patrick asks.

My heart quickens. 'What do you mean?'

'Isn't there a specific way of cooking yams to prevent them from becoming poisonous? I remember you telling me in college that it's all too easy to harm someone with an innocent plant growing in your garden.'

Why is he asking me this? Did I miss something? Did Elle tell him about the tincture? Even if she did, he has no reason to suspect, has he?

'You mean like cyanide?' I tilt my head away from him, pretend to focus my attention on the rows of tables that are now adorned with golden candelabra and mirrored plates.

'Cyanide.' He turns the name around inside his mouth and I can't help but wonder if he's hiding an accusation in there too. 'Which plant does that come from?'

'Hydrangea.' My voice is small, snagging on the growth that has appeared in my throat.

'Like the ones over there?'

I nod without looking. I helped redesign this garden years ago, over the course of a summer when Elle and I would camp out under the willow tree, surrounded by jugs of pink lemonade and fairy cakes smuggled in from the local bakery. While she drew pictures of her future wedding dress, I lay out borders and raised beds, along with a secret garden hidden behind layers of pink and white fuchsia bushes. Unbeknownst to me, she showed them to her parents, who promptly spent a small fortune turning my inner musings into a living, breathing work of art.

The fact that she didn't ask, just took my idea, something that belonged to me, and made it her own, was insulting, but not unexpected. Once a thief, always a thief.

'What's that other one, the famous one from the murder a few years ago?' Frank's joined in now. It's like they're playing a bloody who's who of toxic plants. Batting it back and forth as if it were a game at Wimbledon.

'Deadly nightshade.' Patrick seems to be enjoying the camaraderie with his father-in-law and I will him to stop, to talk about anything, anything at all, other than the ways in which a person can use plants to end the life of another.

'So what's this I heard about a burlesque dancer?' I link my arm through Frank's and attempt to steer him back towards the house, back to the safety of high-gloss tiles and deep-pile carpets.

'Yeah, that's the one.' He's nodding now, like the ridiculous plastic dog stuck to the dashboard of his car. 'But isn't it called something else? Something foreign-sounding?'

Patrick pauses, a line between his brows, and I hold my breath, seeing his moment of realisation as if in slow motion. 'Belladonna.'

My legs buckle underneath me and I sink to the ground.

'You okay?' Patrick's frown now altogether different.

No, I'm not. I'm anything but okay.

'I'm fine, it's just the heat.'

I allow them to help me to a nearby seat, gratefully accept the glass of water that is brought, and bat away their concerns. The thoughts swell behind my eyes, tightening my vision into a single point.

I know how I can weaken her, kill her, but I don't know if I can still use it. Is Patrick trying to warn me somehow? But warn me of what? Surely he can't suspect and, even if he did, why not be angry about it? Why not confront me?

Or is this simply an indicator that I need to be more careful? For even though belladonna doesn't show up on blood tests, there would be signs, indicators that some kind of poison had contributed to her death, should anyone feel the need to perform an autopsy.

I need to be smarter. Find another way.

* * *

As much as I hate to admit it, the marquee looks incredible. Soft-pink linens highlighted with golden thread, antique lanterns suspended above the tables and fairy lights wrapped around the stem of each flower-filled vase. At one end a dance floor awaits, at the other a seating area with plump sofas and low-level tables. Dozens of waiters skim around the guests, refilling glasses without needing to be asked.

I don't need to know where he is in order to find him. It's as if he has some kind of homing beacon recognisable only to me. Years of watching him from the periphery of my vision; the way his eyes crinkle when he laughs, the scratch of chin when he feels uncomfortable, looks heavenward when seeking an answer he can't quite find. I could pick him out from a crowd of thousands, so a few hundred is no trouble at all.

He's in the far corner, elbows on the edge of the table and hands clasped as he exchanges conversation with one of the ladies from what I like to call Jackie's liposuction club. I imagine Patrick is doing his very best to remember whether this is Eileen whose husband spends most of his time in South America, or Beatrice, who fills her days with an online gambling addiction. But his focus is over by the bar, on someone who has been holding his attention from the very first moment they met.

'She's drunk,' my mother says as we watch Elle toss back her head, offering up her throat in sacrifice to the man at her side.

'I know,' I reply, aware of Patrick rising from his table and going over to his wife.

'I'm guessing this isn't a new development?' She's looking at me now. I need to be careful.

'It's not a problem.' My go-to reaction with my mother is defensive. Barriers up, triggers at the ready. Even more so when Elle is involved.

'Patrick doesn't seem to think so.'

He's there now, teeth bared in a false greeting to the man who has been salivating all over his wife. One arm curls around Elle's waist as Patrick tries to convince her to come with him.

Bad idea. Elle doesn't really like being told what to do, even less so when she's being given the attention she thinks she is entitled to. A triangle of light comes between them as she tries to step away, the tension radiates up his arm as he resists. Words are exchanged, the man holds up his hands in resignation as Elle looks from him to her husband, then strikes Patrick across the face. He lets go and she stumbles against the bar, upset glasses betraying the situation as all the room's eyes turn to stare.

'Definitely a problem.'

I'd forgotten for a moment my mother was standing next to me, witnessing the chaos in her own sweet way. She never under-stood their partnership, was as surprised as I when the wedding invitation arrived. I say surprised, but it was more like someone had removed my heart with a rusted fork, then ripped it apart and scattered the still-throbbing pieces in the sewer.

'I might go and see if I can help.'

Her hand stops me, reminds me we mustn't meddle in other people's affairs. Elle's cousin is there now, arms spread wide to shield them both from view.

'Leave me the fuck alone!' Elle's voice dances through the silence, its tone uglier than the words.

Patrick yanks her out of the marquee like she's some crazed alley cat, hissing and spitting her insults, which make their way into the ears of all who sit and listen. His face has lost all meaning, a painted-on mask hiding his secrets. I know that mask, I wear it every day.

'There you are, Jane, thank goodness.'

My mother and I turn as Elle's mother approaches, busy with the jewels around her scraggy neck. The one place the surgeon can't erase her years.

'I was wondering if I could have a word with you both.'

111

'Of course, Jackie.' My mother puts on her own mask, concealing her amusement for another day. 'Is everything all right with Elle?'

'No, I don't think it is. I need your help.'

'Absolutely.' I lead Jackie away without so much as a nod in my mother's direction. 'Anything at all.'

This was all supposed to be behind me. It was stupid to come back. But I never could resist them. I still can't.

* * *

I lie awake, listening to the sounds of the house and talking to him, my baby, my precious boy. I tell him not to worry, that I will figure out a way for us to be together.

My hands trace the memories of scars now stretched tight across my mountainous stomach. Reminders of the pain I had to endure. Reminders of why it is I find myself carrying a child I never knew I wanted.

Is he the key to it all? Is he the reason for all that has happened? Do I need anything more than the chance to love him the same way my father loved me?

Can I find a way to keep him without setting my demons free?

Leave no trace. First rule of how to kill your best friend: ensure there's nothing that could possibly put you under suspicion. Which means scrolling through the internet for ways and means to dispose of a body is out of the question. Along with all the other natural poisons already catalogued, considered and dismissed.

Killing someone's the easy part. Not being found out takes a bit of extra work.

CHAPTER THIRTEEN

Cornflower: Worn by young men in love; if the flower faded too quickly, it was taken as a sign the man's love was not returned

The hate comes out of me with every jut of the spade into the earth, giving way to only the movement of limb, the ache of muscle and the grey-blue light settling into dusk. But he's here, always here, even when all other thoughts drift away.

Patrick. My curse, my millstone, my one and only. I want to love another but my heart refuses to listen. I tried to leave, I could again, but he would keep calling me back, invading my dreams with taunts and false promises. I know I should have stayed gone, but I also know he belongs to me.

I should have killed her when I had the chance.

So why can't I? Why can't I bring myself to do it? There are so many ways, so many, many ways to kill a person and I know them all.

A knife, a razor, a shard of broken glass. All will cut through flesh. A bullet, a car, a baseball bat that could crush and break her skeleton into a thousand pieces. Peanuts. Her own personal poison, slipped into a curry I could cook just for her.

How simple it is to end a life, if only you dare step over the invisible line put there by your own morality. I have examined every possible angle, I see it with each and every step I take. A nightmare that follows me wherever I go, even to the other side of the world. I thought once I was gone the whispers in my mind would fade away, and for a moment they did. Only to come screaming and raging in the middle of a civilised meal between ex-lovers.

'Aren't you supposed to be cultivating those, not destroying them?'

'Hello, Robin.' I stand at the arrival of my brother, look down at the twisted stems that droop from my hands. I let them fall, seesawing through the air to land in a broken heap in the crevice already dug.

He comes over, encircles my waist and turns me around so that one of my feet kicks out behind. It's something of a ritual; after years spent trying to pick up his older sister, since the moment he discovered he was strong enough to do so, he hasn't stopped.

'Put me down.' But the laughter overtakes my words and he spins once more.

'You've been ignoring me.' His voice trails behind then catches us up.

'Seriously, put me down or I'll be sick.'

'Or I'll drop you, fatty.'

I land half a punch on his arm and his mouth forms a perfect O in mock pain.

'Carry those over to the greenhouse, would you?'

He picks up my garden tools and follows me along the path he helped lay last spring, when the earth sucked at the heels of our wellies, complaining at having not been turned over in so long. I look across to the perimeter fence, beyond which lies the river and its perambulating babble that reminds me of idle summer days spent punting while at university. Punnets of strawberries and glasses full of Pimms to be enjoyed as I watched Patrick navigate the waterways, face taut with concentration because he refused to ever fall in.

It all comes back to him. Everywhere I look, every memory I own weaves through my soul and offers one of them up as some kind of demented sacrifice.

'Looks like you've been busy,' Robin says, hanging the spade on its allotted nail and laying the other tools on the workbench next to rows and rows of poppy seedlings. Slice those pods open and out spills a milky liquid capable of doing all sorts of harm. A gift of sorts for my best pal, my buddy. A gift I'm still trying to decide whether or not to give.

'I needed the distraction.' I open one of the greenhouse vents, the stretch pulling around my side, another reminder that I am not as I once was.

Robin watches my movement, sees the reveal of skin between my clothes.

'Am I allowed to talk about it?' he asks.

'Not unless you've something different to say.' Everyone has an opinion on my situation, my decision, especially my younger brother. He laughed in my face when I first told him, helping himself to another round of roast potatoes while both our mothers hovered on the edge of the conversation. When I didn't correct him he put down his knife and fork to look at me straight, the same game I taught him to wheedle out a lie. I didn't blink and he pushed his plate away, which told me everything and more.

'Do you want to stay for tea?' I turn the watering can around so its handle faces the right way, then go back along the path to the house. The kitchen door tuts against the pot of sweet peas propping it open and I lift my face to the darkening sky. Dark curls of cloud slink over the sun, a breeze beginning to stir, and the first droplet of rain splats onto the stone at my feet.

'Depends,' he says, removing his boots and padding over to the fridge. 'What have you got?' He finds the tray of tinctures I was keeping for Elle, taking one out and holding it up to the window.

'That reminds me, I need to get rid of those.' Stay calm. I hang in the doorway, half in, half out.

'Out of date?' He goes to remove the lid and I step forward, snatch the vial away.

'Something like that.'

A pause, a question hovering in the silence, one I cannot have him ask. 'Your mum told me what happened at the party.'

I don't doubt it for a second.

Turning back to the fridge he opens a Tupperware box and tears off a chicken leg, gnawing at it like some kind of Neanderthal. Ever since he was small it has been impossible to marry the amount of food he eats with the distinct lack of fat on his body. A genetic inheritance I am fortunate enough to share with him, but that's where the similarity ends, for there isn't an ounce of malice running through his veins. It would seem I sucked up enough of that for the both of us.

'So is it true? Is the crown finally slipping?'

Robin has never been a fan of Elle. He was about ten when they first met; I took him with me to her parents' house and she was out by the pool, resplendent in a lurid pink bikini. I had assumed that, like all other males of the species who came into contact with her, my brother would be instantly won over, but instead he whispered to me he thought Barbies were boring and asked if he could have a kickabout with Elle's brother instead.

I have adored him ever since.

'So what are you really doing here?'

He wipes his fingers on a tea towel then pulls out a small blue notebook with gold stitching around its edge and chucks it at me.

'Mum found this when she was clearing out the loft, thought you might like to have it.'

'I haven't thought about this in years.' That's a lie. I think about it every time I catch sight of someone who reminds me of my father. Every birthday, every Christmas, every time I want to ask my mother, where did he go? Why did he leave and never come back?

* * *

Twenty-five years ago

'Hello, chicken,' Daddy said as he pulled me to him. He still smelt the same and I had a sick feeling in my tummy again, only this time it felt nice.

'What happened to your beard?'

A low chuckle as he rubbed at the hint of stubble along his jaw. 'Sara wasn't a fan. Said it was too prickly.'

'I liked it. It made you look distinguished.'

'Did it now? I missed you, my clever, clever girl.'

I could feel a smile stretch across my cheeks as he lifted me high and twirled me around and around, my legs kicking free and all the world a giddy blur.

'David?'

An unfamiliar voice cut into our joy and my feet returned to the earth. I leant into Daddy as he led me along the path, a piece of gravel worming into my red-buckled shoes. It pressed against my heel with every step.

The woman in the doorway held out her hand. It was small and soft with a sparkly ring on one finger. Her nail varnish was pink and her skin smelt of freshly cut grass.

When she smiled at me I felt sad for Mummy and a bit naughty as I knew I wasn't supposed to like Daddy's new friend.

'Why don't you come inside and meet Buster?' she said, hand reaching out for mine.

I glanced at Daddy, a question inside of me all bundled up with an idea too wonderful to admit.

'Go on.' He grinned, then gave a gentle shove at my back.

I went into the house, following the trail of gingerbread that had escaped from the oven, teasing me in with the taste that was in my open mouth. I turned the corner to find a neat, square kitchen with French doors open to the woods beyond.

I heard him before I saw him. A gentle *thup, thup, thup* as tail hit basket followed by the shortest of yaps. Hands balled tight, my feet jumped on the spot, my own delight too much for the pup who half-ran, half-skidded over to me, coiling round my legs as I laughed and laughed.

'Is he real, Daddy?' I asked as Buster licked my ankles, his nose exploring my new scents. 'Is he really, really real?' I had asked Mummy for a dog, but she always said no as they were too much like hard work and, besides, you can't put a nappy on a dog.

'Of course he's real,' Daddy said. 'Would you like to take him for a walk?'

'Yes, please.' My brow crinkled. 'But Mummy will be upset if I get my new shoes dirty.'

'Which is why we got you these.' Sara held out a pair of bright-blue wellies, each with a flower painted on its toes.

She knew about the flowers. I looked from her to Daddy and back again. Already I felt like a traitor.

'And when you come back we'll have fish fingers and chips for tea.'

'I'm not allowed chips. Mummy says they make you fat.' I looked at the round ball of her stomach. 'Have you been eating lots of chips?'

She laughed, the sound like hundreds of tiny bells, and I wondered if she was a princess or maybe a fairy Daddy had found at the bottom of the garden.

'Mummy told me you were a whore.' The laughter stopped. 'But I think she's lying.' Yes, I was definitely a traitor.

Daddy and Sara shared a look. One of those grown-up looks they think children don't understand. It meant I'd said something I wasn't supposed to, but they didn't seem upset or angry. If anything they looked pleased.

'Come on, chicken.' Daddy helped me off with my shoes. 'I'll let you hold Buster's lead for a little while.'

I slipped my feet into the wellies and clicked my heels together.

'What do you think of Sara?' Daddy let Buster off his lead and watched him dart into a nearby bush. I hoped he wouldn't catch a rabbit. I liked rabbits.

'She's very pretty.' I held tight to his hand. I never wanted to let go.

'She is.'

'Is she clever too?'

He smiled down at me. 'Why do you ask?'

I kicked through fallen leaves, sending them into the air and watching them twirl back down again. 'Mummy says God never gives someone everything, to make it fair. That's why some people are pretty and some are clever, like me.'

'What else does your mother say?'

He was annoyed. I could tell because he said 'mother' and the word got caught in his teeth. I wasn't sure what else to say so I picked up a stick and began to poke at the ground.

'Careful.' Daddy stilled my hand. 'Look closer and see what you've found.'

I crouched down, damp earth cool on my skin. I breathed in its mossy scent, could taste the rain that had come and gone in the night. A ladybird sat on a leaf, one leg raised as if it was waving.

'She has five spots.' I moved closer and her wings popped out from her back as she took off into the wind.

'Do you want to know her real name?'

'*Coccinella septempunctata*,' I answered, searching for the little bug but losing her in the trees.

119

'Well, at least all that time in the library is good for something.' Daddy whistled and Buster came hurtling back to us, clods of mud under his paws and ears sticking out like propellers.

'That's what I wanted to tell you,' I said. 'I've been writing a book all about flowers and I still have some of the bulbs we were going to plant together. I promise not to forget what you taught me so that I can still be a gardener when I grow up.'

'Oh, my precious girl.' His sigh was deep and rich. 'You could be so much more.'

'That's what Mummy says. But I like flowers. I thought you'd be pleased.' I felt the bubble deep within, the type that would rise through my throat and then burst into a thousand, thousand tears.

'Don't cry, chicken.' He bent down and wiped away my sadness. 'I am pleased. I could only ever be pleased with you. But you shouldn't be stuck in a library, you should be outside in the park, creating adventures with your friends.'

'I don't have any friends.'

Daddy's face went blank.

'They say I'm weird.'

'You're not weird.' He looked angry again.

'But I am different.'

'You are unique and special and brilliant and don't ever let anyone tell you otherwise.'

'But you're not unique. Nor is Mummy. So why am I? How can I be not unique?'

Daddy thought for a while. I could see he was thinking of just the right words to say. I waited for him to be ready.

'How would you like a change of scene?'

I looked around.

'Do you mean go back to your house?'

'Yes. But not just for today.'

The gasp ran into my mouth before I even knew it was there.

'Would you like to come and live with us?'

120

I nodded. Then stopped. 'What about Mummy?'

'Well, I don't think there would be room.'

'Yes, there would. You told me there were three bedrooms in your new house. One for you and Sara and one for me, which means there would be one spare for Mummy.'

Daddy stood with his hands in his own pockets. He was thinking again.

'Sara isn't fat, chicken. She's pregnant. You're going to be a big sister.'

*　　*　　*

That was the last time I ever saw my father. Six years old with all my life still to live. He dropped me home then drove off into the approaching dusk, the rear of his car blending into the shadows that crept out of the woods. I remember feeling scared, as if the sun was going to set right on top of the car and push him into the earth. I remember the cry of a wounded fox, a recurring nightmare that it came into my bedroom and tried to steal me away; the warm milk I was given to lull me back to sleep.

*　　*　　*

Now

The first picture inside is of a cornflower. My father's favourite and the one flower I come back to again and again. It's why I drink Lady Grey tea, the blue petals intermingled with ashen leaves a constant reminder of the void he left behind.

It was my way of staying connected to him. The book, then the tea. I learnt everything I could, wrote it all down in my immature script. Crayon drawings accompanied by rainbows and bumble bees that gave way to wonder about where and when plants were first discovered.

But I was never content with only knowing part of the answer, and over the years my obsession grew as I learnt the ways in which nature could harm as well as heal. That if you only knew how best to manipulate it, some plants were just as capable of killing as they were of alleviating aches and pains.

The notebook is where it all began. I must have over a hundred that line one wall of my workshop, each cataloguing the interest that spilled out into the garden of my childhood home. My mother gave me free rein, understood in her own way that it was something I needed to do. To first pull apart and then rebuild the garden he so loved. As if my talent for horticulture kept me close to him somehow.

I wonder if she knew anything about the plants I grew, that still grow outside her kitchen window. About the truth hiding behind the veil of my chosen fauna. Sometimes I think she's pretending not to see, not to recognise herself in me.

The sky is lifting a little and I push wide the door, tipping my chin to bathe in a shaft of sunlight. The rain has moved on, its freshness mixing with the smell of pickles, cheddar and mayonnaise. My stomach wriggles in recognition and I look over to where Robin is in the middle of constructing a triple-decker sandwich.

'Do you think he'll ever come back?' he asks, adding sliced tomatoes to his feast.

I don't. I do. I don't have a bloody clue. I've turned every single possibility up and over and in on itself over the years, but none of them makes sense.

'He was sick, you have to remember that.' Squatting down, I pick off one of the sweet peas, breathe in its lightness. I pull away the petals from their stamen, let all but one spiral fall to the ground. 'He's gone, we have to accept that he chose to leave us all. Besides, even if he is still alive, why would he come back now?'

'To meet his grandchild.'

'It's not mine, remember?' Soft petal on my lips, soft like his. I ache for him, I am lost without him.

'No? You sure about that?' He bites down, a globule of mayonnaise leaking from between the layers. Like the milky blood of an opium poppy.

The idea first appeared as suddenly as all the others, firing along my synapses as the possibility took shape. Laudanum can be mixed with alcohol, and I suppose its presence in Elle's bloodstream could be explained away as a painkiller addiction. A possibility, but now Robin knows what's growing in my greenhouse and I don't want to make him complicit.

'I'm doing this for them.'

'By them, you mean Patrick.'

A flash of his face in my mind. There has to be something I can do. Something that won't arouse suspicion. An accident? But how?

'I don't know what you're talking about.'

'Sure. Because you haven't been in love with him for the past ten years.'

'Nine.' Nine years, four months and seventeen days, but who's counting?

'Exactly.'

He's always known, understood in that way only a sibling can. Because he is the only one who can make me laugh one minute and want to strangle him the next for coming into my house and emptying the contents of my fridge without asking. He is my blood and one of the few people in this world I haven't thought about the best way to kill.

'You always did know exactly what you wanted.'

I told myself that running away was what I wanted. Because it's something I can never unsee: the sight of Patrick on their wedding day, besotted with her. It's why I fled to the other side of the world. But it was always too difficult, staying away. Because at some point one of them always managed to lure me back into their lives. That's when I realised they could survive without me, that they changed and adapted to fill the space I had left. But I

123

wanted them to need me. Which is the real reason I always came back.

'We keep coming back to each other. Surely that has to mean something?' I trace the contours of the sweet pea's petal, thin lines running from one edge to the other. When I hold it to the light it changes, the lines more like veins underneath skin. If you cut someone they will bleed. Could I make her bleed? Would she do it to herself, or could I at least make it look that way?

'It means you're a masochist. Even you're not completely impervious to her charms, despite knowing that underneath it all she's only friends with you because it makes her feel better about herself. Makes her believe she never did anything wrong in the first place.'

He thinks I'm talking about Elle. He still thinks my loyalty lies with her. Even Robin doesn't know of my wickedness. Of the thoughts I have about so many people, people I don't even know. A stranger on the bus with a crested tie and wiry hair; the woman at the deli counter who can't decide between honey-roast or apple-smoked ham; the delivery boy who still smells of the person he lay with the night before. I have planned for each and every one, but never followed through.

Sometimes I fear I will be like the flowers I surround myself with. That I'll wither and rot before anyone knows any part of me.

'I don't want to be alone.' I toss the petal into the wind, watch it flee from the one who did it harm. I want someone to have touched every freckle, every patch of my skin. To understand me better than I do myself. But that would mean revealing the darkest part of my soul, and who could love that?

Robin wraps his arms around my waist, gives my bump a gentle rub. 'You're not alone and yet for some reason you always try to be.'

'I'm not going to leave again.' I want to. I want to flee to the furthest point from here; to start again, to create an altogether better life.

'What makes this time any different?'

There's a future, with him, with Patrick, so close I can almost taste it.

'I've bought a house, haven't I?'

'So? A home isn't just bricks and mortar, it's who you fill it with that counts.'

I know, I know, I know. Can't you see that's what I've been trying to do all along? Can't you see that I'm trying to make the family fit?

'You can lie to yourself all you like, pretend no one else sees what's really going on, but I know you.'

Not as well as you want to, little brother. There are some secrets even you're not allowed to know.

CHAPTER FOURTEEN

Orchid: Women in Ancient Greece believed that if the father of their unborn child ate orchid tubers, the baby would be a boy

Patrick is trying to say something, but the patio doors are shut so I can only guess at the syllables passing over his lips as I watch. I don't think he can see me as I can him, his eyes following Elle as she moves around the kitchen, collecting her belongings. He goes as if to kiss her goodbye but she doesn't give him the chance, skipping past and out of my sight.

I crouch down behind the oak tree as he steps out into the garden. I should go home. Turn around and retrace my steps back through the woodland that runs across the back of the property. My intention wasn't to come today. I was supposed to follow along the river and into the village to get some liquorice for when Robin and I go to visit Gramps tomorrow. But my internal compass keeps pointing this way, and the chance to observe, to watch him for a moment more, is a lure I'm powerless to resist.

So I slip round to the front of the house, smooth down my

dress so it clings to the swell of my stomach, and slick on a smile as I ring the bell, waiting for permission to enter.

'You've just missed Elle.' The door swings wide and I drink in the sight of him as he blinks away the morning light.

He looks so tired. In need of some attention instead of being neglected by his wife. But then he's not the only one Elle's been neglecting.

'Come in.' He steps aside to let me pass. 'I was just making a fresh pot.'

I follow him along the hallway, the marble tiles a welcome cool on the soles of my feet. I don't need to turn my head to see the pictures that hang from the walls, cataloguing their lives together. I am in there too, camouflaged by their happiness, a memory of how they first met.

The kitchen links into the den, its sunken floor and oversized wood burner hanging from a double-height ceiling more sugges-tive of the Hollywood Hills than the English countryside. A glass coffee table at its centre, on top of which sits a magenta orchid I gifted them last time I was here. I can smell the remnants of Patrick's breakfast: bacon sandwiches with brown sauce, never red. His staple diet along with pasta and toast that final year at university, a diet we shared along with our hopes for the future.

He moves around the kitchen, stacking plates in the dishwasher and rinsing out the teapot before adding fresh leaves. So simple, so everyday a scene, but I blink away the bitterness because it was supposed to be our togetherness, our memories.

'Actually, I'm glad you're here.' I see him pour an amber line of tea from pot to cup, add milk then come over to me. 'There's something I've been meaning to talk to you about.'

I wrap two palms around the china, squeeze tight the burn. 'What's that then?'

His own cup rises, words dulled as the rim touches his mouth. 'What would happen if we changed our minds?'

'Changed your minds about… the baby?'

'It's awful, isn't it?' Cheeks puff full as he shakes his head, eyes darting to mine then safely away. 'I shouldn't have said anything. Forget I said it at all.'

'I thought this was what you wanted?'

A momentary tightening of his fingers around the cup, stretched white at the knuckles. 'It's what she wanted. What she said she wanted, but now I'm not so sure.'

'But you and Elle have been trying for years to start a family.' I'm stating the obvious. He hates it when people tell him what he already knows, but the shock of it, of his admission, has left me somewhat misaligned.

'Exactly. But instead of bringing us together, creating a family, it's pushing us apart.' He sips his tea, smarting at its heat, then sips again. 'Perhaps none of this was supposed to happen. Perhaps Elle and I shouldn't have done what we did.'

This is so much more than I expected. But I need to be sure.

'I really don't follow.'

'The charts have gone.'

Now this is interesting.

'I thought you hated the charts.'

'I do. I mean, it all became so undignified. Regimented.'

'I don't need to know the details of your sex life, Patrick.' I do, I do, I do.

'That's just it. There isn't one. Not anymore.'

Excellent news.

'At first it was a relief. After so many years of only ever being physical because of what it could become, I was exhausted.'

Too. Much. Information. And yet I want to know it all. She's already told me of the arguments about him refusing to leave the office when she was ovulating. Of the rage whenever she began to bleed. Of how sick she became of people asking when they were going to start a family; even more so when the questions stopped.

But Patrick rarely offers up anything quite so intimate. Even to me.

'So what happened?'

He hesitates and I wonder if he's found out more about Harry than I had intended at this stage.

'She accused me of having an affair.'

Pot, kettle, black, but I won't be the one to tell him. Not yet, not when there's so much more fun to be had.

'What did you tell her?' I lean against the countertop, arch my back and look up at him as I sip my tea.

'I didn't,' he replies and I notice his gaze lingering on my bosom. 'The whole concept of me cheating on her is just ludicrous.'

This isn't really about who is or isn't having an affair. This is about Patrick being challenged. About his moral compass being called into question. Something I knew would irritate, would wriggle its way into his subconscious and slowly mutate until it made him question everything about their relationship.

He pours his drink away. Leaves the empty cup on the side, not bothering to wipe away the brown stain that slinks towards the edge. Two hands grip the work surface; shoulders rise then fall before he speaks.

'What if she does change her mind? Or what if I do?'

'You won't.'

He turns then to look at me. 'I wasn't talking about the baby.'

Oh, my. Surely he can't mean…? But what if he does? And there it is once again, my own sinister flash of hope, and I have to push it away, not allow it to take hold for, if I do, it will be too much, too crippling to bear.

'Explain.'

'I have my concerns about her current state of mind.'

The shard of pain in what's left of my heart. For hope is fortune's fool. Nothing good can ever come of wishing for something you cannot have. Yet I am incapable of stopping. Of allowing myself any peace. Why? Why do I persist in this godforsaken longing? Why can't I control the beat of my heart, the pull of my soul?

'You mean the drinking.'

'You noticed.' A pointless smile, like a child admitting a mistake for which it isn't really sorry.

'I'm not an idiot, Patrick.' Sometimes I hate him as much as I do her. For making me feel. For making me so wretched that I allow the darkness to tempt me. It is his fault as much as mine.

'No, no. Of course you're not. And I was going to talk to you about it.'

No, you weren't.

'But then she seemed to be getting better these past few weeks. Since her father's birthday.'

Since I swapped over her tinctures. Ever since Patrick and Elle's father had their chummy conversation about poisonous plants I have been supplying Elle with nothing more than Rescue Remedy. Got to keep up the pretence, at least until I figure out a better way to dispose of her.

'So what's happened?' As if I don't already know. Sometimes it can be so dull pretending not to know it all. A part of me is tired, so tired of the game, but I've never quit before and I certainly don't intend to now. Not when the pieces seem to be falling neatly into place.

'Come with me.' He leads me through to the laundry room, the air laden with tumble-dried clothes, and opens one of the boot cupboards to reveal half a dozen boxes filled with empty glass bottles.

'These are all hers?' I don't remember there being so many. But then again I don't doubt that several of these were shared with someone other than her husband.

'Well, I certainly didn't drink them.'

Does he suspect? Does he see her for what she really is?

'You're sure she hasn't had people round while you've been away?' She has, but not who he would think of, because Patrick would never, even for a second, suspect that Elle would be unfaithful to him. Especially with someone so inferior in every conceivable way.

130

'I asked her, but she was adamant.'

He isn't yet ready to see. Because he knows Elle doesn't like to be left alone for long. Certainly not while he goes on a business trip to the Far East in order to tie up a lucrative deal she pushed him towards. Another chapter in his life all done and dusted over saki and sushi.

'You showed her the bottles?'

'I'm hardly going to confront my wife about her alcohol problem by lining up the evidence in the laundry room.'

My wife. As if I don't know her. As if he's trying to explain her to me.

'So how do you know they're all hers?'

'They were hidden all over the house.'

'Where?'

I know exactly where, because I am the one who set up the game of hide and seek. One of the advantages of working from home, especially as I have a spare key to the house, just in case Elle should ever lock herself out of her castle.

'The gym, the study, even behind the vanity unit in the guest en suite.'

'What made you look?'

He closes the cupboard door, the weight of him sinking into it. 'She's never hit me before. I hated her for it, for how it made me want to hit her back. Something shifted between us then and I wanted to understand what it was.'

Because he always has to understand, just like me. I get it now. That longing, that keenness within that won't go away. To have this child growing inside of me has shown me a side of Elle I could never empathise with before, never see the significance of.

'This is the first time in her life she hasn't got exactly what she wanted and she doesn't know how to deal with it.'

He flinches at my words. 'What does that even mean? I have sacrificed everything for that woman, changed my future in order to make her happy. I even agreed to bleach my feckin' teeth.' He smacks a fist against the door and I dare myself to reach for him, to lay my hand on his.

'You're being too hard on yourself. None of this has turned out the way we expected.'

'Your life seems pretty well on target.'

'Because all I've ever wanted is to be barefoot and pregnant, living in a house by the river with a white picket fence.'

He chuckles, a warm note fighting its way in among all the pain. 'It does have a white fence, doesn't it?'

And a garden big enough for a playhouse, with a winding path that leads you to the river, where he could sit and fish with his son. Our son.

'I've been doing some research.'

'Does this mean you're finally quitting the dark forces of private equity?'

'If only. No, I meant into Elle's condition. Her symptoms don't necessarily tally with what I've discovered.'

This could be a problem. Patrick is nearly as thorough as I am. Then all of a sudden there's a shift inside of me, but not one of fear.

'Oh.' It's him, my baby. He's trying to talk to me, to let me know I'm not alone.

'What is it? Is something wrong?' One arm around my waist, the other against the base of my spine. The concern behind his eyes as they flicker between my own. The love he has for his unborn child so raw, so fragile.

'He's moving around quite a bit.'

'He?'

There. A tiny gasp of wonder and I've got him.

'Just a feeling, but of course I could be wrong.'

'A mother's gut is usually right.'

He sees me as the mother. Does this mean on some level he knows? Or does he remember what happened that night? Oh, how I want him to remember, to relish it, to need it to be true.

'I never expected to love him.' The words tumble forth before I realise I've thought them. It's too much, too close to the absolute truth, and I try to move away, but Patrick takes my hand and pulls me back. His arms come around me and he drops his head to my shoulder. The nearness of him hurts.

'Thank you,' he whispers, and I have to escape, to take his touch from me.

'For what?' He shouldn't be thanking me, wouldn't if he knew what I really wanted. The harm I intend to cause.

'For being you.'

Fear courses down my spine as I put my hands to my belly and close my eyes. My flesh feels cold, like the world all around me. How can I bring a child into my darkness? How can I protect him from me?

'Sometimes I think about how different things could have been.'

I can feel him watching me as he speaks, but don't dare open my eyes.

'In what way?' In so many ways. If only I hadn't left that night. If only I had resisted the temptation of another. If only I had told him how deeply, how completely, I love him. But would that have made it worse? To be rejected? To lose him completely?

'What if you hadn't offered to help Elle, to help us?' His voice recedes a little and I know it's safe to look. He's gone back into the kitchen, is staring across the freshly mown lawn to the pergola that is covered by trailing wisteria, its lilac petals now gone until next spring. At my suggestion they have put a loveseat underneath, where it catches the morning sun. The perfect place to sit with a newborn, if only this were my home.

'Does it worry you?' A line creases his brow and I wonder where he has gone, what pictures are forming inside his mind.

'What?' I go to stand next to him and the garden seems to stir, as if waiting for the moment to change. I can feel the warmth of

133

his skin so close to mine, can taste his scent, hidden underneath laundry powder and shower gel.

'The unknown? The future?' He looks down at me, a slight dip of his chin, and I long to close the space between us, to kiss him, to be lost in him.

'It's all I ever think about.'

Am I afraid of this baby? Or am I afraid of what I will become? Will he love me, the way I love him? I have tried so hard not to love, but it is beyond my control and I am afraid it stops me from being safe. This is a love I do not understand, tangled up with an unfathomable fear of the unknown. Now I see death everywhere I turn, but death that is not of my hand and it is all directed at him. At my child.

The thoughts astonish me. They follow me everywhere and I cannot make them stop.

'Are you all right?'

'I'm fine,' I say, rushing from the room and into the downstairs cloakroom. Locking the door behind me and turning on the taps at the sink before plunging my hands into the enveloping cool.

It reminds me of the night I found Elle, thirteen years ago, when she rang and asked me to go over to her parents' house, saying she needed my help.

* * *

Thirteen years ago

I called out as I entered her bedroom, taking in the unmade bed, the open window letting in the rain, and a trail of discarded clothes leading my eye across to the en suite. The door was shut, but from under it I could see a telltale line of yellow.

I heard the soft flow of a tap turned on. Fingers around the handle, I paused, picturing my mother on the other side instead of my best friend. Door open, I was bathed in fragrant steam that made me think of a wildflower meadow after a thunderstorm, but this rain was hot, too hot even if it were midsummer instead of spring. My gaze fought through the wet to see her, skin as pink as a baby kangaroo with hair stuck to her sweaty cheeks and a near-empty bottle of gin hanging from her left hand.

Plunging my arm under the surface, teeth clenched against the scalding water, I pulled out the plug, watching as the steam unfurled from Elle's naked body. I clasped my hands together under her arms and around her chest, feet slipping on the tiled floor as I heaved the weight of her up and over the rim of the tub.

She began to sob as I covered her with a towel, her body curling in and around. I helped her to stand, aided her hobbled movements into her room and onto the bed. Slowly I patted dry her scalded form, reading her face for any sign of a clue. Her eyes were open but not there, not seeing the person in front of her. Her limbs were as flaccid as a doll, no objection made as I slipped a nightgown over her head and began to plait her hair.

Under the covers she lay, childlike in her slumber, with whispers on her lips too secret to share.

I gathered up her clothes, went back to the bathroom and emptied the last of the gin down the sink. It was then that I saw it, staring up at me from the bottom of the bin. A stick of white with two lines of blue. Two lines that belonged to Harry. Two lines that would map out the future she was so afraid of. A future her mother was preparing her for but that she did not want.

Knowledge passed down through stories of older girls who dealt with their own little problems without needing to involve either parent or doctor. Knowledge that an unwanted child was so easily disposed of when your parents were out of town and your brother was too preoccupied with his own sex life to care about his little sister and all her despair. Knowledge that your best friend would find you before any real damage was done.

135

So I put the offending pregnancy test in my bag, along with the empty bottle of gin, kissed Elle goodbye, then shut the door on all I had witnessed.

* * *

It's one of the reasons Elle has found it so hard to understand why she can't get pregnant. Why she has subjected her body to countless tests in an attempt to reassure herself that, by aborting her unborn child, she didn't unwittingly prevent herself from ever being able to conceive again. Then there's the guilt. The question as to whether she is being punished by an unknown force for ridding the world of a life, for playing dictator when she wasn't supposed to make such a choice.

I could tell. I could let go one of the secrets that bind Elle and I together. But what would be the point of sharing this knowledge, of causing pain that has no consequence other than dulling the memory of first love? Because it makes no difference to where we find ourselves now. Would do nothing but make Patrick feel for his wife on another level. Show him some of her vulnerability, explain why it is she struggles with the idea her body is betraying her.

But there are other, more enduring ways of causing pain than death. For what if it is Elle's baby that I carry? Or even if not, should I hand it over, allow Elle a moment of happiness before exposing her affair? I could watch her heart shatter, wait for her to understand that betrayal is nothing compared to the removal of something once so beloved.

'Time for one more?' Patrick holds up the teapot as I return.

'Aren't you expecting Elle home soon? I don't want to intrude when you barely get any time together, what with all your travelling.'

'Elle won't mind. She's gone to meet up with a school friend.'

She would mind, if she weren't preoccupied. An anticipated

136

outcome, but one that has flourished and developed at a far pacier speed than I dared hope for.

So predictable is Elle. That volcanic ego left to smoulder for too long has, for just shy of a month now, been allowed to bubble away under the sculpted body of her first love. It was all too easy, for Harry is everything that Patrick is not. Brash, brazen and ever so slightly common. The perfect match. Ken and Barbie on steroids. Just like they were at school.

Tonight Harry is cooking her dinner at his place with the promise of something special for dessert. Except he spelled it 'desert' in his email, which I read because she hasn't changed any of her passwords since school. So trusting. So naïve. No doubt he is, at this very moment, feeding her chocolate-covered strawberries and pink champagne, because Elle has always been a sucker for anything sweet.

'Who's she gone to meet?'

'One of the girls, I presume. I'm surprised you weren't invited.'

I'm not. If Elle had been meeting one of the girls, the gang, the 'Famous Four' as they liked to call themselves, I sure as hell wouldn't have been invited. Which suited me fine. I wonder if Elle has shared her dirty secret with any of them? Probably not, for, delectable as it may be, an exciting distraction from their everyday mundanity, it also reeks of imperfection, of a chink in her indestructible marriage.

'I have to go.'

'Stay.' His hand finds mine, the platinum band of his wedding ring scratching my skin.

It would be so easy to stay. To use his vulnerability, his unease, and bring him back to me. For men are inherently weak. Stroke that ego, feed the desire that wiggles away so close to the surface. I want him, I want to steal him away from her. I want to make her feel the humiliation, but I also won't allow her to be the victim, to claim I am the one at fault.

But if Elle dies, if there is a grieving husband and tiny child to consider, then the transition would be so much more natural. I could become the saviour instead of the villain.

'I've been thinking about that night.' He looks at me, then goes over to the sink, begins to rinse out the teapot, swirling around the leaves and emptying their fortunes down the plughole. He is waiting for an answer I'm not sure I know how to give.

'What night?' I reply, aware my whole body has begun to quiver.

Teapot on the side, he dries his hands, leans against the worktop with folded arms, eyes still anywhere but on me. 'There are bits missing. Things that don't quite make sense.'

My heart is racing around inside my chest and there is a knot at the base of my throat that threatens to betray me. 'What are you talking about?'

'You were practically naked.' Now those eyes find mine, as if attempting to prise open my mind, search through my own memories and see if they match his own.

But I have been deceitful for longer than either of them. Able to wear this mask even when at my most vulnerable.

'You were drunk, Patrick,' I say, checking my watch as if there is somewhere far more important to be.

He takes a step towards me, fingers rubbing the length of his jaw. 'You were kissing me.'

I was. At the time it felt miraculous, destined, perfect. Now it feels tainted and raw.

'It's not as if it's never happened before. Once upon a time we shared a bed, a life.'

At this he pauses, gives two small nods of his head, then walks over to the window, leans his forehead against it so that his next words mist onto the slice of glass that separates the outside world, the real world, from the torment in here.

'So the baby isn't yours?'

I give a non-committal shrug, pretend to check my watch once more, unable to tell this lie. Not in all its glory. Because he chose her, and I am fairly certain he would do so again, even over his unborn child.

'I've signed the paperwork, Patrick. If you've changed your mind, you need to speak to your wife. This isn't my responsibility anymore.'

He makes no move to stop me, his pride holding so much inside.

Elle made Patrick feel as if he walked on water. She idolised his brilliance in a way I never did. I pointed out his faults, argued over who was right, while she pretended no one had ever made her feel the way he did.

Deep down inside, men want women to look after them in the same way their mothers did. To stay home, raise the kids and be grateful for what they provide. It's the old hunter-gatherer theory. In many ways we haven't really evolved over the intervening millennia. The world is still ruled by alpha males who think they're better than everyone, especially women. But women are so much more resourceful.

History books may have been written down by men, but it's the mothers, the wives, the mistresses and the whores who have suggested and influenced more than any sword ever could. And that's where I went wrong. I underestimated Elle. It's my fault because I didn't protect him. I treated him as my equal instead of my superior and I never saw her coming.

CHAPTER FIFTEEN

Marijuana: To dream of using marijuana implies that you're trying to escape reality

'Are you sure I can't change your mind?' I look across at my brother's profile, at the stubble along his jaw that doesn't tally with the child I still remember.

His head turns as he checks the junction for traffic, accompanied by a noise somewhere between a scoff and a raspberry. 'Why would I want to spend my evening with a bunch of egotistical snobs who love nothing more than swapping stories about how much money they've got? Besides, she's your friend, not mine.'

'Fair point.' I lean my head back against the leather upholstery, listen to the low hum of the engine as he navigates the stone pillars of the gated entrance and steers the car up the driveway.

I've never learnt to drive. I pretend it's because I don't see the need, that I'm perfectly capable of either cycling or taking the bus, but really, I don't trust myself to be able to ignore the voice that reminds me how easy it would be to mount the pavement and take out whoever happens to be standing in my way.

'But won't you at least come to keep me company?'

'I thought you loved nothing more than the opportunity to remind all of Elle's friends how completely inadequate they are?' His lips curl up at the edges, a tease behind the smile.

'And I thought you enjoyed watching me do it.'

'Not anymore.' He parks the car and gets out. It's because of what I've done. Because of what he thinks is a very bad idea. He comes around to my side, opens the passenger door and offers me his hand. Ever the gentleman, even when he's pissed off with me. 'So who's the lucky recipient of your charms this time?'

'Why do you say that as if it's a bad thing?' His eyes narrow, but there's a lightness behind them. His resolve is faltering. He's never been able to stay mad at me for long.

'Commitment isn't one of your strong points.'

'Pot, kettle, black.' He bumps hips with me and I know I am once more forgiven.

'I can be committed.'

'Touchy, touchy. Those hormones are making you even more irritable than usual.'

I reward him by flicking the side of his neck.

'Hey, careful. Don't leave any marks. I want to be pristine for later.'

'By later, you mean when you've stripped your date of all his clothes.'

'We're here now, so just leave it.' He glances up at the old stone building, as if we can be heard from behind its glass doors.

'Gramps loves you. I don't understand why you won't tell him.'

'Because he knows all your secrets, I suppose?'

I ignore him and press the button for the intercom.

'How is he today?' Robin asks the nurse behind the front desk. I hear the suck of air as the automatic doors slide shut behind me, the click of the lock put in place for the patients' well-being.

'He's good. Not so chatty, but he's sleeping again.'

'What about the tremors?' I cover my nostrils with my sleeve. The stench of antiseptic death seems to stretch into every corner and my stomach turns in objection. Everything is more at the moment, as if my senses have been multiplied by the new life inside of me.

'A few.' The nurse observes my discomfort, and understanding follows as her eyes sweep the curve of my midsection. 'But not as persistent as before and his hands are showing signs of improvement. He's mostly managing to feed himself, which is good for his mood.'

'He always was a stubborn old thing.' Which is being kind, for Gramps isn't the sort of man who likes being told he can't do something. No matter that after Nana died he struggled to get dressed in the morning, couldn't make his fingers behave themselves for long enough to grip the kettle without pouring boiling water all over himself and the floor. He saw letting someone else, a stranger, take care of him as an insult.

'I swear you must have some magic in you. Ever since you came back he's like a different man.' Arms crossed over her chest, the nurse looks at me as if expecting some kind of confession, an explanation as to why it has taken me so long to return. I don't need any more guilt laid upon me. My brother is more than capable of doing that without any assistance.

I hear the click of Robin's tongue against his teeth. The reminder of my family duty, the constant questioning about how I could leave Gramps, abandon him by fleeing to the other side of the world?

'Psychology has a lot to do with any illness.' I ignore my brother and begin to walk along the corridor to the dayroom where Gramps will be waiting. Seated by the window so he can look towards the ocean, a mug of tea and today's newspaper on the table by his side.

'Of course, but this is different. Usually patients with Parkinson's get worse instead of better. Thirty years I've been a nurse, and I've never seen anything like it. Whatever your secret is, you should bottle it. Make a fortune, you would.'

Robin and I exchange a glance as she shuffles away, wide hips rocking like the hull of a boat. We know all about the progressive nature of Parkinson's, hate that there is no cure. We understand all too well how, at some point, Gramps's body will be unable to function; the tremors, pain and rigidity too much to bear. He's gone from sailing on the Solent and creating beautiful, hand-carved furniture inside the workshop at the bottom of the garden to being spoon-fed by a never-ending round of nurses. It turned him inward and he lost the passion that made him so much more than just a carpenter.

Which is why, once a week, either Robin or myself visit our grandfather and gift him a bag of liquorice. Sweet treats I personally inject with cannabis oil, the dosage small enough to take the edge off the symptoms of his illness, but not so great that he becomes noticeably high.

Personally I don't see what the problem is. Cannabis has been used both medicinally and recreationally for centuries. A 2,700-year-old grave was found in China containing the skeleton of a shaman and a bowl filled with the plant; in Germanic culture it's associated with the Norse love goddess Freya, and even Shakespeare is thought to have smoked it. More importantly for Gramps, the cannabinoids found in cannabis, specifically tetrahydrocannabinol, have been clinically proven to reduce the chronic pain and muscle spasms commonly associated with Parkinson's.

But if we get caught, Robin and I will no doubt be prosecuted for growing, distilling and distributing an illegal plant. A plant that allows our grandfather to enjoy life once more.

'There you are.' The creases by Gramps's eyes deepen as he sees us approach and we take turns to hug him, breathing in the familiar scent of Old Spice and tobacco hidden in the cuffs of his shirt. 'Isn't it a glorious day?'

We follow his gaze across the lawn, over the treetops and down to the break of water. Sailboats interrupt the line of the horizon, coloured triangles pointing into the morning sky filled with gulls.

It seems like only a whisper ago that we were out there, salty droplets on our skin as he steered us towards the lighthouse, hollering over the waves when we had to come about.

Only once did I succumb to the whip of the boom, tossed into the sea as punishment for not paying attention. The pull of the water all around, threatening to take my soul away, to claim me. I listened to its call, to the end of life it was promising, but I wasn't ready and kicked back with my legs, stretching to the surface before being hauled back onboard.

Robin had squeezed me tight, fear seeping from a face too ghostly and still. Gramps eased us apart, sat Robin between his legs, then told me to pull in the sheet and trim the sail, ignoring my chattering jaw and frozen limbs. He made me take us back to shore, made me understand that death is to be challenged, not revered.

'We brought you some more liquorice.' Robin hands over the paper bag, semi-circles of grease collecting in one corner.

'Only one a day,' I remind Gramps as he peers inside, one caterpillar brow raised.

'You don't need to tell me every time. I haven't got Alzheimer's as well.' He extracts one dark coil and pops it in his mouth. The muscles of his jaw creak as he chews. 'God this stuff tastes bloody awful.' He reaches over for the mug beside him and takes a long sip of what is no doubt lukewarm, stewed tea with two spoons of sugar.

'Gramps,' Robin hisses at him as he looks around, weight shifting from foot to foot. He's always been too morally decent, but even he understands that this is a secret he cannot spill.

'It's not me you have to worry about.' Gramps points the mug at Robin. 'If anyone ever asked you I bet you'd start singing like a canary. Good job you didn't end up in MI5 or the whole country would be falling apart.'

'I'm going to get us some fresh tea.' Robin skulks away.

'You shouldn't tease him, Gramps.'

'He's too sensitive.'

'He's never going to stop hoping.'

'Well, he should. I know he was your father, but that doesn't mean he was blameless. At some point Robin is going to have to accept he wasn't a saint and that he's never coming back.'

Robin used to have a fantasy that our father was a spy. That he was on some secret mission, deep undercover somewhere, saving the world, which was the only reason he couldn't come home. When he shared his theory with Gramps he was rewarded with a bellow of laughter that rocked Gramps backwards off his chair and saw Robin flee to the safety of Nana's arms.

Gramps isn't exactly a hearts-and-flowers kind of guy – he's loyal and fiercely protective of those he loves, but he could never pretend not to hate our father for what he did.

'So are you ever going to tell me the real reason you're doing all this?' A nod to my belly, no need to explain his disapproval.

'It's complicated.'

'No, it's not. Not with you.'

'I thought you always said we should stand up for those we love.'

'Yes, but not at the expense of our own happiness.'

'Not even for our children?'

'But this isn't your child.'

He sees the twitch of my face, the curl of fingers that press nails into my skin, and I have to move away from his gaze, from the mind that understands me all too well. Because I don't want to lie to him, don't think I could, even if I tried.

'You came back for them.'

Not for him, or Robin, or my mother. Did I miss them when I was gone? Of course, but safely, because in a way I knew they would always be there for me. And my mother didn't blame me for running, for being like my father. It was like she knew I needed to go, even though I don't think she has ever in my entire life actually sat me down and asked me how I'm feeling. Gramps is far more direct, so she can't have inherited her bedside manner from him.

'It's complicated.'

'You've said that already. Children aren't a bargaining chip, Jane. I see too much here that confronts people with imper-manence. A reminder that people can leave this world as easily as they arrive. A child is supposed to be a promise of a future, but you don't seem to care that you're giving it to someone else.'

'That's kind of the point, Gramps. They couldn't have a future without me.'

'Never known you to be such a martyr. With all their money they could have paid someone else to carry their child. Hell, they could have just bought one from Africa.'

I can't help but laugh at this. The notion of Elle descending on an African orphanage like some kind of ethereal being, sweeping a dozen or so children into her arms and running off to a waiting helicopter.

'Why do you all have such a problem with what I'm doing?'

'Because we're your family. Not them.'

And there it is. Family. What it all boils down to. The only thing any of us ever has to leave behind in this world. Gramps has always thought I walked away too easily from the people who raised me, loved me, cared for me, despite all the turmoil that bubbled inside. Because you forgive your own for just about anything. But I don't think even he could forgive me for what I have done, what I intend to do.

'You've always been such a contradiction of light and dark. The temper you try so hard to keep locked away battling against all the goodness.'

'What goodness?'

'Remember when Robin fell out of the tree?'

'Of course she does,' Robin says as he approaches, three cups clutched between his hands. 'It was her fault.'

146

'You say that as if I pushed you.' I accept his offering, cradle it in my palms.

'But you did try to poison me.'

A slop of hot liquid over my knee at his choice of word and I hastily wipe it away. 'I never meant to hurt you.'

'No, you simply wanted to put me to sleep for a thousand years.'

'Now, now, you two, play nice.' Gramps grins at us, ever the referee when it comes to his grandchildren.

Although secretly I think he always enjoyed watching us spat. Marvelled at the back and forth of insults and taunts that changed over the years, as I learnt to accept Robin for who he was and not blame him for being one of the reasons I grew up without a father.

Part of me used to believe it was easier for Robin. Our father left before he was even born, which meant he had no memories of him that weren't titbits gleaned from photographs or stories told by someone else. Because surely it was impossible to miss someone you never even knew? Surely it was harder for me, the child who could remember the sound of his voice, the way he would always shave his face from left to right, then let me wipe off the last of the soap with a flannel and fetch his aftershave from the cupboard.

I understand more about family than Gramps gives me credit for. But I want what I didn't have. I want my child to grow up with both parents instead of only one.

'What was it that you gave me?' Robin takes a bite out of a chocolate bourbon biscuit then hands me the packet. I take two, put one in my mouth, then go back for another.

'You say that as if you don't remember asking me on every possible occasion for the past twenty years.'

Like some kind of fable, the story of how I used Snowberry essence to poison Robin when he was six years old is rattled out at every family gathering. With every telling it becomes more embellished, more dramatic, with me being portrayed as a veritable witch, locked away in a dungeon with my cauldron, concocting vicious spells against my innocent little brother.

In truth, I thought I was helping. Robin was a terrible sleeper, never going more than a few hours as a baby, and then, when he was older, repeatedly waking with nightmares about various creatures trying to eat him. His mother had tried everything from night lights to a superhero bunny complete with homemade cape that would attack the baddies if they ever dared enter his room. She had been told by the doctor that Robin simply had an overactive imagination, that when he started school he would be both physically and mentally exhausted and so would begin to sleep. Except Robin didn't play by the rules and continued to wake his mother most nights with tales of dragons and ghouls and things that go bump in the night.

So I thought I'd give him something that would help him sleep. Unfortunately, this was at a time when my experimenting was in its early phases and I didn't understand that giving a small child a couple of berries could not only make him sleepy, but potentially kill him.

Luckily for me, Robin's mother is an extremely forgiving person with a very dark sense of humour. It's the only reason I can think of why she and my mother became friends after my father left.

Gramps rests his hand on my knee, looks up at me with crinkles in his cheeks. 'You carried his little body all the way to the village, hollering at the top of your voice for someone to dial 999.'

'I thought it was to the police station?' Robin shakes his head, tiny crumbs littering his chin. 'Didn't she fall to her knees with arms outstretched, announcing that she had brought me to an untimely end?'

As I said. The story has changed somewhat over the years. But the moral of this particular incident in my life is that it made me realise I had space left in my heart to love someone other than my father. Space I should have been more careful of.

'Okay, fine.' I hold up my hands in defeat. 'You've got me. I am the black sheep of our tortured little family.'

'But everyone has cruelty within them.' Gramps holds my gaze, his voice stern. 'It's what we choose to do with it that matters.'

This is the same lesson he taught me that very first time. When he caught me letting go of my demon and showed me how to put her back on her leash.

* * *

Twenty-five years ago

Sand-swept hair curled around my eyes as I fashioned a miniature town, created from broken-down relics of the beach. I picked through the accumulated treasure, seeking out the knobbly star Daddy once told me used to live in the sea. The idea of a living star was exciting. Had it dropped from the sky, or was there a whole other world beneath the waves that I had never seen?

Turning it over, I stroked its belly, silently wishing it back to life before placing it atop the tower where the mermaid princess lived. I remember wishing the star could tell me if the princess was as beautiful as I imagined.

'What are you doing?' An older boy approached with his taunting words and I looked back to see nothing more than a rather clumsy sandcastle.

'What does it look like?' I hoped the sun was bright enough to hide the blush that speckled my chest.

He eyed me maliciously, the beginnings of a smile threatening to tug at his thin lips. Without warning he lurched forward, snatching the star from its precipice and used his other arm to shove me sideways.

I watched him at a right angle, his long, ungainly limbs making him appear like an unmastered puppet as he ran towards the sea. He stopped and looked back, ensuring his audience was fully alert, unaware of the seaweed caressing his ankles.

I saw him lean back and stretch his arm like an archer teases an arrow with his bow, and then the star was once more in the sky. Holding my breath, I watched, half-believing it would soar ever upwards, out of sight until the night woke up. The traversing arc broke and the star joined the sea in a gloomy plop, the water it disturbed like raindrops in reverse.

It was my star. He had taken my star and tossed it away like it didn't matter. Like it wasn't important at all. Just the same way everyone at school used to taunt me, tell me I was weird and a freak and no wonder my daddy left.

My hands curled into two tight fists and the sickly feeling in my belly came back, the one that happened whenever I thought of Daddy.

It's his fault.

A whisper. An idea. One of the voices that snuck into my mind during the darkest of nights, telling me things about the girls and boys at school. Telling me they were stupid and stinky and wet the bed at night. Voices that told me to put dead mice in their backpacks and slugs in their plimsoles. Voices that told me the boy on the beach was the one who should be thrown away, should be made to hurt.

The boy turned to me, triumphant. I hadn't moved but he did not seem to notice. Picking up a stick he turned his attention to jabbing a jellyfish that had dared to invade the beach.

Make him hurt.

I stood for a moment and thought of the star, floating above the mermaids and lighting their way. Then I padded across the sand towards him, snatched the stick from his hand and rammed one end of it into his leg.

I remember wondering if he would split apart like the jellyfish, little particles of goo clinging to the wood. I smiled at his tears, at his pain, which made me do it all over again.

My grandfather lifted me from the sand, ran away with one arm around my waist, skinny legs dangling as I watched the boy pressing against the bloody gash on his thigh.

'Take him with you,' I whispered to the sea. My weapon of choice lay indignant beside him, evidence of both attacks being washed away by the approaching tide.

'What made you do it?' Gramps asked later as we sat, side by side on the back step to the house. Nana was in the kitchen, peeling potatoes for supper, but we had been put in charge of the fish. I followed his neat, precise movements with the butter knife as he ran it from tail to head, scraping away scales that flicked rainbows when they tumbled through the air.

I shrugged.

'Did he hit you first?'

My pigtails bounced as I shook my head, no, watching as he took the fish to the garden tap, allowing it one more swim in the water. He bent his head down and around, seeking out my eyes.

'Did he deserve it?'

I couldn't answer, because I wasn't sure whether he would agree.

'Everyone has bad thoughts,' he told me, picking up a different knife by the blade and handing it to me. 'It's what we do with them that matters.'

My insides were smiling but I knew not to show how happy I was at his forgiveness. Instead I pressed the knife into the fish, feeling its flesh give way as I sliced it open all the way up to the gills. I lay down the knife, using my fingers to wriggle inside and pull out the wormy guts.

'Not squeamish at all,' Gramps said. 'Just like your mother.'

*　　*　　*

Who knows who we really are, underneath all the lies, the pretence and the social niceties?

I have an idea, but I also understand it's too dangerous, too tempting to try. For it only ever left me temporarily. That disgusting desire to harm. So I bury her, the her I want to be, beneath the acceptable version of myself.

151

Part of me loathes myself, the other holds me up in all my twisted ways and wonders at the beauty of it all. For isn't death as almighty as life? The only true eternal? The basis of all religions is death. The incompatibility of time at its end. Something beyond all our control. And yet... To be able to control it. To decide when the curtain finally falls. There's something poetic about that. To choose. It's so easy to choose.

At any given moment I could have taken the pen I was writing with, walked over to my teacher and stabbed her in the eye. Watched as it fell from a bloodied socket then thrust the pen back through the hole into her brain.

Except I wouldn't, neither then nor now, because so much about violence is just that – violent. And I wouldn't consider myself a violent person. I don't want to bring harm unto others. I just can't stop thinking about how, if I ever did want to kill someone, I would go about the final act.

152

CHAPTER SIXTEEN

Nasturtium: Conquest, victory in battle

Katya, Isadora, Clarissa and Elle. The Famous Four. Reunited under the pretence of nothing more than a get-together, a catch-up over three courses and several bottles of wine. But Elle wants to show off her new, or should that be old, lover, all the while pretending they're just good friends. The secret is becoming too much and I sense she is close to sharing. She was too excitable when I arrived, cheeks flushed and fingers twitching about her neckline, fussing over which perfume to wear.

It reminded me of all those afternoons spent watching while she preened herself to perfection as I sat on in silent admiration. Pretending not to be affected by her beauty while I dutifully recited notes from our revision books, her unpaid tutor. But I watched and I learnt, and slowly, ever so slowly, I used those same tricks on myself.

'I have to tell you something.' She looks at me from the safety of the dressing-table mirror, as if its reflection can somehow lessen her sins.

'No, you don't.' She can't tell me. Not yet. I am the keeper of her secrets. Her fears, insecurities, even the petty thefts from her mother's purse all those years ago. I know what makes her cry. I know how easy it is to hurt her. It makes me strong, but the knowledge scares me too. For when I start letting them out, like puppies they will tumble and slip over one another, eager to be free. Then it will all come out, too late to try and contain any of it.

She rises from her stool, her trimmed-down figure hugged by cloth that could have been spun by Midas himself. It's amazing what a touch of lust can do for a woman.

'Trust you to know so much more than anyone else.' There's a sigh hidden among her words and I can't figure out if it's one of sorrow or disappointment. She's slipping away from me and I need to be careful. I need to be ready to run.

'If you tell me, I have to tell him.'

She opens a box of jewels, holds two teardrop emeralds up to her cheeks. 'Because, of course, you've only ever told him the truth.'

I go over, pick out instead a pair of diamond earrings shaped like daisies. 'Don't make me lie for you, Elle,' I say, handing over the gems that catch the light as she tilts her head to fasten them tight.

'What about Patrick?' She slams shut the mirrored box, one sharp snap of annoyance. 'Have you lied for him, covered up his betrayal?'

'Don't make this about me,' I say as I lean towards the mirror, push back my eyelashes the way Elle taught me years ago. 'I've told you before, he's not having an affair and I have no desire to be part of your little revenge game.'

Elle watches my reflection. I see her eyes skate over the blush on my cheeks, the subtle wave in my hair, the new swell of my breasts. 'I'm not doing this to make him jealous.'

'Then what?'

'It's more than that, Jane,' she says as she turns away. 'You of all people should understand. Harry adores me.'

A confession without actually saying the words. As always, Elle is so very good at making sure the finger of blame cannot be pointed at her. Because if I were to tell, all the shame would fall onto me, for knowing, for conspiring.

'This isn't about taking sides.'

A narrowing of eyes as she checks her reflection one last time, then brushes past me and out of the room. 'No, you've made it perfectly clear whose side you're on.'

'We grew up, Elle. People change.'

She pauses at the door. 'What if I'm not ready for it all to change?'

'Change is the only constant, you know that.'

The chime of the doorbell announces the arrival of her troops and she shakes her head at me. 'Why do you have to be so metaphorical about it all?'

Wrong choice of word, but I get what she means. She's irritated she didn't have the chance to share her good fortune, to relish the moment when she finally got to tell me something I didn't already know.

Should I have allowed her to tell? Then I could have asked her about the baby. Where did he fit into her new life? Did she still want him? Did this free me from the responsibility for her death? Was it really that simple?

The questions, the possibilities, mutate in front of me, but there are too many. With one click of a finger she has sent me scurrying around my conscience and I know not what to do.

I follow her downstairs, watch as she opens the door to her friends, the people who shaped her, influenced her and think they know her better than anyone. Two kisses that never reach the skin on cheeks heavy with rouge. Heads that swivel to allow the owner a better look around, at the costumes they are all wearing, the jewels, the shoes, anything new they need to be jealous of.

The husbands follow, arms wide, slapping the backs of men

they only associate with to keep their wives happy, all the while wondering whether they are all just as desolate and alone.

Women put so much energy into themselves, energy that men would far rather was being put to use on them. It's as if we can never be sure of our bodies, are baffled by them instead of revelling in our own power.

But men don't care. They love each and every way our hips curve. Which is why I learnt to get my revenge in the easiest of ways.

'I didn't realise you were going to be here,' Katya says, and then all eyes move up as I come into focus, the light from the oversized chandelier in the hallway only highlighting the glow of my skin. Several glances at my swollen bosom, and not just from the men. For I understand the toll bringing a child into this world can take on your figure. It can lead some women down the same path as Elle's mother. Preserving themselves through the surgeon's knife. I like to imagine their skeletons in years to come, implants perching atop their bones, all that beauty rotted away.

'So lovely to see you again, Katya, Isadora, Clarissa.' I kiss them each in turn and we all know I'm lying.

'You too,' Clarissa replies. 'Pregnancy suits you.'

Their looks stick to me like molten lava. I see them from the edge of my eye, watching, waiting for me to make a mistake, to reveal the snake as I shed my skin.

'Do you think?' I turn to the side, emphasising the curve of my stomach.

'It's all rather odd, though,' Katya says through a smile too thin. 'I mean, I would have happily stepped in to help, if only I'd known.'

I love that they despise me for being the one Elle confided in. For being the only one who discovered a way to edge ever closer to the queen. Because they don't understand, not really. They think they do, but they see me for what they want me to be. A social climber, a geek who has somehow managed to better them all. Not least because, despite their best efforts, Elle remains mine.

'Dinner's nearly ready.' Patrick bestows his own greeting on Elle's friends. With a tea towel draped over one shoulder and a sprig of rosemary in his hair, he is like Aphrodite, rising from the sea with garlands of the herb wrapped around her naked body. I reach up to remove it, find Katya watching. Let her look. Let her stare. Let her wonder exactly how close the three of us really are and what made them pick me instead of her.

The doorbell chimes once more and Elle rushes to get there first. She looks over at me and I watch as she smoothes down the fabric of her dress and flutters her hair. Her palms will be moist, her heart tight and her thoughts befuddled. It will pain her to try not to reveal it to us.

I know because it's the exact same way I feel whenever I see Patrick.

'Harry.' A swallow, a sleight of hand. The pause, the flicker of eye. All of them betray her, hint at something more.

'Elle, thank you so much for inviting me.' He allows himself a moment longer to look at her before turning to greet us all in turn. More air kisses for the women, handshakes for the men, including the man whose wife he is screwing, but Patrick still seems to believe he is nothing more than a friend. Katya looks less convinced. Or perhaps it's too painful for her to remember? Another party, this time when Harry was drowning in the absence of Elle. A night when Katya took advantage of his inebriation but forgot to lock the bedroom door so that I witnessed her treachery in all its glory.

How quickly a rumour can spread. Like fire on the dry grass of a summer meadow, catching and scattering in all directions, too quickly to put out the flames. Of course she doesn't know it was me who struck the first match. The convenience of such parties is everyone is so drunk they can't accurately recall how they got home that night, let alone who whispered to them what was going on upstairs.

Such a shame Harry doesn't remember. But I do, and so do all the people who gathered in the doorway, commenting on the size of Katya's arse.

Elle claimed to find the whole incident hilarious, but the seating arrangements at lunch the following term told a different story. All she needed to do was place her bag on the seat Katya was trying to occupy and a teenage world imploded.

My legs jiggled under the table as I listened to Elle describing to the group in excruciating detail all of the sexual conquests she had accumulated over the summer. Giving them marks out of ten for effort and bonus points if they were particularly useful with their hands.

Telling us all how she was relieved to have broken up with Harry, that sex was so much better with someone who knew what they were doing.

Her comments were accompanied by a lingering stare across the table. There had been a moment's pause before Katya jumped up, her white plastic tray and all its contents spilling the length of her skirt. I could almost hear the words she wanted so desperately to speak, to argue her case before judge and jury. But no matter how compelling her testimony, no matter how many others were on her side, we had all known it was pointless to protest. Instead, she simply picked up her bag and walked away, accompanied by the whisperings of her classmates.

All the unspoken things, the words we are too afraid to say. They mean so much more than the filtered-down conversations we have.

'Right, let's go eat,' Patrick announces, and he leads us like the Pied Piper into the dining room, lit by candles and set for a feast.

Katya circles the table, waiting to see which seats will be filled first. Her husband, Leo, sits as far away from her as possible, which she notices but doesn't comment upon. She is waiting for Harry, but I ease into the space between them, accepting the chair he holds out for me.

'Are these nasturtiums?' Harry prods at one of the flowers on his plate.

I nod my reply.

'They're perfectly edible,' Patrick calls over to him. 'Nothing to worry about.' I told him this. Is it a warning? Telling me how he is a witness to my plan?

'At dusk the petals emit tiny darts of light, but in actual fact it's the contrast between the vivid orange of the flowers and their green leaves that causes a reaction in the human eye.' I can't help it. The words seem to run out of me, matching the fearful beat of my heart.

'Fascinating.' Katya rolls her eyes at Harry.

'So what else can you tell us about our supper?' Katya is goading me with the same sickly sweet smile she has been practising since she was fifteen.

The salad is simple but delicious: rocket, figs, Parma ham and chubby balls of mozzarella that split into shards of creamy heaven, all topped off with a sweet chilli dressing. It's more than edible, but I seem to be the only female allowing anything of substance to pass over my lips.

'Rocket was banned in monasteries during the Middle Ages due to aphrodisiac properties.' I help myself to another slice of bread, slather it with butter and allow a little moan as I take a bite. Katya is watching, they all are, and I can almost hear their empty stomachs complaining.

'Really?' Leo leans closer and Katya's smile dampens ever so slightly. Leo has a bit of a reputation. A reputation she knows I am privy to, and she hates me all the more because it was common knowledge at the bank where Leo and I both did our graduate training. It wasn't the first time he strayed, but the only time he admitted to. It's not so well-known that I became one of his mistresses, although I like to make her speculate.

'And chilli is often laid around crops in Africa because elephants don't like its smell.'

'I forgot how much you like plants. What else have you prepared for us all, Elle?' This is Harry now, enjoying the opportunity to look at her. Except she's not the one who did all the work. She can barely boil an egg, let alone produce a restaurant-standard meal. 'What are we having for dessert?'

'Saffron ice cream with caramel sauce and lavender biscuits.' Lids lowered then raised once more as she caresses the side of her mouth with her tongue.

'Everyone knows about saffron,' Katya chimes in, eyes flicking from Harry to Elle and back again. 'It's expensive, which is why Elle likes it.'

I wonder how quickly she would bleed out if I used my knife to slice open her throat.

'And caramel's not even a plant.' Clarissa, also quick to try and show some level of intelligence and failing.

'But sugar cane is.' Patrick can barely hide his amusement.

'Lavender was used in mummification.' We swap smiles. Two kindred spirits engulfed by ignorami.

'Do you mind, I'm trying to eat,' Clarissa complains.

My God, they're just ridiculous. It's like having dinner with a group of children. Why some people are allowed to reproduce is beyond me. There should be some kind of screening process. A simple test to future-proof our world from such vacuous creatures.

'Wasn't it used to protect against the plague?' Leo breaks away from his assault on Patrick's wine collection to offer up something resembling intellect.

'What's that song?' Clarissa looks around the table, as if somewhere behind her friends' painted faces the answer to her question lies. 'Ah, yes, "Lavender's Blue".' She says it like it's the solution to world hunger.

I could correct her, but what's the point? She's thinking of 'Ring a Ring o' Roses'. Besides, it was all merely superstition. There are not, nor have there ever been, any plants in existence capable of staving off infection from the bubonic plague.

Like some kind of talent-show audition, the four of them start singing the nursery rhyme, out of tune and heads swaying like a troop of rag dolls. I feel my toes curl into the carpet, tension reverberating all the way up my spine. How easy it would have been to slip some poison into the dressing. To purge myself of their utter inadequacy. The bread knife glimmers, taunts me with its potential, but I would probably only manage to dispose of a couple of them before I was overcome.

'"Lavender's Blue" has nothing to do with the plague, it was just a folk song about fucking,' I say, aware of Leo edging closer, his napkin no doubt hiding a flimsy arousal.

'What's the plant that mutates?' Elle smiles across at me, cheek resting in her hand. 'You know, the one that changes back into cabbage.'

Turns out some of the time she was paying attention. I stand and begin to clear away the plates. No one makes a move to help. 'Brussels sprouts, broccoli, kale and cauliflower are all types of cabbage.'

'But I hate Brussels sprouts,' Katya complains like a spoilt brat. 'Elle, please tell me there are no Brussels sprouts.'

'There are no Brussels sprouts. Now shut up and listen, would you? You might learn something.'

A smile teases my lips as I move around the table, stretching over to collect their dirty wares. 'If you grow them within close proximity of one another they will eventually all revert to their wild cabbage cousin.'

'Sounds like one of my cousins.' Leo's comment is rewarded with schoolboy snorts from the other end of the table.

'So what you're saying is that you can't escape your roots?' Isadora chooses this moment to address me for the first time since we exchanged false greetings. Dark eyes watching me from over the rim of her glass.

Of them all, Isadora is the smartest. Managed to scrape herself a place at Oxford to study anthropology, although we were never supposed to ask exactly how large a donation her parents made to the college in question before she was offered a place. She openly admitted that she was there to 'marry well' rather than use her brain, and it infuriated me that she would take the place of someone so much more deserving, someone who wanted to better themselves without relying on their parents to do it for them.

Still, the ruse paid off and she is now married to Oliver, who is bald, overweight and stupid, but Isadora doesn't seem to mind, given that his parents own half of Yorkshire.

'Are you still sailing?' Oliver turns to look up at me as I pass. Every single pore on his nose is blocked and there are dark hairs escaping from his nostrils. I have to try very hard not to picture the two of them during the act of reproduction.

'That's right, you came with us to Cowes one summer.' Isadora's smile is as crooked as her morals. 'Said you could sail, but I seem to recall you've never actually owned a boat.'

'She does now.' Elle stands, takes the pile of plates I have collected and walks out to the kitchen. Moments later, Harry follows.

'Really?' Katya's interest is piqued by the mention of money and turns to her husband. 'Perhaps you should have taken the position in Hong Kong before they offered it to her.'

'I didn't realise you were in the running?' I smile at Leo and he at least has the decency to look a little abashed.

They never offered it to him. He's only at the bank because of who his father went to school with. But go ahead, Leo. Tell your wife the lies to make her think you're worthy, to make her think you actually know how to do your job. She needs something to stop her from leaving because, from what I recall, there's very little else about you to keep her satisfied.

Sometimes I look at the shells of their existence, the gloss and polish in their private-estate houses, and wonder what it was I

162

used to admire. But I also understand what I really wanted. To prove I was better. That the only thing between us was money. And now I have more than any of them and they hate it, which only makes me bathe in their resentment even more.

'We should all go out on your boat sometime.' Leo's arm creeps closer to my skin and I resist the urge to bite off one of his fingers. After all, I think his wife deserves a little more uncertainty about what really happened between us.

'That's what we should do for your birthday.' Elle comes back into the room carrying an oversized silver platter piled high with succulent slices of marinated lamb. Her bottom lip is a little swollen and the strap of her dress is askew.

'I don't see the need to celebrate...'

'Oh, shush, you know how much fun it will be.'

It won't. It will be horrendous.

'But is she allowed, this far into the pregnancy?' Patrick says. 'I mean, Elle, think about her condition. Plus I won't be there to help sail. I've got to go back to the Far East next week.'

A shrill little laugh followed by a wave of her hand. 'I forgot.'

She forgot. She forgot about the baby.

'I mean, couldn't Robin come too?' she says, looking across at me. 'You can still swim and it's not as if we even need to go that far out? Please say yes, it will be great.'

Perhaps the boat isn't such a bad idea after all. So many accidents happen at sea.

'Dammit,' she says. 'I forgot the couscous. I'll be back in a sec.'

I decide to follow her. If anyone asks, I needed a glass of water.

Harry is perched against the kitchen counter, legs splayed, attention all on her. She leans into him, chin dipped, and he uses his thumb to follow the line of her jaw. Eyes up, she sees me enter the kitchen, and steps away from Harry reluctant and slow, but I make sure to focus on the other side of the room, to allow her that moment of belief that I did not see.

'Do you need any help?' I ask as Elle shakes her head, flaxen tresses all a-quiver. Then she picks up the forgotten serving dish and disappears, leaving Harry and I alone.

'It's funny.' Arms folded, he watches me go over to the fridge and take out a bottle of water. I move across to the island, take a knife from its block and begin to slice into a lime.

'What's funny?'

'None of you has changed a bit. Even you.'

'What's that supposed to mean?' I grip the lime a little tighter to stop my fingers from shaking, to stop myself from plunging the knife into his overly inquisitive eyes.

'Oh, I think you know.'

I can't help it. My head whips round to confront the accusation and he sees me. He sees what lurks, waiting.

This is going to be a problem.

CHAPTER SEVENTEEN

Monkshood: Beware its beauty,
for a deadly foe is near

A seagull swoops low over the river, a flash of white against the blue, then up and over the mast, soft caws calling out to its flock. The sun hangs high above our heads, altocumulus clouds doing little to block out its warmth, but there is a scent in the air that brings with it the promise of rain.

Gramps used to bring us sailing along here, all the way from Beaulieu and out to the sea. He taught us to tell the difference between the buzzards and hawks that skimmed the sky, the little egrets and mandarin ducks that lived in the reeds next to kingfishers and redshanks with their yelping cries. Sea trout that returned each year to lay their eggs in the shallows, eels and pike and so much more. Fish I would impersonate as I dove beneath, allowing the coolness to envelop me and wash away my sins.

Robin told himself our father was a spy, but I held on to my own private fantasy – that he was an explorer who sailed out to sea and never returned. Forever reaching for the horizon until he came across a new and magical land no person had ever before set foot on. It was filled with windmill palms, monkshood and flowers that forever smelt of summer, a new type of Japanese aralia he knew I would love. He was trying to find his way home, but one day I would captain my own boat and venture out to rescue him, to bring him back.

The fantasy died but my love of the water remains. The oceans hold more secrets than any human could possibly imagine, so much that is unknown hidden in the breadth and depth of blue. I wish I could bury my secrets down there, hide them away under lock and key, a buried treasure without a map. To be free of what I know about them all, to be rid of all the lies and the pretence. To just be.

I always sleep better on boats. The rock and bye of the tides take with them the monsters and demons, lulling me into dreamless oblivion. Eyes wide shut I always knew I was safe, that nothing would come and steal me away in the night. More and more I find myself here, alone.

Robin's at the helm now, the same seriousness etched into his face as always. He sees himself as the boat's commander, the one in control. But for me the boat understands better than I, and it is about letting go, about giving in to a power altogether more. Sailing is probably the closest to godliness I will ever get.

This is my place, the repetitive lap of the water against the hull of the boat my private hypnosis. So why did I bring them here? Why did I, once again, find myself powerless to resist her demands?

'Do you ever wonder what it would be like?' Her face is tilted to the sky, lids closed so I have the freedom to simply stare. I understand that I love and loathe her in equal measure, that in such moments it is easy to forgive, to forget.

'What do you mean?' When she is still, my thoughts become disjointed from my mind, running around without anyone to tame them, and I have to remind myself to focus.

'How our lives can be so drastically changed because of one

166

moment, one decision.' She turns, leans back against the railing and looks at me. Really looks at me, with steely eyes and no hint at what lies beneath.

Did one of my thoughts run into her? Did she see the torment I battle with on my merry-go-round of despair? Every single moment I have ever spent could be blamed for what has occurred. There is no way to go back, to undo or even redo what came before, but that never stops me from wondering at what point it changed. At what point it will end.

I look past her to my brother, one hand raised as he steers us along the Solent. She returns his greeting, although I know it would have been directed at me, then eases herself away from the railing and skips her way over to him. I watch as he steps aside, allows her to take the wheel, her hair whipping out in the wind like the shards of golden thread Rumplestiltskin so craved.

Everything about her is straight out of a fairy tale. The beauty, the glory, the happily ever after. It's as second nature to her as carrots and mince pies are to children on Christmas Eve. She simply accepts that this is the way her life is meant to be, so why doesn't she ever seem satisfied?

There's this idea I have of people being wrung out by the world they build around them, never stopping to appreciate what it is they have. Elle is chasing something that's never going to fit and it's meant that Patrick has become a desiccated version of himself, because of her, because of everything he is trying to be to keep her happy.

She thinks it's simply a matter of changing her mind, that she can flick away her marriage like a piece of lint on her silken shirt.

And yet...

If she were to leave Patrick, the risk would become hers alone. He would be so bereft, so vulnerable, that I could take him in an altogether different manner. No blood would need to be shed, or at least not by me. Perchance he could be convinced to do the deed himself. It's an idea that has been floating around in my mind ever since she claimed to have forgotten about the baby at dinner.

This is what happens when you fall in love with someone. And I don't mean the love we are bombarded with in storybooks. I mean the kind that hurts each time you breathe.

I've built this whole existence in order to prove to the world that I don't need Elle, or anyone, to help me. That I can do it by myself. But the truth is I miss her, I miss what we were before Patrick, and I hate myself for it.

I need her. I've spent so long being a certain way, shaping my life around her, that I no longer know how else to be. It's what's preventing me from changing the life that stretches out in front of us, of being the one to tip the scales, to unseat us all and free us from her clutches. Because it is she who is responsible for all of this. It is she we are all incapable of removing from our lives. It is she who is holding us all back.

So why can't I bring myself to do it? Why can't any of us get rid of her?

I tried running away, to form a future away from her, but some invisible rope kept tugging me back and I never could say no whenever she asked for help.

'So you've never been jealous?' I turn to see Harry approaching, two tiny reflections of the sky in his wraparound shades. A swig from his bottle of beer, legs spread wide to counterbalance the gentle rock of the boat.

'Of what?'

'Patrick and Elle.'

The statement is heavy with intent, a reminder that he has guessed more than most. I have been mulling over the problem that is Harry every night before I close my eyes. Have imagined the ways in which I can dispose of him, and not necessarily in the physical sense, for psychology is just as powerful, as deadly as any bullet or poison. That I was the one to reintroduce him into the fold makes my torment all the more irritating; like a paper cut, he seemed insubstantial, but the sting is far too real.

'I ended up with two best friends, which is more than most people can ever hope for.'

'So there's nothing more to it?'

Is he asking or suggesting? It's difficult to tell which way his suspicions have fallen and there's every reason to believe that others have tainted him with their own misgivings about how close I am to both husband and wife.

'Look, I understand you and Elle have reconnected over the past month or so, but if you think she's ever likely to actually leave Patrick for someone like you...' The fact I speak what it is I am hoping for may be ironic, but that doesn't make it wrong.

'Someone like me?'

Yes, you, with your year-round tan, gym-honed physique and spiffy clothes. The convertible Porsche with its personalised number plate, the penthouse apartment with a view of Tower Bridge, and all your famous friends. It is so far removed from the man she chose to marry, and yet I also understand that Elle and Harry are the perfect match. So why am I punishing him instead of helping him achieve his own dirty ambition?

'If I even have to explain, then you clearly don't know Elle at all.'

'Oh, I know her.' His lips curl up in the imitation of a smile. 'In ways you never will. Which drives you mad.'

A laugh escapes my mouth at the sheer incongruity of what he is implying and the smile turns upside down.

'It's not exactly a secret.' He's wrong-footed, having assumed I would profess my love for her, that it was she I wanted in my bed. I suppose he would think that, assume that only Elle would be worthy of anyone's lust. 'Everyone at school knew you were obsessed with her. It's not natural the way you would follow her round like a lost puppy, desperately hoping she'd be friends with you.'

He was exactly the same, but is conveniently forgetting to mention that.

'Says the man who's trying to steal her away from her husband.'

'And you're not?'

His arrogance makes my insides fizz.

'No, I'm not.'

'I don't believe you.' He juts his bottle at me. If only I had a sword with which to answer his challenge.

'Believe what you want, but do you really think they would be having a baby together if they were having problems?'

'Elle's pregnant?' Eyebrows appear over the top of his sunglasses and I can't help it, I grin like a loon at his total ignorance. Oh, this is too easy. Way too easy.

'She didn't tell you? No, I don't suppose she would. Why ruin all the romance by telling the truth?'

'But I would have noticed.'

'She's not pregnant per se.' I rub my stomach, watch as his eyes follow the movement. The beat inside of me is strange, fast but halting. I can feel him and his presence is astonishing, this invader, this wonder that grows beneath my skin.

'That's hers? But why? I mean, it's all wrong.'

'Wrong how? That I'm giving my best friend the one thing she's always wanted? The child she's been trying to conceive for years?'

'So you slept with Patrick?'

I did, I did, I did. It was wonderful, perfect and true.

'No, you idiot, I'm the surrogate.'

'Of course you are.' He drains his drink, unable to look at me. 'Can't help but interfere with her life at every given opportunity.'

So she's told Harry what I did when we were at school. That I was the one who encouraged her to break up with him. That he was too clingy and she didn't need to be tied to one person when there were queues of hot guys lining up for her. Never mind. His heart should be used to the pain by now.

'You have absolutely no idea what it's been like for her. It was Patrick, not you, who comforted her every time she bled. Went

170

with her for the endless rounds of tests. Held her hand when she injected herself with hormones in the vain hope that each time it would be different. Watched her heart break every time one of her friends announced their own pregnancy.'

'You sound like her keeper rather than her friend.'

'And you sound like a fool. You're nothing more than escapism to her. She is using you to forget about the fact that I am doing what she cannot. The very second this baby enters the world, you will be discarded, just like the first time.'

This last one hits the mark.

'She loves me.'

'Oh, don't be so fucking naïve. Elle always gets what she wants and you are not part of the plan.'

He wants to hit me. I understand that look all too well. Part of him is struggling with the desire to crack fist against bone, to use me as a way of venting his horror at what he has just discovered. He knows I'm right, that Elle has no intention of committing to him. She never saw him as anything more than a dalliance, as someone to make her feel better about herself.

'What if I said I was willing to raise the child as my own?'

'Now you sound delusional. But I'll tell you what…' I point behind him to where his lady love approaches. '…Why don't you go ask her right now? See what she says.'

'There's something not quite right with you.'

Of course there isn't. But that doesn't mean there's anything wrong about me either.

'And there was I, hoping we could be friends.'

Elle looks between us, sensing the upset but not yet ready to confront it.

'Robin says we can make it to Cowes in time for lunch.' Her arm trembles by her side, as if she is struggling to contain the urge to wrap her limbs around him.

The original plan was to do a quick sail up and down the river, then head over to The Master Builder's House for some food,

171

but, of course, now Elle has a different idea in her mind we will all have to follow suit. Robin would only be thinking of the time on the water, because I normally don't let him captain all the way across to the Isle. But he should know I want to spend as little time onboard with these philistines as possible.

'Why didn't you tell me?' Harry shifts away from Elle and I hear her intake of breath at the unexpected slight.

'Tell you what?' she asks, rolling onto her toes and back down again, unsure as to whether he will allow her close.

'Don't pretend to be innocent, Elle.'

Then again, I can happily watch as this unfolds. Nothing wrong with a little bit of drama to liven up the day.

'It's not that I didn't tell you.' She bites her bottom lip, angles her body towards him. A seemingly innocent gesture, and yet so loaded with intent it's a miracle he doesn't start undressing her there and then.

'No? That would seem to sum it up nicely.' He stands with his jaw clenched and hands tucked under his armpits to prevent them from straying.

'Harry, please, I can explain.'

She takes one step closer and he nearly loses his resolve. A pause, then a swift shake of his head. 'I don't think there's any need. You lied to me.'

He walks away and she watches to see if he will come back.

'What did you have to go and do that for?'

'Seriously? This is my fault?'

She whirls round, frustration brimming in among her tears. 'Of course it's your bloody fault. You told him about the baby.'

'Well, pardon me for not realising it was a secret.' Although, if I'd known, I would have shared it with him sooner. Saved myself several sleepless nights.

'Jesus, why can't you just be happy for me for once? Why do you always have to spoil things?'

'Spoil things? You're the one having an affair.'

'As if that wasn't what you wanted all along.'

Her insight is quite unexpected, but I don't think for one moment it goes any further than mild irritation at having been discovered, instead of being the one to share her juicy bit of news.

'So that's it? You're just going to walk away from your marriage? Not to mention the child I'm carrying.' I can't say it's for her. I can't. I can't carry on that lie.

'Well, maybe I don't want it anymore.'

'Maybe you don't… You're unbelievable.' She's talking about the baby as if it's an order placed at a restaurant. A side salad she no longer has any appetite for.

'No, you are. You've never approved of me and Patrick.'

She's right.

'You never thought I was good enough for him. Or for you.'

Right again.

'You think I don't see the way you two look at me when I can't understand what you're talking about? You think I don't hear the sniggers and sighs behind your fake smiles? I'm fed up of being made to feel like I'm stupid and inferior and altogether not worthy.'

So it would seem there is comprehension hiding underneath all that spit and polish. A level of understanding I simply didn't believe her capable of. But I can't have her turn this around on me. It would be oh so easy for her to create a scenario where she ends up the victim. There are too many players all willing to lay the blame on my vulnerable head.

'For heaven's sake, Elle, at what point are you going to take responsibility for your own life rather than expecting everyone around you to do it for you?'

'So you finally admit it. You think you're better than me?'

Do any of us believe we're worthy, or do we all hide a darkness within? If we are but animals, only the strongest will survive. In which case I have just as much right to play the game as her. But I'll make sure I win.

173

'There's nothing to admit. I will say it again. I am carrying a baby. The baby you said you couldn't live without. That you claimed would complete you, would make your very existence worthwhile. And yet now you tell me you've changed your mind because you've started fucking some simpleton?'

There's a shift behind her eyes, a shift I have seen time and time again in the face of my mother. I should be careful, but I doubt this wildling will ever actually pounce. Besides, part of me wants to fight, to vent. So long has it been hibernating, so long have I wanted it to wake.

'I was going to leave him. I was all ready to tell him when he got back from Hong Kong, but then he told me about the wonderful plan the two of you had concocted and I couldn't bring myself to ruin his happiness because it meant you were coming home.'

What have I done? I gawp at her, at the revelation I missed. Myriad alternate outcomes flash before me, but I cannot allow myself to linger on even one of them. Because then I would have to admit that this is of my doing, not hers.

'I did this for you.'

'No, you didn't. You did it for yourself. As a way of finally getting back at me. But guess what, little miss clever clogs? I only married him to piss you off.'

It was like cutting into a piece of meat and realising it was rotten from the core. As if she hadn't already ground the shards of my battered heart into me over and over, now there was a whole other level of pain to discover.

'You were my best friend but then he came along and ruined it all. You were supposed to be mine, not his. It was so easy to take him from you. Always so fucking grateful to be around me. It makes me sick just to look at him.'

I hit her across the face, nails raking skin that will bear the marks of my anger in days to come. In return she shoves me, hard, in the chest, and I take a step backwards. One step and everything is broken.

My ankle collapses under the extra weight I now carry as my body turns in an alternate way, useless hands reaching for something they cannot find. Another stumble, another fall towards slippery steps at the boat's stern that lead down to the sea.

On hands and knees I look along the horizon, see we are at the point where the river stretches wide as the end of a wave tumbles through our wake. I go to stand, one leg lifting, when the ocean betrays me, catches me unawares, and over once more I go, down the steps onto the landing platform at the boat's stern.

Without my extra weight, without the internal movement that has shifted my centre of gravity, perhaps I would have been able to stretch out one arm and clasp hold of the railing instead of being tossed into the river. Perhaps I wouldn't have been disorientated, swum away from the boat instead of towards it. Perhaps the hull wouldn't have struck first my side and then my skull, causing me to spiral into obscurity.

Perhaps, perhaps, perhaps.

CHAPTER EIGHTEEN

Deer: Piety, devotion and grace

There's a mass inside of me, spreading out to every corner of my body, holding tight and forbidding movement.

Do I sleep? Or only dream? This is not the world as I know it, but familiar still. What is it that I know? I am me, he is not she. Memories or wishes, I cannot tell.

Someone has turned off the light, too dark, too bright. Turning, swooping, all around, but no more sound. Faces, places, where they be? Stretching, calling, run from me.

Then a picture. A sight once seen. It appears as a pinprick, gaining, gaining, until there it stands. Proud and true. A deer. A doe. An animal I once did know, until she took it, made it all gone.

Fear wretched on its face as the car slams, brakes, makes it bleed. My mother, hurrying, swooping from metal into the air.

The creature lain on tarmac oozing life from a slash of wound. Eyes find mine, looking, scared. Does it see me? Does it know what comes after? A rock. A crack, then more oozing as eyes turn dead.

Cold glass on my cheek as my eyes seek out the murder. Sweet breath on my neck as my mother tells me not to look.

No more fear. No more nothing. Hand on my arm, pulling, fleeing. Engine roaring, someone singing about love and a boy far from home.

Moaning sirens, lifting, falling, turning me over and right once again. Faces, questions, words unheard of, a rip deep within then cold, so cold. Up and down and through my soul. Hands inside me, searching, stealing. Who ripped out all that I know?

A cry, not his, not the cry of life. But my own wailing, pain ascending. Take me too, I have no desire to stay.

Water, water, all around me. Let me go, let me go, let me go.

* * *

'Jane? Can you hear me, Jane?'

Who is here with me? Too bright, the light streams over my head, flashes of colour and sounds I do not know.

'You're in hospital. There's been an accident but we're going to do everything we can to help you.'

I manage to nod my head. I'm rewarded with a sensation that feels as if someone has shoved a very long, very sharp instrument into my ear.

'I can't feel my legs.'

'We've given you something for the pain.'

My hands flicker at my side as I try to move them over my stomach, but the nurse holds my arm still.

'We're nearly there. Hold on a moment longer, okay?'

There's a quiver to her voice that I don't want to have heard. It means something's wrong. It means something more than what she is allowing me to know, and the pain in my head is replaced by an idea so terrifying I want it gone, never to have been considered, even for a second.

'The baby.'

She looks down at me, the outline of a smile at the edge of her mouth and I know then it is anything but good. 'The doctors are going to take care of you.'

'I need to go with her.' A more familiar voice, the last one I heard before falling, falling, and it takes me back to that place of ever-reaching dark. Of turning, always turning, but finding nothing that could save me. Nothing that could save my boy.

'No,' I whisper. 'No.'

'You can't come any further,' the nurse says to Elle. 'We have to take her into surgery.'

The nurse never takes her hand from my own as the trolley pushes ever onward, not stopping as it sends me crashing through double doors. Not stopping to listen to Elle calling out after us.

'You have to save her. Please.'

Too many people. Too many people whose faces are hidden behind surgical masks. Whose eyes don't ever quite meet my own. I try to grip tighter to the nurse's hand but she slips away, tells me not to worry.

'Jane, listen to me.' A new voice. Male, assertive. Looking directly at me as strangers lift me from the trolley onto another slab and I try, oh I try very hard, not to see the puddle of red left behind, staining the sheets with my poison. I am just a piece of meat they intend to slice and dice. Just a collection of skin and bone they are allowed to cut open.

'Jane.' Louder this time and I look back as he lowers his mask, allows me to see more than just the slit between it and his pale-green cap. 'There's been a placental abruption. Do you know what that means?'

My body is a lump of flesh that they are moving about at will. A screen is being placed over my torso and I feel someone removing what's left of my bloodied clothes.

'We have to get the baby out, which means it's necessary to perform an emergency caesarean.'

'No, it's too soon. He can't come out now, it's too soon.'

But they aren't listening. There's a coldness seeping up my arm and I turn to see that someone has stuck a needle into it, is pushing clear liquid into my veins, and I have no recollection of

178

when this happened. A beat inside of my head, persistent and loud, a level of pain I never before thought possible, but it means something. It means I am still here.

A tug of my body that only registers because my arm twitches. I can't feel anything below my chest and I am haunted by the idea that they could cut me in half, like some sick magician's act, leave a gap between the two parts of my body, stitch me back together in a way that doesn't fit. Make me more of a freak than ever.

The sight of something being lifted, of hands shielding something from my view. A doctor's back, a swathe of green as they move away from me to the side of the room and I try to see. Stretch out my arm to try and reach him.

My boy. My boy is here, in the world with me. My heart beats in a way it never has before. Doubles in size, squeezes tighter than tight, pushing out all the love that was stored away for this very moment.

Another stranger goes to join the doctor holding my child. I see their bodies moving, hushed words I cannot hear.

'Is he okay? Why isn't he crying?'

The nurse is back. Her eyes are wet. She tells me not to look but I have to. I have to see him, to hold him. To tell him he is all I have ever wanted, I know that now. Nothing else matters other than him.

'What's going on? For fuck's sake, why won't anyone talk to me?' The doctor's movements slow. The dip of head, the slump of shoulders before he turns his eyes to the nurse by my side, then me, then back to her.

'I'm sorry,' she says.

Two words. No more, no less.

'No. No, you don't say that. You don't say that because it means there's something to apologise for. You told me he would be okay. You told me you would take care of him. You told me…' And then my mouth stops working.

I hear a series of unidentifiable clicks and then a raised voice, an urgent voice, a voice that is asking for help. I feel hands, once more moving around inside of me, pulling me this way and that. The speed with which the nurse leaves my vision, goes to the other side of the screen, to where my body is open to the world, tells me once again that nothing good is happening here.

The breath catches at the back of my throat, tiny gulps of air that don't seem to be doing what they should. My heart is straining against its frantic pulse, pushing out yet more blood, stealing it from my mind so that, all around, the edge of my vision is being peeled away, revealing the darkness behind.

I move my eyeballs, feel the tendons stretch as I try to angle myself so that I might see his tiny body once more.

Then no more to see. No more movement, no more sound, just acres and acres of nothing as someone turns out my light.

CHAPTER NINETEEN

Lily of the Valley: Tears of the Virgin Mary

I don't want to open my eyes. I don't want to see what I can hear in their muffled words. Wondering what to say. The fact they're whispering, or think I can't understand them, tells me I want to stay asleep. To lie in obscurity, because to come back to the light, back to the world, is to accept that it is over.

He's gone.

My hands lie limp, no need to stray to my centre to feel his absence. The stench of death hangs heavy and true.

Go away. Go away, all of you. You demons and devils and dastardly creatures who pretended to care. Who sucked me into your tornado of false hope and promises and made me believe that I too could have a life.

But no more. All is undone. Everything broken and stale and rotting.

Oh, where can he be? My child, my unborn. Hidden in a box somewhere for no one to see?

The knot inside of me is too much, it needs to burst and spread and disappear. The sob I is not enough to encapsulate

181

all I am feeling, all the horror that I know will never let me be.

'Miss Young?'

The voice is unfamiliar, accompanied by the creak of a chair and cushioned footsteps edging away.

'Miss Young, it's just you and I now, you can open your eyes.'

I do as I'm instructed, blinking away the blur of colours and light that settle into a young face surrounded by startling white hair. A mad professor of sorts, with gentle blue eyes and a stethoscope that hints at a level of intellect his age contests.

'Do you know where you are?'

I manage a dip of my head. I find that I don't want to look away from his eyes, I don't want to see the room beyond. Because if I see, then I will know that I am not on a ward with other mothers. There are no children here. No newborns. No hope.

'Do you remember what happened to you?'

At this I feel something inside of me give way, my body curling in on itself and a shard of ice forcing itself up and through my gut, then splintering and shattering what is left of my heart.

The sound that escapes my lips is nothing even close to a word, more a letting go, a keening, a mourning for what I know is obsolete.

'Try to stay still. You've undergone surgery and you need time to heal.'

Heal. As if there will ever be a day when I don't remember this moment, when my body won't feel this ache.

'Make it go away.' The whispering torments in my mind that won't let me forget the sight of his tiny body being wrapped up and taken away.

'I'm very sorry for your loss.'

'No!' Don't say the words. I don't need to hear them to make it so.

'Miss Young, I need to talk to you about what happens next.'

'She said no.' The voice of my mother allows me to crumple as she pushes the doctor aside. Strong arms come around my

182

shoulders, cradle me to her and I disappear into the folds of her blouse.

'I'll come back in a couple of hours. Check how she's doing.'

'Yes, you do that.'

I hear their exchange, the sounds enter my ears, but I cannot focus. I cannot see or process or feel anything other than the emptiness inside of me. The space where he should be.

'My darling,' she murmurs as she strokes my head. 'My poor, poor darling.'

I know not what to do with her emotion, the tenderness that she kept concealed for so many years. But I want it, I need it, to be that little girl gently held in the arms of her mother. Allowing her to make it all better once more.

'I want my baby.' One little slip of the tongue and I've shown my secret. She pretends not to have heard, but it will be in there now, swimming around her mind and making her wonder what it is that I have done.

'Shh, lay back. Let me call for the doctor, see if they can give you something to help you sleep.' She picks up a plastic cup of water, presses the straw to my cracked lips and waits for me to drink. I take a few swallows then swat it away, the cannula in my arm pulling at my skin. One more pain to bear.

'Can we come in?' Jackie's voice draws near, her question not waiting for an answer until she's there, staring down at me. And her. Hanging back, arms folded, then uncrossed once more. Fingers restless, eyes unsure.

'I really don't think now is the time…' My mother tries to shield me from them, but Jackie simply sets her malnourished backside on the edge of the bed.

'Oh, nonsense, we want to make sure she's okay. You're okay, aren't you, my love?' She gives my arm a gentle pat, as if this one movement can make up for everything that has happened. I half-expect her to invite me on a spa weekend, to make some remark about how I'll feel like myself in no time at all once I've had a

183

good scrub down with Balinese kelp. It's her go-to solution whenever any kind of scandal threatens and I wonder how she plans to explain away this little scenario to her circle of friends.

'Jackie, please, she needs time to rest.' Mum busies herself with plumping my pillow, a territorial gesture both sweet and annoying. I don't need her pretending to play happy families. I don't need anything at all, other than to be left alone. I don't want this. I don't want them picking around me, as if their attention is enough to put right what is so, so wrong.

'Mum, perhaps we should come back later,' Elle says, eyes landing anywhere but on me.

That's probably the best idea she's had in her entire waste of a life.

'Why?' Jackie looks back at Elle, her frozen brow attempting to wrinkle in confusion.

'Because she's been through enough already.' She's waiting to see how much I am willing to divulge. Wondering if I am to point the finger in her direction.

'And you haven't? It was your baby who died.'

'Mum…'

'Don't you "Mum" me. That was my grandson.'

'Where is he now?' I can't help but ask the question.

Elle comes closer, sneaks a hand out to take my own. I stare at it. Waiting for some kind of reaction to her touching me once again. 'We named him Conall, after Patrick's grandfather.'

'That's nice.' I move my hand away. It's not nice. It's the most ridiculous name I've ever heard. He wasn't a Conall. He was a little boy with green eyes and dark hair that curled at the nape of his neck. I used to talk to him, tell him stories about his parents, his family, what we would all do together when he was born. How we would celebrate Christmas and his dad would teach him to ride a horse and I would teach him to sail. He would be brilliant at maths but also see the world in a new way, and he could teach us about how to love, how to be a family.

184

No, he wasn't your Conall. He was mine.

'I'm sorry.' The catch in Elle's voice reveals the guilt behind her apology. For which part does she claim to be sorry, I want to ask, but another part of me does not care. She can't even raise her head, as if I am too much for her to look upon.

'Elle, you've nothing to be sorry for,' Jackie says. Defending her child. Defending her family. 'If it wasn't for you going in after her they'd both be dead.'

She jumped in after me. Didn't wait to see who else would come. It was Elle who chased me through the swell and torrent of the sea that tried so hard to claim me. It was she who pulled and heaved me upward, trying to save not destroy.

Would I have done the same? Or allowed all of her secrets to drown?

'Don't cry.' Jackie reaches into her bag and pulls out a packet of tissues.

I don't understand. I'm not crying. Then I see that she's talking to Elle. Comforting her. Putting her arms around her and giving her all the affection. As if she is the one who deserves to have people feel sorry for her.

'You can always try again,' Jackie says.

'What did you say?' My mother replies, and I sense the creature stirring, see the whites of her knuckles as nails push into palms. But Jackie doesn't know of the danger, of the pressure cooker that stands so close.

'I mean, this was horrible, of course it was. But there's no reason why Elle and Patrick can't still have a baby.'

'Get out.' My mother's voice is quiet but full of warning, and though it isn't aimed at me, I shift away to the other side of my bed.

'Really, there's no need to be so rude. We are all in this together.'

'What is it with you people? You think that because you have all this money it somehow makes you better than the rest of us?'

'Well, I have never...' Jackie reels back at the force of my mother's wrath, one hand seeking out her daughter. Elle looks at my mother in astonishment, then the attention slips over to me. I see her from the corner of my eye. The questions no doubt building, about all the times she asked me what was the matter and I couldn't answer.

'I'll tell you what, you have never…' My mother stabs at the air with her forefinger, each thrust accompanied by venom-laced words. '…You have never even stopped to consider what this has been like for her, for my daughter. You have abused her generosity from the very moment they first met. She has been nothing but a loyal and trusted friend to Elle, and all you can do, all you can do after she has sacrificed her own chances of ever having a family…'

'Wait, what?' What does she mean? What else could I have possibly sacrificed?

'They didn't tell you?' Jackie takes a step towards me.

'Don't you touch her! Don't you lay a finger on her! Just get out, get out and leave us alone!'

Elle guides her mother from the room, the hiss of air as the door slides shut behind them. I wait, count my breaths and give my mother the necessary time to regain control before asking.

'Mum?'

She sits next to me on the bed. Smoothes an absent hair from my face then cups my cheek. She is crying, which is more terrifying than her anger could ever be.

'They did everything they could, but you were in the water too long and he didn't get enough oxygen.'

'But you said…' There was more. I know this isn't the end of my punishment. There is more to come and I know I deserve it, but I don't want it. Don't tell me. But I need to be told. I have to hear what it is I have been dealt.

'You were losing too much blood. They had to perform an emergency hysterectomy.'

The lump in my throat is like an abscess. The delayed movement of my Adam's apple grating the soft tissue and reminding me of when I had my tonsils removed as a child. Oh, to have that pain. To swap this for that and go back again.

'So that's it then. I can't have children.'

And then it all fades to nothing. I turn my head away, eyes open but unseeing. Chest rising but no breath will ever be enough. Heart beating, but no longer does it carry the love I so craved. I have become nothing more than an empty vessel, alive but not living.

It was my fault. Everything they ever said about me is true.

* * *

'I don't know what to say.' Robin appears in the doorway, a wicker basket hung over one arm, no doubt filled with more of my mother's pastries

His voice brings me back, but the honesty hurts more than any lie. I can't speak. Not yet. I don't want him to be kind to me.

The rustle of paper as he lays something on the bed beside me, along with the heady aroma of lily of the valley. I can't help but smile at the irony of him bringing me a highly toxic plant. A plant that was thought to have sprung out of the ground when Mary cried at Christ's execution. But I guess all Robin remembers is that I grew vast quantities of them on my balcony in Hong Kong.

'I'm sorry I never called you back.' I lift the blooms, bury my sorrow in the tiny white petals. Think how easy it would be to take my own life.

'Given the circumstances, I think I can let that one slide.' He bends down to kiss my forehead and, even though I don't deserve it, even though it is the last thing I should feel, I can't help it, it makes me glad.

'Is she okay?' Another voice, so familiar it hurts, pulling me back down to where I now belong.

'Patrick.' I drop my hand. Feel the knot inside of me return. He looks as wretched as any man could possibly be, and that too is my fault.

'Why are you here?' Robin asks, the crossing of arms betraying his dismissive tone.

'I'm the father.' He clears his throat, fiddles with his collar. Looks across at me and then away. 'Was. I brought you a book of Sudoko.' He holds it out, arm crossing the gulf between us, and I move as if to take it, but am forced back by the searing pain across my stomach.

Robin snatches the book away, turns it over in disbelief. 'You brought her what?'

'Numbers relax her. I would have thought you'd know that.'

'It's because of you she's in here.' Robin tosses the book on the bedside cabinet. 'If you hadn't asked her to be the surrogate none of this would have happened.'

'He didn't ask. I offered.' The betrayal laid bare.

'You offered?' The hurt behind his words. The fact I never told him, allowing him instead to believe I needed to return for Gramps, for my own family. Not to help the two of them start another.

'Yes.'

'Why?'

There are no words that could ever make him understand why I did what I did. To say them would be to admit it all. The love, the hate, the envy, the desire. Everything so connected and yet so completely at odds that I have never fully understood what it is that drives me, that makes me do the things I do.

'Because I thought it was the right thing to do.'

'Because you thought… That's not the point. He should have said no.' He turns back to Patrick. 'You should have said no.'

'I know.' He hangs his head, as if he has anything to be ashamed of.

188

'Out. Now.' Robin sets the basket down on the edge of my bed and proceeds to lay out a picnic made for two, complete with individual pork pies and homemade apple chutney. My stomach reels at the thought of all that food. I don't deserve the pleasure of eating it.

'I assure you it was never my intention for any of this to happen,' Patrick says, his weight shifting from each foot as he looks from me, to my brother then down at the floor.

'You really need to get out more, Patrick. Learn how people in the real world practise the art of conversation.' Robin doesn't even bother to look across at him. His disapproval of Patrick was barely concealed even before he chose Elle over me.

'I'll come back again in the morning.' Patrick's kiss lingers at the edge of my mouth, but I can't bring myself to respond. I must not feel. I cannot. Not anymore. He and Robin exchange glances before he leaves the room.

Robin hands me a pork pie and then pours a stream of hot tea into a china mug. It's one of mine, with a picture of honeysuckle creeping upward from the base. There's a bee painted on the inside, with silvery wings and one leg missing. He's been to my house. He's been through my things. What else did he find?

'Why is Patrick here and not with his wife?'

There is more here than a simple accusation about Elle's marriage. More that Robin is assuming I will confide in him. More that he suspects me of but h knows better than to push. He knows there is too much hidden under the surface of my pretence, never truly dormant, always threatening to be unleashed. I see him look down at my wrists, at where my nails have once more begun to scratch. I allow his hand to remove my traitorous fingers, keep them away from my skin. But we both know the monster is lurking, waiting to reappear.

He adds milk to my tea and passes it over. It's Lady Grey, the tiny blue petals lurking under the surface. It makes me think of

189

my father, of how he could be lying at the bottom of a river somewhere, all alone, not knowing how much we miss him. I put the cup aside.

'Enough,' I say, not ready for all this platitude. This assumption that tea and cake makes everything all better again.

'Okay. I'm sorry. For everything. I wish I could make it all go away.'

I look at him then, properly, for the first time since he entered the room. There's no need to tell him the truth; on some level he already knows. 'He's dead, Robin.'

'I know.'

'I don't understand how this could have happened.' How did it get to here? My whole body begins to shake, pain rippling upward and inward and scratching at each tiny piece of me. I need it. I need to be punished, to be reminded every second of every hour of what it is that I have done.

'It's not your fault.' He takes hold of my arms, squeezes hard enough for me to feel him more than myself.

'But it is.' Tears block out his face, creating their own river of blame as they fall, one onto another, onto another. 'I did all of it. It was my idea.'

'An idea built out of love. Nothing wrong with that at all.'

Except there isn't anything right with it either. I did it out of love, but not for Elle, or even Patrick. I did it out of a selfish desire to have what I thought I wanted more than anything else in the world. How could I have been so ignorant to think that was all there is? That the basal desires of man and woman are what makes being here of any importance?

The structure of our DNA is so inexplicably unique, so complex, so magnificent. But it is fragile and fleeting and completely insignificant. Take a step back, look at the blood, the face, the family. Further still, the house, the street, the land. Even more, the world, the galaxy, as far as we will never be able to explore. What is it all for? Why do we even bother?

The very purpose of our existence is to reproduce. That is it. To pass on our seed, our genetic make-up and ensure the survival of the species. We are not important as individuals, we are only worth what we can continue.

And now I can't even do that.

CHAPTER TWENTY

Asters: When the Greek goddess Astraea wept at the absence of stars, her tears fell to the ground and turned into flowers

Lilies. Their spicy aroma finds me before I see them in all their garishness, littering every surface of the church. They wouldn't have been my choice of flower, too obvious, too demanding of attention. Something more dignified, quieter in their beauty, like asters, whose dainty heads were laid on the graves of French soldiers as a gesture of loss and longing. A loss incomparable to anything else ever known.

But then I wasn't asked anything about my son's funeral. The only courtesy extended was an invitation slipped through the letterbox. I heard someone on the other side of the door, could picture a hand raised as its owner decided whether or not to knock.

My mother thought I shouldn't attend. That it was a mistake to show myself so soon. As if I were the one with something to hide, to be ashamed of. That the sight of me would be too painful for those who were actually grieving.

Happiness is fortune's fool. The idea that it could last forever a cruel trick dreamt up by whoever created us. There cannot be a God, or if there is, be he but a tormentor, a trickster who likes to watch the players of this world fret and weep. For how could he show us such beauty, create the layers of enchantment that can be held by our hearts, then watch it be taken from us? What cruel manifestation must he be to make us feel at all?

Patrick and Elle are stood before the altar in a scene disturbingly reminiscent of another to which I also bore witness. Only now it is all so altered. Black not white. Remorse not celebration. But I am the one to feel the full force of it all. Real pain. Real absence of anything significant other than what I must endure.

Murmurs of apology, of meaningless words that people offer up in sympathy, all the while secretly thankful it's not them pretending to be grateful for the crowds who have shown up to bear witness to their tragedy.

'Jane.' A hand on my arm, familiar fingers curling around to let me know I have gone too far. 'You shouldn't be here,' she whispers, and I can't help but wonder if the fear I sense in her voice is for me, or for the family at the front of the church with eyes on a tiny wooden box that contains the beginnings of a life that never was.

I try to move away but she escorts me to a pew at the back of the church. Hidden from direct sight behind a vast stone pillar.

Robin slips in on my other side, turns my face to him as the vicar's words pour into my memory, coiling around inside and ripping out another part of my heart. I didn't know there was anything left to give, any more of me that could escape, but from somewhere it reels up again. The rage, the unfathomable fury that this has come to pass, spews forth as some kind of primal howl that reverberates around us, bouncing off the solemn walls and landing on the couple sat in the front row, heads bent into one another so that no light passes in between.

She is the first to turn. To seek me out, eyes as wet as my own, shadows of remorse underneath. Then his head lifts, follows the direction in which his wife now looks. A moment's pause as this is not a situation for which any of us is prepared. No one knows what to do next.

I would like to destroy them. To rip, to tear, to obliterate their world. Lock them inside of here and burn them all to hell. Hear their tortured screams and watch as their souls try to fight their way free. I want it all gone, every part of what has happened, all memory, all knowledge of what I have done.

Instead I have to watch as she sits, like some fucking deity to whom they all bow down. The space around her like hallowed ground on which only the chosen few are allowed to tread. What is it that she pretends to mourn? She knew nothing of what it felt like to have him grow inside of her. Was willing to cast it all aside for her own selfish desires.

The plan is undone. Not just my child but everything that went with him.

'He was my son, not yours. Mine and mine alone.'

I do not realise the words are out, do not remember choosing to let them go until I see them hit her perfect features. See the effect they have on her. And him. See how he battles with the memory of that night, of what he chooses not to remember.

Of how I was always just a means to an end. And now the end is here.

He rises from his seat, snatches back the hand Elle is trying to hold, then strides up the aisle with jaw set and fists clenched tight.

'You need to leave.' He spits out the words, unable to control the way he is shaking as he leans against the pillar.

'I have every right to be here,' I say, treacherous tears blurring the sight of his disapproval.

'No. It's too much. All of this is too much for Elle.'

'Oh, fuck you.' I throw the insult as hard as I can. 'Fuck the lot of you and your condescending ways. Except you couldn't do

194

it without my help, could you? Nothing wrong with renting my womb as long as it served your higher purpose, was there?'

'Jane, please,' my mother urges. 'Not here.'

'Then where?' I whip round to face her. 'What will it take for them to realise they're no better than anyone else? That no amount of money or beauty or anything at all makes the slightest difference because, in the end, we all die and no one gives a shit about what happened when you were alive.'

My mother grabs me then. The squeeze of bone around my arm, urging me to stop. Before I have a chance to respond, Robin pulls her away from me and suddenly I am running. Legs taking me out of this holy place and away, for if I stay they will consume me, suck me into the belly of the world, turn me to cinders and bury me deep.

I am aware of her voice, calling me back. What for? Death claims us all and we have no control over when. I want them back, my father, my son, I want what I cannot have.

How long must it take before I can make sense of what I now am, what I have become?

A murderer.

It does not terrify me, though I fear it should. I am not sad. I am resolute. I wanted to end another's life, her life, but instead he was taken instead. Did it happen because of some kind of karma, punishment for what it is I thought I so desired?

Be careful what you wish for.

A sudden flash of colour as a child scoots along the path in front of me, followed by a woman pushing a buggy. I watch them head towards the one place I have fastidiously avoided since leaving hospital. The invisible perimeter fence embedded in my mind whenever I have summoned the courage to venture this close to civilisation.

Ducks on the water, squabbling over the morsels they are thrown. Brightly coloured climbing frames and an ice-cream van filled with promises of sticky faces and sugar-crazed children. It is wonder and horror all rolled up into my own personal package of jealousy that I have tried so hard not to witness.

Sing-song voices yell out to one another in a language I now have no need to learn. Children climb and swing and twirl, over and under and back and forth. Running to their carers, shouting out their woes, then turn around and off again to explore, to play, to grow.

The mothers, the nannies, the stay-at-home dads, gather at the edge of the playground. Small clusters of everyday people, swapping stories about tantrums, vaccinations and the need to put your child down for the best school even before they are born. Others pay more attention to their phones than their offspring and I want to shake them, wake them, make them see. For why is it that they are special? How did they manage to have a baby? How did they get to have what I cannot?

Unable to move, I watch as one mother deposits her child in the sandpit then turns to another woman standing beside her. Neither of them pays any attention to the attempts at interaction their offspring make, instead complaining how tired they are, how bored of the monotony that is parenthood.

I need to leave. To retreat from this fake paradise and return to the safety of my childhood home. It is not reasonable to be here, when my mind is swimming with images of the ways in which I could make them understand.

The strap of a bag can be used to strangle out life, to make eyes bulge and fingers scratch. A buggy becomes a weapon instead of a shelter. A metal frame hard enough to hurt. Push them over, smash their skulls, or hold them under the water, have them watch the ducks' legs kick as they swim away.

I should leave, but there is something here that calls out to me, draws me near. There, under the shade of a sycamore tree, lies a baby all alone.

Go on. Go look see.

It is one of those old-fashioned prams, with large silver wheels and a dark-blue hood. It is jiggling, alive with his frustration, the noise of him echoing through the world. So why can no one else hear him? Why does no one come? Looking around, all is as it was before, no mother running over to scoop up her fractious child, no nanny half-heartedly doing her job.

Two steps more and the cries grow louder, more fretful. It is as if someone has taken hold of my insides and yanked, hard. I feel his pain. He is crying out for me.

You need to comfort him. He needs his mother.

His face is as pink as a boiled lobster. Eyes no more than slits, bare legs pumping and dark hair slick with frustration. My hand slips neatly underneath his middle, the other supporting the back of his neck as I bring him to me. His scent is sweet and ever so slightly musty, a unique combination I recognise in an instant.

He is mine.

'Shh,' I whisper, feeling his heart beat frantically against my cheek. 'It's okay now, Mama's got you.' The gentle to and fro as I rock him into quiet, the whimpers slowly fading as I drink in his deliciousness.

'That's my baby. She's got my baby.'

There is someone hurtling towards me. The woman from the sandpit. I look beyond her to see her child still content in his game, then try to see who it is she thinks has him.

She stops a few feet away, arm stretched out, her whole body shuddering. He stirs, lifts his tiny head and emits a gentle belch.

'Good boy, what a good boy,' I say, placing a kiss on his head.

'Give me back my baby.'

Why is she talking to me?

'I haven't got your baby.' I incline my head back towards the sandpit. 'Isn't that him, the one you've abandoned in the sandpit?'

'Are you crazy? That's my baby, you're holding her.'

She moves closer and I step away.

'Please, don't hurt her.'

'I'm not going to hurt him, I love him.'

197

'Please, I'll do anything, just let her go.'

Others are moving in now and I recognise the looks on their faces. Just like at school, staring, accusing, whispering their loathsome thoughts.

'Leave me alone.'

'I'm begging you, give her back to me. She needs me, she needs her mother.'

'What are you talking about? I am his mother.'

At this he begins to cry once more, a tiny circle of lips as he calls out for me to run, to take him away from this place and these horrible people who don't even know how to look after their own children, let alone give advice to me.

'He's hungry,' the woman says with a hiccup.

'I know that. I'm a good mother.' I lay him back in his pram, place my palm on his belly. A sudden grip on my arm, pulling me away, and I turn, see fury in the madwoman's eyes.

'Get away from her, you crazy bitch.' She flings the insult at me, which is all the ammunition I need.

It is all too easy to fight back, to protect my child. I push her away, but she bounces up and throws her body into the attack, arms raised, teeth on full display.

Do it.

The sensation of bone on bone is staggering, a wave of feeling from fingertip to shoulder. It is something. It is amazing. So I do it again. To see the way her face contorts as my fist makes contact, her weakness only igniting my desire.

More. Do it once more.

Two arms encircle me, drag me away.

'Stop. You have to stop.'

Robin's voice, but he should be fighting her, not me.

'No, she's trying to take my baby.'

'That's not your baby,' he says, and I watch as the stranger runs to my child, picks him up with shaking hands and brings him to her swollen face.

'Don't touch him,' I scream at her. Why won't Robin let me go? His grip is too tight, I cannot break away.

'That's not your baby,' he says, and I want to yell at him to stop repeating falsehoods, to let me go. 'He died.'

'No.' No. No. The word is not enough to convey how wrong he is.

'Who died?' The stranger speaks, her voice gone soft, anger fading as she looks over at me, at the melancholy clothes I am wearing, at the agony stitched across my face. 'You lost a baby?'

No. He is there. She is holding him.

Told you you were stupid.

'This is my little girl, Maisie.'

She is still talking to me but I don't understand what it is she is saying. The baby she is holding is wearing a pink babygro with daisies stitched around the neck. The same babygro Elle was looking at all those moons ago. That is not my baby, that is not who was in the pram a moment before.

'What did you do with him?' I search the crowd that has multiplied, all of the little ones clutching hands or being held tight. He is not here. He is gone.

My legs buckle underneath me, my spine liquified and no longer able to do what it was designed for.

'It's okay, I've got you.' Robin scoops me up, presses my face into his shoulder so I cannot see them watching me as I let him take me away.

CHAPTER TWENTY-ONE

Lotus Flower: Rebirth, new beginnings

'Hi.' She's there, waiting for me as I return from my morning amble. No doubt expecting me to have shown myself before now, asking for absolution. Honey-coloured limbs stretch out on my front porch, one hand curled around a post, the other shielding her eyes from the setting sun. Waves of heat rise from the earth, blurring her outline.

Two hands wrapped around a pink china mug. The same one she always chooses whenever she calls by. One that sits in a cupboard above the sink in the kitchen. One she has access to because best friends trust one another with the spare key to their house, with all their worldly possessions. For a moment I wonder if she has explored beyond the kitchen. Seen more than I would want her to.

I walk around the side of the house, collecting a spade along the way.

Humans can only process something by linking it to a memory, a thought. It is the repetition of life that is comforting, that grounds us, tells us we're not completely insane. It feels as if all

200

of my memories are about her. My mind attaches significance to everything, but only in relation to her.

'I thought it was about time we talked, face to face,' she calls out, following me to the back garden.

There is nothing I would like more than to smash her face in with this spade. To carve her skull in two and spread her brains out among my plants, feeding them with her stupidity. But I do not know if she deserves death. If she is worthy of its finality.

'I brought you something.'

I turn, looking not into her face, for I know it would unsettle, but into the offering she has brought. It is a lotus flower. White. Not a single mark on its silken petals.

'I spent ages trying to decide what would be the right one.'

As if there could be a right flower for this moment. For this attempt at an apology, a treaty of peace. I take the flower from her and walk across the lawn, sit down on the curved garden sofa and place a cushion on my stomach. She stands a distance away, on the other side of the battle line I have drawn.

'I looked it up. Buddhists see it as a sign of faithfulness.'

Interesting that she chose to focus on the Buddhist beliefs. Hindus see the lotus as representative of wisdom and spirituality. As representing someone who goes about their life with little concern for any reward and without attachment to possessions. Does her choice of flower relate more to her or to me?

'They also see it as a sign of purity, of rebirth,' I reply. 'The lotus is considered to be the womb of the world.'

She has the decency to be shocked by my words, at the reminder of why I have hidden myself away.

'Why are you here, Elle?'

Her hand passes over the cup from which she has been drinking and I see it is filled with Lady Grey tea, my favourite. I take a sip, feel the lingering heat slip down my throat as she replies.

'Because you refuse to speak to me, or to Patrick. I wanted to know how long it would be this time.'

This time. As if it's a schoolgirl spat that can be forgotten in a matter of moments. A disagreement about who was going to wear what to prom. The first time I tried to purge myself of her existence was after I learnt how she had broken the unwritten rule: thou shalt not steal away thy best friend's boyfriend.

After that I refused to speak to either of them for six months. Was only inveigled back into their lives by Gramps's accident. By my inability to ever say no to her, to ever find the strength to walk away and live my own life.

It was always the same. Me forgiving her for something that tore away a segment of my soul, putting it in a box, hiding it away and pretending it never happened. Because when Elle was at her best, she made you feel as if there was no one else in the world. When she wasn't obsessing about the size of her hips or whether her colleagues at work took her seriously, she poured all of that beauty onto you. Made it seem, if only for a fragment of time, that you were worthy of such a gift.

No more. I will not be swayed by the sight of her, because for some reason she thinks losing a child deserves less time apart than the destruction of trust. Because it is always, always, about how it affects her, and punishing her is unjust because Elle always struggles to come to terms with her own culpability, with how she too needs to bear the weight of what has come to pass.

'Please, Jane, tell me what it is that you want me to do?'

As always, expecting someone else to sort out the problem. Because by passing the baton to another it relieves her of the guilt, the responsibility for whatever it is she has done.

'So you're here for enlightenment?'

'Don't patronise me. I was part of this too.'

'Of course you were. Our sordid little threesome just doesn't seem to function properly when one of us is missing, out of sorts, not playing the game.'

Like warriors we face one another, sizing up our opponent.

No doubt she is surprised to find me like this, without compassion and challenging her rule. I have no reason now to bow, to placate, to serve.

'You were the one who said you never wanted children.'

Even when she's supposed to be apologising she can't help but make this anyone's fault but her own.

'And now, thanks to you, I have no choice.'

'It was an accident. You fell.' Arms folded, she looks fifteen again. Daring someone to fight back, knowing they never would. But that was a lifetime ago, and even the mighty must fall.

'Yes, after you pushed me.'

'You hit me first.'

'Because you were cheating on him.'

There. I've said it. Given voice to the truth that we both knew all along. That I value him more than her. She doesn't question it. She already knew. Is this why she took him from me in the first place, as punishment for changing my allegiance?

'Patrick and I are having counselling.' She sits on the far end of the seat, hands around the edge and the tips of her feet perched on the ground, not yet certain I have given her permission to join me.

'How sweet. Are you making any progress? Or are you still supplementing your marriage with Harry?'

'No, that's over.' She tilts her face to the sky and I see the tears that hover. 'I only did it to get back at Patrick.'

'What for?'

She shakes her head, lets go a long sigh. 'I thought it was you. I thought you were the reason he'd been distant, working late. Making promises he can't keep. That fate was turning what I did back on me, putting the two of you back together because you always did make more sense.'

'Patrick and I aren't having an affair.' I see now it would never have worked. Even without Elle. Because he always had to be the best, and so did I.

'I know. I think he's simply bored of me, of this life we have created. A life he only ever agreed to because of me, because he thought it was what I wanted.'

'Then what do you want?'

'If even you can't see it, how can I expect anyone else to?'

She's crying now. Soft tears that do nothing to diminish her beauty. Tears that contain a secret she isn't willing to share and I want to reach out and brush them all away, to taste what it is she is hiding, for once upon a time we told each other everything.

'He wanted that job more than even he would admit,' I say, thinking back to the night it all fell apart. When I realised there were other things in life he wanted more than me. 'He wouldn't have taken it for anyone but himself.'

Being part of the hedge-fund elite played to his ego, allowed him to lay down his brilliance at the feet of others just like him. People born into the assumption that they would be powerful and rich. An assumption I have always had to fight against, purely because of what lies between my legs. He still loves her, but Elle has always needed something more.

'Does Patrick know about Harry?' I hate that I still care, that I cannot banish him from my thoughts.

'No. And I would prefer to keep it that way.'

The truth will out.

'So this is a bribe as much as a gift?' I push the flower towards her and she stops the movement by placing her hand on the seat in between.

'Telling him wouldn't do any of us any good. You know that. He'd blame you as much as me.'

'Because I knew.'

'Because you knew.'

I look at her, only to find her eyes already upon me. They have turned a darker shade of violet around the edges. She is genuinely upset and I expect to feel something in response, but all I can muster is indifference.

'What else doesn't he know?' And despite myself, despite it all, I want to understand what has happened to them now I am once more removed. If what has happened was for anything or nothing at all. There has to be a reason, a significance to it, otherwise what was the point?

She doesn't reply. Takes hold of my wrist and turns it over to reveal the sharp, red lines that criss-cross my skin. Lines that run through an outline of small black dots. Dots that link together into the shape of a sun. A sun whose twin sits in the small of her back. United in ink, a symbol of what used to be.

'You once told me our friendship is what made the voices go away.'

'It did,' I reply as she lets go and my skin feels strange, as if it misses her touch. 'You did. But they always find a way of coming back.'

* * *

Twelve years ago

We were sat by the pool of the Hotel Martinez in Cannes, sipping chilled Sancerre and rotating our bodies like chickens on a spit. Heat rose off the ground, distorting the air and sucking against the wet sheen of people as they emerged from the water.

Elle looked like a forgotten movie star, all bronzed limbs and oversized sunglasses. Every so often she would pick out a cube of ice from the wine cooler and run it over her skin, each of the waiters falling over themselves to check her every need.

'You're nervous,' she said, nodding to where my fingers were scratching at old scars.

'No, I'm not,' I replied, crossing my legs and staring out at the never-ending blue. I remember thinking about how it would feel to dive beneath its surface, to lose myself to the darkness beneath.

'Yes, you are. You only ever do that when you're worried about something. Promise me it's nothing more than pre-university jitters.'

I looked over at her. Knowing she had nothing to fear because wherever she ended up in life people would adore her. She would fit in. Make friends. Be one of the popular crowd. I also knew she would forget me, and once more I would be alone.

'Ever since my father left I've been afraid.' I closed my eyes and turned my head away.

'Afraid of what?'

'That it was because of me. Because of something I did.'

'That's ridiculous.'

For so long I would go over and over that last day. Trying to figure out what it was I said or did that convinced him to go. Wondered what I could have done differently to make him stay. If it was all because he knew what lurked inside of me and wanted to run as far away as he could from.

'I get these thoughts, Elle. More like voices, really. Telling me to do bad things.'

'What kind of things?' I heard her shuffle in her seat to sit a little straighter, felt the air shift as she leant close.

'Hurting people.' The words came out as a whisper, but not so quiet that she wouldn't hear my confession.

'And have you? Ever hurt someone?' Like a child hearing a ghost story, she wanted to know how this one would end.

'Only once.' On a beach. A long time ago. Before Gramps showed me how to contain my demon. Before I gave it any reason to take control.

'Did it make the voices go away?'

'No.' I turned my head to face her. 'The only person who's ever done that is you.'

She looked at me for a moment. Those eyes that could rip a soul in two. Could make a person forget all about themselves, lost in the glare of her beauty.

'Come on,' she said, draining her glass and seizing me by the wrist.

'Where are we going?' I called out with a laugh as she dragged me through the hotel, past designer stores and women carrying tiny dogs in their bags. Past expensive cars and cafés that took up half the pavement. Not stopping to notice all the heads that turned her way, until we reached a glass-fronted building with a ruby-red awning and flickering sign above the door.

'What should we get?' she asked, peering inside to where dozens of designs were hung up on the walls. Pictures of roses and dragons and poor imitations of famous faces, all of which could be emblazoned on your body for nothing more than an hour of pain and a few hundred euros.

'We?'

'A flower? You love flowers. But roses tend to look a bit naff, don't you think?' She was stood so close I could smell coconut in her hair and alcohol in her smile.

'Why are we getting a tattoo?'

Her hand slipped through my own, squeezed my fingers tight. 'Because then, whenever you get, you know, the urge, instead you'll see something that reminds you I will always be here for you, no matter what.'

'That's so corny it hurts.'

The only reply she gave was a laugh. One that made me forget all of the twisted doubts that had been circling my brain for months. All the nights I had lain awake thinking life as I knew it was coming to an end and I would never again be happy.

We chose a sun because it was constant. The promise of a better day still to come. It was romantic and childish and wonderful all at once. We held hands through the pain and afterwards went out dancing until dawn, then sat with our toes in the sea as we watched the sun rise once more.

* * *

Now

'I'm sorry,' she says. 'I should have told you how I really felt from the start.'

An unexpected moment of honesty, one I didn't see coming. 'Would it have made any difference?'

A hesitation, a letting go of breath before she speaks. 'What was really in that remedy you gave me?'

I open my mouth, a reflex that is altogether pointless, for I have absolutely no idea how to respond to her question.

'You know what,' she says, filling in my silence. 'Never mind. On some level I probably deserved it.'

She did. Or at least I thought she did, but then I couldn't bring myself to actually go through with it. No matter the many, many ways it would have been possible to dispose of her, to wipe out her existence, none of them ever seemed quite right and I cannot help but think it was because I knew it was wrong, that perhaps she didn't deserve it after all.

'Patrick knows I was going to leave, before he came back from Hong Kong.'

Was he sad or angry? Was he relieved it could now be over? Did she simply come out and tell him, or was this part of a richer conversation? I see now that there are so many moments I will never bear witness to. So many shared experiences I cannot influence or change. Why did I think it would be possible to bend them away from one another, to steer him back to me?

'He said he had his suspicions. Said he could see the distance between us growing greater every time…' She pauses, looks away.

'Every time you failed to get pregnant.'

'Our therapist says it's a natural reaction to that amount of pressure on a relationship.'

'She sounds wonderfully wise.'

'It's Doctor Franks.'

I remember her from the assessment I had to undergo as part of the surrogacy process. For a shrink she's actually pretty spot-on with her assessments. Shame she wasn't smart enough to see through my lies. Would have saved us all a lot of trouble. Still. My grave and all that.

'She thinks it would be good if you went back to see her too.'

'I don't need anyone to tell me what the problem is.' I use the corner of the spade to dig out some weeds from between two paving slabs, toss them into the flowerbed and notice a bright-red lily beetle, taunting me with its presence.

'There's nothing wrong with asking for help.'

'I don't need your help.' I swat at the beetle with my foot, only for it to scurry down under the earth. Safe for now.

'It doesn't have to be me. But if only you would show some vulnerability, let someone in, then it could be a little easier.'

'Nothing about this is easy.' My grip on the spade tightens. 'You have no idea, no iota of reasoning to come even close to understanding what it is that I am going through.'

Part of me wants to tell her. To have her understand what it is to have your child, your unborn, be ripped from you. For her to know that he was conceived in the most natural of ways, with me riding myself to ecstasy as her husband filled me with his seed. A seed that swam towards my egg – mine, not hers. That we created life inside of me in a way she will never, ever get to experience. Nor will I.

'He was my child.' She is trying to lay claim to the grief, as if it too belongs only to her.

'Who you said you didn't even want.'

'What? I never said that.'

'Yes, you did, on the boat. You said you didn't want him anymore.'

She has the audacity to laugh and the anger that balls inside of me, that aches to be released, makes me shiver, as if my body and mind are fighting over what happens next. Do I kill her, here? Now? Yes, no, which path to choose, which fate to seal, which sin to give in to first?

'You thought I meant the baby? I was talking about Patrick, you stupid, stupid woman.'

Oh. My grip on the spade's handle slips and it clatters to the ground.

'Jesus, how fucked up do you think I am?'

There is no answer to her question. Too many others are showing themselves to me and I cannot quite process, cannot quite see. What is real, what is imagined, what does any of this mean?

'Is that why you've been so distant all this time? Why you've treated this whole sorry mess as if it's my fault?'

Yes. And so much more besides.

'I have wanted a child, ached for it, known nothing more than waking up every morning and wishing upon wishing that I could get pregnant. So for you to accuse me of even thinking for one second about leaving him behind… Wow. You really don't know me at all, do you?'

It would seem I may have made just one small mistake. One tiny misunderstanding that led me to altogether the wrong conclusion. And then I lashed out, made her return my anger with her own. Anger I created, anger that cost me so much more than I ever thought I wanted.

She takes hold of my hand and it is only when she touches me that I realise I am crying.

'How did we get here? What happened to us?'

I cannot bring myself to answer, nor can I let go of her hand.

'I am so, so sorry. You have to believe me.'

I do, which only makes it all the worse. Hot tears splash in my lap, collecting in the soft pleats of my deflated belly, like the droplets of blood that still leak from me as a cruel reminder of all I have lost.

'He quit his job.'

If Patrick has quit his job then it means something between them has shifted. I am being sucked back in, tormented by the two of them in a way I have struggled to control, to step away from. I have to make something new out of all the madness, but I cannot do so if they won't let me be.

'He wants me to quit too. For us to start again somehow.'

'You're leaving?'

'No. That's not what I do.'

The deliberate stab at me.

'I was so focused on having a baby that I forgot to pay attention to the one person I love more than anything.' She takes my hand again, looks at me with those doll-like eyes, one more tear caught on the edge of her lashes. She is mesmerising, which only makes her all the more dangerous. She thinks I am listening, beginning to forgive, to come back to her, to be cast under her spell once more. But all I can think about is how much I want to be rid of her, of all she has made me do.

'But now it's as if we've been given a second chance,' she says. 'A new perspective on life. It's as if his death will allow us to try again.'

My vision starts to blur. She thinks his death can be turned into a blessing, a promise of another turn of the wheel. As if this is all a game that is to be won or lost; as if his life was only ever worth anything if it was of benefit to her.

'Let me help you, Jane. You're the reason why, now, we have a chance to make things right.'

I have no words, no thoughts to convey how wrong this is. How completely false her reasoning is. How utterly worthless her hope is. Because I cannot allow them to heal, to grow, to flourish when my baby is no more. I will not permit them to have the happiness I was so close to finding for myself. They will not get to have what I do not.

'I need more time.' I need to think.

'Of course. Patrick and I are going back to Ireland for a few days. I've agreed to go with him on some bat thing he's been harping on about. So I'll see you when we're back, okay?' She leans in, places a tender kiss on my cheek, and it's all I can do

211

not to whip my face around and bite away her affection.

I am aware of her leaving the garden, of her silhouette on the boundary of my vision, but I cannot watch her go, cannot move from the place where I sit. It all has come to this. Me, myself and no one more. Alone, and of my own making. Because no matter what I do, she always wins. He will always go back to her. That my child's death has brought them back together feels tainted, untrue. Yet I realise that if it weren't for my intervention, none of this would have occurred.

She said she was going to leave Patrick, way back when. And then what would have transpired? Would he have come to me? Would our child have been created under the canopy of honesty instead of tangled in this stinking pile of bile I have fed and watered every day for as long as my memory can allow?

It is all of my doing. All of it. And nothing has changed, except for the tortuous absence inside of me. He is dead, he is dead, he is dead, and yet all around me life continues. Life I have created, life I have nurtured and watched and perfected, and for what? Why does this get to thrive and he does not? Why have I been allowed to believe there is beauty in a petal, in a scent, in a fucking tree, when he is dead and buried and rotting in the very ground from which they now spring?

The spade sighs at me. It knows what must be done.

I feel the stretch across my scar as my arm aims high. Clods of earth dance with flower heads, tumbling down to create a mosaic of horror on the grass. I slash and whack over and over, red wetness on my shirt as my stiches break free. The blood of another runs through me, but no amount of transfusions could make my demons lie down or leave me be.

Stepping back I assess the broken and wounded soldiers scattered all around, turn to walk away when brightness bounces into my eye. Sunlight flares on the greenhouse windows, shining its mirror back on me. I see her now. The monster that lies beneath. The truth of what I am.

212

Metal on glass, two sharps colliding, a fight that neither can win. Splinters on my skin, more red rivers running, as the building gives way to my assault.

Over and over I lash out, destroying all I have built because there is no one here to share it with. There is no child to teach, to follow where I lead, so I will smash it and break it and leave it in a heap on the ground.

No more can I create, no more will I try.

Shadows cling as I step into the kitchen. They wiggle through my wounds, filling my veins with their filth. White light bathes me as the fridge door gapes open, vials shivering in anticipation of what it is I must do. I gather them into my arms, shush away their fears and return to the garden once more. Neat lines they make on the wall, all standing to attention, ready and willing as the fading sun hides behind a welcome cloud, not wanting to bear witness to this brutality.

The first vial creates an unsteady arc through the air. I stand and wait for gravity to destroy its flight, then delight as the smash and clink confirms its demise. One by one they soar through the sky, higher, ever higher, as each tries to outdo the other, to see how far they can go. The last sits atop the brick, waiting, and I curl my palm around it, slick with blood and dirt that pollute the surface. I don't need to read the label to know what hides within. Belladonna may not have done its duty with her, with Elle, but bring it to my lips I must. Let it do its calling, let it take at least one of us away.

Block them out. Block all of them out, the faces and places and all I must escape. Take me to obscurity, for this world is too much, and altogether not enough.

And yet I cannot do it. Cannot bring myself to drink the poison I myself learnt to make as some sort of twisted tribute to my father. Because what if it doesn't work, just wrings out more pain and despair?

Nobody loves you.

It speaks the truth I have been hiding from ever since my father left. It has always spoken the truth, but I pushed it away, told myself I could change. Be better. Become something more.

Murderer.

'Leave me alone,' I roar as the vial splinters against the wall, a jagged piece in my palm that I use to slice open my wrist. To create a fresh line of red, so slick, so comforting, like a trusted friend that always does what you expect. No surprises here.

So I make another line. And another. Watch as they find a path along my arm, moving together into a waterfall that seeps out of my veins. The shard of glass is my trusted companion, my way out of this world in which I do not fit.

Then it is gone. Snatched from me by a warm and loving hand.

'What did you do?' I turn to find my brother, wait for him to see the chaos I have created. He drags me to him, uses his body to shield me from view. His breathing ragged, heart matching my own with its fearful beat, and in his voice I hear both his question and understanding.

'Oh, Christ, what did you do?'

CHAPTER TWENTY-TWO

Begonia: Dark and unpleasant thoughts that distract you from happiness

Being back in my childhood home is strangely comforting. Here in the room where I would invent new worlds within which to play, talking to my dolls and reading books aloud so I could pretend not to hear my parents arguing downstairs. It seems to fit so much better than any other I have ever slept in.

With its slanted ceiling, peeling paintwork and the floorboard by the radiator that creaks, I know every tiny crevice, have examined it all. The brass latch on the window is still loose, spinning full circle whenever it is opened. It was on my father's list of things to do, a list he never got to tick off.

I am sitting, propped up by faded patchwork cushions, on the window seat that bears both my father's and my initials, scratched into the lid after I helped him paint it cornflower blue. It feels safe up here in my tower, at the edge of the woods where I can stare over treetops that stretch towards the village. Now more than ever I am thankful my mother never sold this house, though I often struggled to understand why. Even when I had paid off

215

the mortgage, when she had no financial reason to stay, she said it was her home.

She has sat down there all afternoon, underneath the wilting jasmine that provides little cover from the heat of the day. Rain still has not fallen and the lawn is yellowed, crunchy underfoot. The garden is a tangle of thirst, with cracked soil and struggling fauna, but I have lost my desire to heal, to bring it back to life as once I would have. For what is the point in nurturing something that is only going to die?

I hear the car before I see it, the gravel lane that curves around the old oak tree giving its arrival away. The clunk of door and lolling footfalls as he approaches the house, turns as my mother calls out her greeting to him, invites him to join her for iced tea and a slice of lemon tart.

With all the will in the world I cannot bring myself to move from this spot. I am not ready to face him, to face the possibilities that Patrick could bring.

Wisps of conversation dance upward, seeking out my attention, but I don't need to hear the words to understand what is being said. She bats away his concern, tells him I am doing fine, but need time to recover from the physical impact a miscarriage can bring.

It's what they don't tell you about stillbirth. Those who are left behind must bear more than simply the emotional ramifications. My body believed I had given birth, that I needed to provide sustenance for my child. So three days after he was taken from me my breasts swelled, full of mother's milk with no one to suckle. The pain was like a sharp instrument slowly being inserted into my chest, then turned and turned, searching out a non-existent screw.

The nurses encouraged me to pump, to bleed my body dry and pass on its life force to other babies whose mothers were unable to feed them. But I relished the pain, found solace in its reminder that he had at one time existed.

Now my breasts are flaccid, my stomach slowly shrinking as this body betrays the idea it has ever done anything remarkable at all.

'He's gone.' She is sitting with eyes shielded by a battered old sunhat, the rim of which looks as if it has been munched on by a goat. But, like everything else, she will not throw it away until its use is well and truly no more.

In the centre of the table sit two brown paper packages, tied up with string. I sit down at the opposite end, stare at the empty lane where a dust cloud still lingers, no breeze to blow away evidence he was here. 'I know.'

'Why are you avoiding him?' The hat is tossed onto a chair and she leans forward, her arms forming a triangle on the table's surface, fingers aimed at me.

'I'm avoiding everyone.' There is no need for me to look to picture the hardness in her eyes; eyes that seek mine out, looking for clues, looking for information. I hear the scuff of heel against stone, the rat-a-tat of fingers on metal. Telltale signals that she is choosing what next to say.

Reaching out, I bring the parcels to me, pull at each end of the string to reveal a caddy of Lady Grey tea and a clear bottle of liquid with a sprig of juniper swirling through its centre. I know without opening it that it contains gin.

'He seems to genuinely care for you,' my mother says as she nods towards the offerings Patrick has left. She approved of him, once. Thought him charming and sophisticated and a world away from who she thought I would end up with.

Except I know the gifts come from another. One who asked me why I drank tea with blue petals, who learnt it made me remember my father. A teenage girl who encouraged me to steal a half-empty bottle of gin from my mother's cupboard to take to a party. Who mixed it with vodka in an attempt to appear sophisticated, then spent half the night retching all over a begonia bush while I held back her hair.

I look over at the cacophony of pots gathered at the edge of the patio. Shrivelled petunias hang pitifully over the rims, their fragrance long since burnt away.

'He chose Elle, Mum. No point trying to pretend otherwise.'

At this her mouth draws itself into a tight circle. 'I'm just saying he could be good for you.' Nothing is ever straightforward with my mother. She can never simply say what she means, always needing to layer it with subterfuge so that, even if its intention is misunderstood, she is never to blame.

'This is hardly the time to be thinking about who I should be screwing.'

'That's not what I meant.'

'Then what did you mean?'

She sucks her teeth through her lips. A habit she knows puts me on edge. A habit she uses to demonstrate just how irritated she is with my behaviour. 'You need to leave the house.'

'I'm outside now, aren't I?'

'Oh, don't be so belligerent. You know exactly what I mean. It's not healthy, it's not normal.'

'Since when have I ever been normal?'

A sigh.

'When your father left…'

'Oh, here we go.' I can't help it, I roll my eyes, feeling like a teenager once again.

'Don't be flippant with me, young lady. I am still your mother.'

'How could I ever forget?'

'When your father left…' She checks to make sure I'm not going to interrupt her before continuing. '…I had two choices. I could either wallow in self-pity…'

I seem to remember her doing exactly that for close to a year, but probably best not to point this out when she's in the middle of one of her pep talks.

'…Or, I could dust myself off and see it as an opportunity.'

'Explain how losing my baby can be an opportunity.'

She ignores the possessive reference, has done so with all of my attempts to tell her the truth. No doubt she knows, but chooses to ignore it in much the same way she has anything that threatens to shatter her perfectly preserved existence. If she doesn't acknowledge what I have done, it's easier to pretend it never happened. Easier to point the finger of blame elsewhere, and it makes me wonder what else she is hiding, from me as well as herself.

'You can start again. Make good what went wrong and decide on an altogether different kind of life.'

'There's nothing wrong with my life.'

She gives me a withering look. No need to express her disdain for the choices I have made. How time and time again I chose to put my own life to one side in order to help Elle, to come back to her and Patrick, no matter the personal cost to me. This time I agree, but I'm not yet ready to admit that to her, to give her the opportunity to gloat, to rub in yet another one of my shortcomings.

'The night Dad left…' I pick at the crumbling pastry on what remains of the lemon tart.

'What about it?'

'Did you argue?'

She stretches her arms above her head, arches her back like the gymnast she once was, before me, before I took over her life.

'That summer was even fiercer than this. We had to walk to a standpipe at the end of the lane twice a day as the water supply got cut off.'

I remember. Skipping out of the house to collect battered metal buckets. Filling them from the pipe that splashed icy water over my bare toes. Wishing upon wishing I could dance through the droplets, have them rain down on me and push rainbows into the sky.

I also remember the look on my father's face when I arrived in the kitchen and trod on a piece of broken crockery, the remnants of a casserole my mother had been preparing smeared on the wall by the back door. A shard stuck up between my toes and I dropped the bucket I was holding, washing away my blood into the cracks between the floorboards.

Was it better that he left? Is that what my mother wants, to spare me the pain she herself suffered when he chose another over her?

'You're so much like him.' My mother is staring at me now, at the navy-blue eyes and raven hair I inherited. At the long limbs and double-jointed fingers, the wide mouth and bony knees.

'And yet also so much like you.' I urge her to see, to understand, that I am terrified to leave this house for fear of what I might do.

'Nonsense.' Gathering up the tea tray she disappears back inside.

Her dismissal of me brings with it such a fury, a reminder of all the times I needed a mother but found her non-committal. Of the nights I would lie awake, wondering what had happened to my father because she refused to entertain any other notion than the one she told herself. He left and never looked back.

I follow her into the kitchen, taking with me Elle's gifts, then discover the room to be empty and so I sit alone at the table. Stare out at the swing that still hangs, unpainted and lopsided, from the tree in the back garden. The bottle of gin opens with a pop, clear and slick liquid cracking ice as I pour. Bitterness that kicks against my gullet as I swallow over and over, trying to remember, trying to forget.

'What are you doing?'

As always, my mother arrives unannounced, without warning.

'I'm crying.' I am stating the obvious, although I don't think she was actually asking me a question.

'You don't cry.' She crosses over to the sink to refill the kettle.

I don't answer, but listen as she busies herself with emptying the teapot and opening a fresh packet of tea. No doubt it will be Elle's offering. Her way of ensuring she is never far from my thoughts. I drain my glass of gin, refill it once more.

'He left a hole in the world where all my love fell through.' Even I'm not sure who I'm talking about. Which 'he' is responsible for this constant ache that pulsates through me with every breath.

'It's strange that when something is no longer there it can hurt so much. That nothing can be everything.' She is standing with her back pressed up against the sink, eyes on mine but focused on a time long ago. I want to ask if she is talking about my father, but am scared in case she tells me otherwise. My mouth opens a little, a question forming on my lips when she spins back around, pours steaming water into the pot and gives it a stir.

'We all come apart eventually, it's what we were designed to do. But you have to put yourself back together somehow.' She takes two mismatched cups from the dresser, a single finger looped through both handles. 'Stop hiding from what has happened and face it, fight it, be more than the person who sits and cries and regrets what is done.'

'It's all my fault.'

'Bullshit.' The teapot crashes onto the table, brown liquid sloshing onto the cotton cloth. 'Nothing is anyone's fault. It's how you react to what life throws at you that determines what sort of person you are. Not people, not circumstances, only you.'

She is angry, but not at me. At herself, for not steering me along the course thought best? At my father, for creating the problem in the first place? Or, more simple than that, at life itself for never being what we hope it will be?

'I want more.'

She picks up my glass with a flick of her hand, dismissal and approval in one swift movement. 'Then do something about it rather than waiting for it to happen. I thought I taught you better than that.'

CHAPTER TWENTY-THREE

Iris: Symbolic of hope, wisdom and passion

Robin and I sit above the rooftops of London, surrounded by raised beds made of railway sleepers. In the far corner, next to a delicious kitchen garden, are nestled a pair of hives. Drunken bees weave their way through the abundance of plants that are fed and watered, only to later be served up on china plates to the restaurant's paying guests. I sip my gin cocktail, tasting the bitterness provided by the leaves of the lemon verbena that grows behind me. Robin sits close, swirling his own drink.

He is relaxed. He is relaxing. I understand that he has brought me here, away from what waits back home. All the reminders and questions and fear. Being among people once more is not something I would have chosen, but he sees that I need to feel normal, to not be judged or recognised anymore.

Words are simply the vocalised form of communication of what is happening in our minds, but they can never convey what it is we are really feeling, even if we want them to.

I was living inside a cell from which I knew not how to escape. He has given me back the space to think, to move outside the confines of my mind. I used to think that because plants didn't bleed, didn't betray, they were all I could give myself to. But he is trying to show me another way, another idea of who I could be, if only I were willing to try.

'I've been offered a position in South Africa.' He finishes his drink, the blue chicory flowers melting out from the ice cubes they were trapped within.

'What?' My fingers tighten around my own glass. I don't want him gone.

'They want me to go out there, for some meetings, but you could come with me? We could take a road trip out to Kirstenbosch. It has over 20,000 native plant species, including a rather magnificent baobab tree.'

'Twenty-two.' I move aside as the waiter places my starter on the table in front of me. The plate is dotted with purple sage, which will perfectly complement the pear and walnut salad I have chosen. Robin has picked this restaurant, this hidden garden, with me in mind.

'Sorry?' He frowns over his own starter, no doubt wondering if the flowers on his plate are edible or merely for decoration.

'Over 22,000 species, but who's counting?'

A moment's consideration, to hide the hurt he is trying not to show at my glibness.

'The Mohawk Indians have a saying, that when a child falls into the rapids, the one who rescues her will share in her new life forever.' One hand laid, palm open, on the table between us. 'Let me rescue you.'

I stare at his hand, inch my own towards it and touch the very ends of my fingers to his. 'I don't know if I can.'

'You won't know if you won't try.'

'It's not that.' I look at him, then away once more. He doesn't know what really happened with Patrick and Elle. I don't think he wants to know, but he is hurting from the untruths, the subterfuge and the deceit I have handed him.

'Then what?'

I slide my fingers away, clamp them together in my lap and turn my head away. 'He died because of me.'

'He died because of a stupid accident. No one's fault.'

Even if he suspects, I can never allow him to see. What would it do other than break us all apart completely?

'I'm afraid of caring, because it's too painful.'

'So you don't care about me?' The hurt in his voice makes me look, makes me see him as a tiny baby once more. Cradled in his mother's arms as she introduced me to my brother. A brother I resented because he looked so much like the father who abandoned us all.

'I do, but nothing lasts forever. Nothing. So why do we even bother? What's it all for?'

'It's because nothing lasts that we have to grab on to the moments, the people who make us happy, even if only for a second, to make this all worthwhile.'

'Now you sound like Gramps.'

'That may be, but think... what is it that makes you feel?'

Water. The ocean. Sailing with Gramps that very first time. Running through the woods with Buster, dirt between my toes and grass stains on my knees. All the things that happened before I started to try and be something other, something more. Someone other than me.

'Everything, that's the problem.'

It was true. And for every moment I was happy came a hundred more when I was not. Every conversation, every decision, was loaded with purpose and I couldn't ever just sit and savour. Except with him, with Robin. Because he knew who I was before. Before I met Elle. Everything always comes back to that very first morning at school when she sat next to me, and my entire existence faltered.

'I don't see it as a problem. It's one of the things I love about you, your capacity to feel.'

'You love me? Even now? Even after everything I've done?'

224

'Of course, you're my sister. No need to sound so surprised.'

But it is surprising. The notion that I am loveable. That I am worthy of it without having to fight and claw and steal the emotion I so crave. And I do crave it, long for it, desire it in a way I cannot explain. But I always wanted it from him, from Patrick, so to hear those words from another is like an unexpected gift I am afraid to open.

I sit and look at him, really look at him. At the way his eyes are set so deep within his skull that when he laughs they all but disappear. At the sliver of scar on his top lip that betrays the surgery to correct the cleft he was born with.

'I'm your family and will love you no matter what happens tomorrow. You deserve a different life, a life where you can be whoever you want to be.'

He's right. But it feels like I would be running away, again. Running from everything I have done, everything I am capable of doing. Can I put that on him?

All I can manage in response is a sigh. Then I push back my chair and rush away before he can see me cry.

I press against the iridescent tiles of the washroom wall, close my eyes and wait for the cool to register on my skin. To feel something other than this knot of fear that is spinning inside of me. Perhaps this night is the very end of my suffering? Perhaps I too can be given another chance, to prove I can be someone, something, other than the monster I gave in to, listened to, believed.

Such a need, such a keenness to hope, which makes it all the more dangerous, for if I were to fall again, I do not think my heart would survive.

Breathe in, breathe out, calm down the fractious beat inside of me. Then a quiver of recognition, of a perfume so linked to one who has worn the scent of irises ever since I first gifted her a bottle of *Apres L'Ondee*, and suddenly the rhythm of the room is changed. The energy of my mind spinning, fingers balled tight, for even here I am not safe.

'Jane?' I hear her laughter as she approaches, smell her skin. 'I can't believe you're here. I mean, I'm really glad you are. I've been in the downstairs bar with some of the girls. Come and join us later?'

No. No. No. Not here. Not now. Why can't the Universe leave me be? Give me just one night without her.

'Jane…' Elle says my name once more. 'Are you all right?'

'I'm fine.' I cross over to the sink, turn on the tap and run the cool liquid over the pulse that frets at my wrist, push down on the spout of a mottled glass bottle, watch a line of soap curl into my palm. I try not to look, to see the strapless top that highlights the new glow to her skin. The curl of hair that falls over one cheek. The painful beauty that has such a profound effect on me.

'What's the matter?' She steps closer, one arm outstretched, and I twist myself away.

'Don't touch me.'

'Okay, okay, I'm sorry.' Hands raised, she backs away.

It infuriates me, this look of innocence, this assumption that I am the one in the wrong, that she is merely trying to placate a madwoman. Then her face shifts into something altogether worse. Pity. As always, looking upon me from up above, from her fucking pedestal that makes her so much more than I could ever be, and she knows it. She knows how much I have craved her, envied her, loved her. How much she has taken over my every thought, every deed, and for what? For me to be here, hiding in a washroom instead of accepting the love of someone who seems not to care about all of my demons.

She doesn't deserve you.

'No, she doesn't.' She doesn't deserve anything anymore.

'Who are you talking to?'

'What do you care?' Water slips between my trembling palms, washing away the temptation, sending it down and away. Do not give in. Do not be the darker side of your soul. Do not become what you know is there waiting.

226

'Of course I care.' She has the nerve to look offended, as if I am the one to have done her a disservice. 'You're making no sense.'

'Oh, I'm making perfect sense. For once it's all become so fucking crystal clear I could cry.'

'I really don't follow…'

'No, I don't suppose you would. Too preoccupied with your own precious existence to see how you're destroying mine.' I wish I could go back. Do it all over again. Find that one moment when I chose a different path and tell myself it would end in this, a style of pain that has no meaning. That I needed to choose someone other than her.

'Is this about Conall?'

'Stop calling him that!' My fist smacks against the porcelain basin. 'His name was not Conall. He wasn't your baby, he was mine.' I find her eyes in the mirror. 'If it weren't for me he never would have existed in the first place.'

'And if it weren't for you he would still be alive.'

The soap bottle skims through the air before I even register having picked it up. It explodes into tiny fragments that spit glass and soap all over the wall, some of which settle on Elle's shoulder.

'What the fuck is wrong with you?'

'I hate you.' I pick up another, take better aim and send it hurtling towards my prey. 'I hate you for what you've done to me. For everything you took from me.'

She ducks a moment too late, a look of disbelief as the bottle makes contact with the side of her face.

'Jane, please. Stop.'

'Why? Why should I stop? Why should I do anything at all that you tell me to?'

'Because I love you.' She closes the space between us, clasps my hands.

'Stop saying that.' I try to pull away but find I cannot. That even now I don't have the capacity to resist her. 'You have no

227

idea what love is. What it means to give yourself to another. Completely and without thought for your own fragile heart. How it feels to have it all stolen away, but still be there, so close yet out of reach. You cannot talk to me about love because you have never known what it is to lose.'

'No,' she says, her pupils dark as night. 'I mean, I love you, love you.'

Air catches at the back of my throat when she bends her head to mine, mouths touching, lips parting as she deepens the kiss. Just like a night so long ago. A night I never forgot but completely misunderstood.

* * *

Twelve years ago

'Come on,' Elle urged. 'You can't make me go up there by myself.'

'Yes, I bloody can,' I replied, neck tilting backwards as far as it would go, making my mouth hang open as if it were waiting for something to drop down my gullet.

'Please?' She clutched at my hands as she hopped from foot to foot. 'I promise not to ask for anything else, ever again.'

Of course I would agree. Despite my reluctance, due to an over-powering fear of heights, I knew even before she pleaded that I would succumb. So I climbed in beside her and attached the flimsy chain that was supposed to prevent anyone from falling out of the side of the carriage as the Ferris wheel spun us up and around.

White lines stretching between my knuckles, the pinpricks of light at the edge of my vision pulsating as the circle pulled us towards the heavens. The fairground spread out before us like one of those miniature villages. Except this one contained living, moving creatures that flung up their voices to where the air still held a sickly taste of candyfloss and cheap cider.

The end-of-school farewell. The celebration that marked this part of our lives as over and declared we were ready, willing and more than able to become adults, thank you very much. No more did we need supervision from teachers or parents. No more did we need curfews and revision timetables because we were beyond all that. No more did we bow down to the pressure to conform, to behave, to fit in with convention.

So of course we chose to recognise this moment in our collective histories by consuming vast quantities of alcohol and trying to shoot down as many paper targets as possible in order to win an oversized teddy bear.

Except I was the tag-along. The third wheel. The personification of social gooseberry, for, while everyone else had been paired off for months, the invitation to go as another's date had never quite reached my door. Which meant I was there with Elle and Harry. Forever witness to their suffocating romance, which as far as I could tell seemed to involve little more than exchanging bodily fluids. No scintillating conversations or musings about their future together, just a basal meeting of orifices.

They kept coming back together. No matter how many other boys lined up for her, she kept going back to his bed. But she knew that to be tied to someone so early in life would prevent her from discovering what else was on offer.

'I can't believe we're leaving.' Elle placed one end of a joint in between her glossy lips then held up a lighter to the other. I watched the fire take hold, tiny circles of amber that spread as she inhaled. Saw her eyes close, her features relax as the drug hit the back of her throat.

'We'll be back.'

'You won't,' she said, passing the joint to me. I hesitated, not wanting to release my hold on the railing, even though I knew it would make absolutely no difference as to whether or not I would tumble from this fragile seat to the ground below.

'Is this about Harry?' I asked, blinking against the fumes that always made my eyes complain.

He wanted her to reconsider going away to university. To stay in London with him. But that would only end in inevitability, which Elle seemed so intent on avoiding yet did absolutely nothing to prevent from happening.

'No. Yes. Maybe? I just feel as if everything that's waiting for me is nothing to do with what it is I actually want out of life.'

'Then what do you want?'

She blew a long line of smoke into the sky, grey mixing into navy as if it were never there at all. I imagined stoned little insects breathing in her air, unable to find their way home. 'I have no fucking idea.'

Another drag, another plume of smoke as she tilted her head back and blew upward. I watched the rise and fall of her Adam's apple. Wondered what it would be like to kiss it.

'Isn't that the point?' I took the joint from her, sucked in the delirium, felt it swimming around my brain. 'That we're young, free of all responsibility, which means we can do exactly what we choose?'

Is this what we all do? Put up a futile fight against the gods? For they have already determined the exact way our lives are going to pan out. Is the rebellion we cling to as teenagers, on the cusp of adulthood and all the weight of accompanying responsibility, just a momentary glimpse of freedom that doesn't really exist? Does this mean there's no point fighting to be anyone other than who you were from the very beginning?

A giggle passed over my lips as I realised this was not your typical weed, but an altogether different kind of beast. No doubt procured for this very night, when all bets are off and we knew it would become a memory to be revelled in when we were old, wistful and in mourning for our youth.

'Easy for you to say.'

'Coming from the resident princess.' I looked up, tried to form the stars into something resembling the constellations, but all I could think of was how they looked like the scales of a mermaid's tale.

'You don't have any expectations to live up to,' Elle said and I righted my head, saw her turning her hand over and back again, looking for something that wasn't there.

She had no idea about the mountain of pent-up frustration my mother had reminded me of every single day since my father left. Of everything she'd sacrificed because of me. Of all the other paths she could have walked down, qualifications she could have earned. Respect she could have gained for being something, anything, other than a mother. Because as soon as you have a snotty little offspring attached to your bosom, people see them before they see the person who created them. Comment on their beauty, their intelligence, the fucking colour of their poo, because anything is more interesting than a sleep-deprived being who can't even remember what day it is, let alone argue about the state of the world's economy.

My mother was desperate for me to be something more than her, which only made me terrified of what would happen if I failed.

'Have you told Harry?'

Elle dropped the end of the joint over the side of the carriage, watching it spiral to the ground. 'I figured I'd wait until after tonight.'

Which meant she didn't want anything to tarnish her memory of this, our last farewell to being a teenager, the moment when we were expected to grow up and forge ahead on our own. It was both liberating and debilitating, this possibility of what lay beyond the bubble of school, and I understood her need to cling to it as long as she could. For here she was, the top of the pyramid, the person everyone either wanted to be or wanted to be with. But would that power remain or be stolen by another when she ventured out into the world where there were creatures as beautiful, as alluring as she?

I knew there was so much more out there than the scraps she would send my way. A life in which I wasn't always walking a

231

few paces behind, waiting for the opportunity to prove my worth. But for Elle the unknown was as terrifying as waking up to discover all her hair had fallen out in the night.

'You're so beautiful. You have no idea what it's like to be outside of everything.'

'I think you're just scared of the truth.' Hands either side of my face, her forehead touching mine. Pupils wide open, the sweet scent of marijuana on her breath. My thoughts were all a blur as she kissed me softly, those lips that were coveted by so many against my own.

A fraction of a moment that stretched infinitely through time to last forever and a day. A single action that would never be undone, never not remembered; that would create so many questions and feelings and torments now cemented in my heart.

When she pulled away the returning air felt cold in the space left behind. There were no words I could speak, no sense to what had just happened, but before I had a chance to respond she began to climb onto the tiny metal seat and reach her arms into the night.

'Elle, get down.' I grabbed at her dress, tried to pull her off the seat, but that only served to make the tiny carriage rock more violently.

'Fuck you, life! Fuck you and all your lies!'

The couple in the carriage in front turned round, screeching at the sight of Elle, who was completely oblivious to the attention she was once again commanding. I wrapped my skinny frame around her calves as her torso bent back and forth, like one of those wooden toys where you have to push against the bottom to make it move.

'Think of the freedom, of choosing how it all ends,' she said, grinning down at me. 'Of dying before you have the chance to fuck it all up, to be a disappointment.'

A crowd had gathered at the bottom of the wheel, arms pointing up to the chaos. Calls of alarm, cheers of encouragement, the flash of a thousand photographs as each of our spectators made up their mind about the story they would tell.

The angry cry of the ride's supervisor, demanding that Elle sit back down immediately.

'Fuck off, you controlling bureaucrat!' She laughed back at him as she tried to shake off my grip.

'Elle, please. You have to get back down.'

'You don't understand.' She was crying, all the bravado melted away.

'Understand what, Elle? What is it you're not telling me?'

A sudden lurch as the wheel came to a stop, the unexpected absence of motion forcing her sideways, away from me.

Time doesn't slow down in the event of a tragedy. It's not as if you're watching the world through a slow-motion camera. There's not even a second during which you can stop, assess and decide. One more thing we cannot control.

It was the chain that saved her. That tiny, insignificant looping of metal that stopped her from disappearing out of sight, breaking her incredible self on the giant spokes of the wheel and landing in a heap of bloody mess.

That night will be embellished and distorted and retold over and over in so many ways by people who weren't even there but claimed to have witnessed the moment when Elle Hart nearly fell to her death.

Nearly, but not quite. Because of me.

* * *

Now

'I can't.' My head moves away and I see pain mirrored in her eyes. A pain just as real, yet so different to my own.

'I know.' She offers up a half-smile and it breaks me, crumbles me into a million pieces of misunderstanding and regret.

'Why didn't you tell me?'

'Because I didn't want to lose you.' It is her turn to cry. I want to reach out and wipe her sorrow away, but there is a new line drawn between us and I am not yet decided which side I wish to stand upon. Too much remains undone. Too much remains of the agony I still feel.

'So instead you stole the one person I thought could make me happy?'

'I'm sorry.'

'That's not enough.' Will anything ever be enough? Or is it all now too much? This knowledge, this affirmation of something I must have suspected somewhere along the way. Playing along because of a desire to be so close to her. Seeing it as an opportunity not to be missed. Could I really have been so totally ignorant? Or did I choose not to see?

'Forgive me.'

'I don't know if I can.'

This time I am the one to walk away. To leave her there, trapped in her loneliness, trapped in her lies and deceit, trapped by a future unknown.

This time I am the one who gets to choose.

CHAPTER TWENTY-FOUR

Deadly Nightshade: Deception, danger and death

I'm standing in the doorway to my father's shed at the bottom of the garden, by the edge of the wood and as far away from the house as it could possibly be. For months after he left, it remained abandoned, held in a perpetual state of limbo, until I stepped inside one frosty morning and decided to claim it for myself.

From here I can see the uneven shelving that holds up the walls as much as the other way round. They are still littered with his research books along with treasures unearthed on any one of our adventures into the unknown. A rock in the shape of an old man's face; a miniature dining table and chairs that Gramps hand-carved for a doll's house I never played with; and rows and rows of bottles and vials. But it is not these that have caught my eye, rather the top shelf that is now lined with nearly three dozen glass bell jars, each containing one of my early experiments.

I drag the stool closer and climb up, still feeling a little unsteady on anything other than solid ground. My finger draws a line through the dusty glass, revealing a piece of coral, chipped like

235

a broken tooth. My father brought it back from Egypt when he was a student, diving into the Red Sea and smuggling home all that he could. Next to it is a duck egg I pickled in formaldehyde, retching against fumes that clung to the back of my throat. I remember wishing I had left it alone, that by trying to change it into something other, I ended up taking away all of its beauty.

The wind lifts, bringing with it a promise of change, much like the arrival of Mary Poppins. Something more, a scent so familiar, yet today it does not seem to have the influence on my heart it once did.

'Your mother said I might find you in here.' Patrick stops a lifetime away, skin warmed by summer sun and stubble all the way along his jaw and down his neck. He looks so like the student I once knew that for a moment I am taken unawares, transported back to an autumn afternoon in the college library. One blink is all it takes to show me the clearer picture, of how much we have both camouflaged our true selves for the sake of another.

'I'm surprised she let you in.' I clamber down from the stool, aware of his uncertainty as to whether or not he should be assisting me.

'She was reluctant.' Patrick steps inside, peering at the gathering of trinkets and picking up a half-empty bottle marked *citronella*, swirling the lemony contents my father swore kept the bugs at bay better than any carnivorous plant could. The first man I ever loved, the first one to break me, the first one to leave.

'It's like an old-fashioned apothecary.'

He moves around the small space and his proximity is unsettling, but not in its usual guise. Now I find myself on edge, wishing I could be here alone, to rediscover what I thought was lost. His presence once would conjure up such intense longing and desire that it was all I could do not to press my skin on his, to imagine him undressing me, running his hands all over me, kissing me against the wooden wall. Now I want him gone. He is a distraction I can no longer bear.

I see him leaning closer to an object tucked away behind a tortoise shell and old gardening gloves.

'Don't touch that. It belonged to my grandmother.'

'What does it do?' He cocks his head to one side, neck stretching out as his eyes try to make sense of something unfamiliar. I can almost see the workings of his mind, the consternation at not knowing the answer to his own question.

'She used it to distill her own gin.' Perhaps I should start up her tradition once more. Give these hands something better to do, for the bottle Elle gave me is now empty of its ware. The self-induced coma in pursuit of a dreamless sleep, a haze that lingers even when I wake because any kind of feeling is still too much.

'This feels more like the real you.'

'What do you mean?' I look over at him, see his eyes darting all about.

'This...' he says as he gestures around him. 'The shed. The chaos. The experimenter. No clean lines and perfection.'

'I've always been a bit OCD.'

'Your room at college was anything but tidy.' He scoffs, the beginnings of a laugh that doesn't quite take shape. 'When did you become someone else?' He's staring at me, as if I am a riddle he needs to solve. 'Your clothes are different, even your hair. It's as if you've been smothering the real you, but now you're not.'

There it is again. The prod, the nudge against my subconscious that reminds me how, underneath all the money, he is a decent, intelligent human being. That I chose him as my soulmate, saw so much more than the moth-eaten jumpers and scruffy hair. How I told him about the real me, the one who hunted for bugs, went fishing and planted a magnolia tree at the entrance to our driveway, hoping it would somehow entice my father back home if ever he were to pass by.

It is because of them that I was forced to hide, to change, to be better, to be more. To never decide for myself what it was I wanted, but rather try to imagine what he would want me to be. But for all my efforts, all my abilities, I never won the ultimate prize, the prize of true love. Because the fairy tales never tell you about the one who is left behind, the one who loves the prince but isn't chosen. The one whose dreams are smothered for the sake of another's happiness. The one who stopped believing in happily ever after.

'Every time I get close to being happy one of you fucks it all up again.' I take down a book, open it, then slam the cover shut.

'One of who?'

How is it that neither of them can see what it is they have done? Or what I have done, for them.

'The world does not turn just for you. You are not the reason stars shine, or a bee makes honey, or a forsythia flowers during the leafless season.'

'Now you're just rambling.' He tucks his hands into his armpits. 'You never ramble.'

I'm not rambling. I am perfectly in control of my thoughts, but I find myself pacing, only a few steps before I reach a wall and have to turn and go back again.

'No, of course not. Because I have to be controlled and sensible and an overachiever, because…'

'Because what?'

'Because I'm neither her nor him.' My voice bounces around the small space and my hands come out as if to snatch back the words I've been so scared of admitting. 'Without him she never gave me the chance to figure out who I actually wanted to be.'

'Okay, I'm still confused.' One quick shake of his head, to get rid of the unwanted perplexity. 'Who are we talking about?'

'My father.' The realisation comes out in a sigh, a release from where it has been trapped deep inside of me. 'Everything I ever did was either because I was trying to be like him, or not. To be better so that my mother wouldn't be disappointed.'

My whole body is shaking, and I wrap my arms around my

238

stomach in a weak attempt to stop everything from pouring out. The years of regret, of trying to make her love me more. To fill the abysmal void my father left in my soul when he decided I wasn't enough to make him stay, to make him want to be part of my life.

'Will you show me how it works?' He points at the small copper distiller then leans against the workbench, fingers tapping out an uneven rhythm.

He's trying to distract me by bringing me back to what he knows I love. It's one of his better qualities, his ability to read people, to understand them even if he cannot always relate to them in the more conventional sense. My arms slowly unravel, fingers finding the air and guiding my body over to the workbench where the copper pots stand, awaiting my attention.

'My grandmother used to put lavender in her gin, but the process is pretty much the same no matter what you use.' I show him inside the largest round pot and am rewarded with a thousand memories of when I would do this very same action. Over and over again. Experimenting. Learning. Trying in some way to become more like my father, when now I see I was simply being myself.

I remember the first time Nana showed me how to use it. She had allowed me to pick the juniper berries that would be mixed with vodka and turn it into gin, but I wanted to know what was in the small, glass bottle she was adding to the blend. Opened it and breathed in the powerful scent. Asked how she did it. How she managed to capture the smell. Was she a witch? She laughed and took me to the shed that leant against Gramps's workshop. Unlocked the door and welcomed me into a whole new world of intrigue and possibility. Then she gifted me the distiller, said it was my turn to transform and enhance what nature first created.

My father may have loved plants, but it was my mother's side of the family that showed me versatility. Of surviving no matter the odds.

'So you can distill anything at all?'

'Within reason. Usually something that has oil in it, but it can also be used to purify water. I tried it with pine cones, bark, even a dead mouse.'

'Eau-de-mouse doesn't really have the same kind of appeal as roses.'

The smile appears first, pulling apart his lips to set free his laugh. A deep belly laugh that has him close his eyes and rise up on his feet, then sink back against the bench once more. The laughter stops, but still his body convulses, only now I see that it is sorrow causing him to move, to push tears from his eyes.

I've never known Patrick to cry. Never known him to open up to his emotions in such a blatant way.

Maybe this is what grief looks like when you have lived a charmed and healthy existence instead of being dark and twisted from childhood. Maybe this is normal, but I don't like it.

He lifts his head to look at me. Sorrow, raw and open, contorts his face into one I don't want to look upon.

Why should he get to be normal? Why should he claim this sorrow as his own when he knows nothing of what real pain can do to a person? The way it can rip wide your world and stuff it full of the worst imaginings you can ever have. The way guilt follows you round like a ghost only you can see, whispering its accusations, sniggering at your pathetic attempts to justify what it is you have done.

No. He does not get to have such a blessing. He does not get to feel in such an easy and uncomplicated way.

I stretch out my fingers in the direction of the house, make sure he looks to where I point.

'Do you know what that plant is, growing up against the wall over there, next to the holly bush?'

'No. Why do you ask?' Confusion that sits neatly in his brow, at why I am not joining him in his grief.

'*Solanum dulcamara.* Otherwise known as deadly nightshade, or belladonna.'

Will he see the connection? Will the dots slide together to form a memory of the conversation he had with Elle's father? A conversation that made me stray off course. A conversation that had everything to do with what happened next.

'I don't see what this has to do with…'

'The flowers are glorious. Deep violet with dots of green near the stamen. They open like lanterns, hanging from vines of toxic leaves. But it's the berries you need to be careful of. Did you know they both look and smell a little like tomatoes, which is why you have to be particularly careful not to let any children ingest them, although some experiments seem to suggest they're only poisonous when immature.'

'Why are you telling me this?'

I'm telling him because he needs to understand that, just because something is beautiful, it's folly to assume it's safe.

'It's one of the first plants I ever successfully distilled. Right here, in the back garden of my childhood home, waiting for my mother to pay attention to me. I deliberately chose it so that if I ever decided to kill myself, I would be absolutely certain to succeed.'

His silence shouts at me. The sensation of the world moving ever onward while we face one another, trying to figure out what it is we are each trying to say.

'Do you still have any?'

'No.' Which is true.

He glances at my wrists, watches as I turn them from view.

'Do you still want to do yourself harm?'

The way he phrases things. It used to be endearing, because it made him different. Now it's ridiculous and arrogant, as if he knows better than any of us how best to speak, to converse. How can I have allowed myself this infatuation? With him, with her, with it all?

'I don't want to make any more mistakes.'

We're so scared of saying the wrong thing, but what are words

241

other than a poor imitation of what we are truly feeling? The only thing worse than saying the wrong thing is saying nothing at all. Which is exactly what he does, turning around and walking away with hands clasped behind his back, long strides taking him towards the swing, where he stops, spins around and rages at me.

'Conall was not a mistake and I will not allow you to tell anyone, even yourself, otherwise.'

'I wasn't talking about my baby.'

'For God's sake, you were the one who offered to be the surrogate.'

'And you could have said no, you should have said no.'

His jaw twitches, reveals the internal battle over whether or not to push.

'I know what happened that night.'

Pain. Sharp and fierce at my centre, then rushing up to my heart, where it sits, waiting. I can't speak. I don't trust the lie to work anymore.

Shoulders slumped, he sighs, then strokes back his hair. 'It's not just your fault, Jane. I could have stopped it.'

Not with the dosage I gave him, but now's not the time for semantics.

'Elle and I were falling apart long before you came back. I think we told ourselves you were all we needed to make things right.'

Which part of the chaos do I fear the most? And who am I trying to hide it from? He remembers that night. Has carried the secret with him as my belly grew fat. Perhaps wondered at the depth of his own betrayal. Questioned whose child his wife was expected to raise.

I wanted him to know, to remember, to see how complicit he has been in everything that has transpired. Because if it weren't for him, Elle and I would have stood a chance of being happy. If it weren't for him, we might have dared tell one another the truth.

'Does she know?'

'No.'

I need him away from here. I need to think, to breathe, and I can't do that when every time I inch closer to a semblance of a normal life, of figuring out how to be, they come back. I need to cut clean.

'Are you going to tell her?'

He doesn't reply, just stands there, staring, as the sky starts to fade into grey. I look up, see that the sun has been shut out by cloud and the wind has sucked the heat from the day.

'I think you should go.' I skip past him towards the house. A movement behind the kitchen window tells me my mother has been watching and I wonder how much she has been able to discern from that distance.

Patrick reaches out for my hand, but I dodge the offering, try not to hear what he says as I walk away.

'It feels as if we're saying goodbye, all over again.'

This time it's my turn to be silent. Not trusting the words to come. Never the right words, never the right moment. Is that all life is? A series of random moments we hope will somehow collide and make us happy? Why do we even bother if there is no way of knowing whether the outcome of all our efforts will be worth it? At what point do we stop believing and just resign ourselves to whatever shit gets thrown our way?

I close the kitchen door behind me, not turning to see if he's still out there.

My mother's over by the sink, hands busy with something, always busy, never resting, never content to simply be.

'Is he gone?'

'I don't know.'

She raises her gaze to mine, eyes narrowing a fraction as she takes me in.

'Well, instead of standing there, come and make yourself useful.'

I do as I'm told, go over to the kitchen counter and take the stand from my mother's outstretched arms. Six silver tiers, decreasing in size as they climb, with a glass pole running through the middle. I take it over to the table and place a lace doily on each circle.

My mother comes alongside me, puts down a box full of vanilla cupcakes with criss-crossed wrapping. Then another box of bell-shaped cakes topped off with pale, pink frosting. Yet another contains bone china cups in which she has baked cappuccino-flavoured sponge. It will be my job to pipe on the icing then top them with spirals of sugar designed to resemble steam.

We work around and around the stand, trussing it up like a maypole for all to wonder at.

'Find someone who thinks he's lucky to have you, not the other way round.' She says this as she ties a white satin bow around the cake that sits proudly on top, covered in royal icing that hints at her reflection. I expect it has been decorated to complement the blushing bride's own gown.

'You mean someone other than Patrick.' I pass her the first in a line of handcrafted sugar roses, which she sticks to the top of the cake, then waits for me to pass the next.

'I do. Patrick knows you're better than him. That he could never compete with you, so he would come to resent you for it.'

Everyone thinks it's Patrick my heart breaks for. I did too. Until I realised that I miss her more than anything. I miss the way she accepted me for who I was, even if I was unable to see it for oh so long. For the simple fact of being my friend when no one else would. She didn't have to talk to me, didn't have to include me. I made no sense, didn't fit with the rest of her world, yet she chose to love me, chose to let me be part of all the memories we created together.

'Elle is breathtaking, but she isn't right for you either.' She stands back, bends down to inspect her creation from every possible angle. Avoids my astonishment, refuses to explain why she knew but never told.

'She was never right for you, but until you see that you can never be happy. Don't compromise yourself for anybody. Just be you.'

If only it were that simple. If only I actually knew who I really was.

CHAPTER TWENTY-FIVE

Turmeric: Purity, prosperity and generosity

The window is open to a night heavy with heat, stuck in air that refuses to move.

Night-lit, the kitchen waits, bright white covering me as I open the fridge and take out a frosty bottle. Milky waterfall into the pan, a sprinkling of turmeric that becomes a swirling mass of lines staining the liquid copper.

I perch at the open window, lean into the ebony night from which no breeze stirs. The endless heat of summer we know not what to do with. All is still, all is as it has been, yet altogether other, for I am changed. My entire existence has been upended so I am not what I was before.

A whirring of cogs announces another passing hour, the clock in the hallway stripped bare of bells ever since it prevented me from sleeping as a child. My head turns to the noise, as familiar as the scent of my mother's skin; the absence of either would make this house feel wrong. The dresser against the wall calls out to me, makes me look upward, to where cobwebs link it to the ceiling. Sat atop is a small cardboard box. A box I had forgotten but now know all over again.

Cup put down, I go over, begin to climb the same way I always did, when something needed to be hidden, away from a brother too inquisitive, too keen to be grown like me. A simple box that once contained a pair of black plimsoles in which I would hide my secrets.

I remember Robin's howl as he watched me climb, place my treasure up high. Chubby arms reached out, dotted with glitter and dirt. Always fiddling, always hunting for things that didn't belong in the arms of a toddler. He was always here, never there, with his mother whose eyes stayed ever half-closed. Weekends were supposed to be my time to roam, to dig, to explore the garden my father left for me – me, not Robin – and not the reminder of how he left us more than once.

Box open, I inhale its reminder of a time no more. All that remains is a piece of broken pot, undone by my own hand when first he left. The remnants of a butterfly's wing painted at the break. A creature that is born a certain way, then cocoons itself from the world so it might transform into something beautiful. But such a fragile kind of worth, for touch its wings even once and no longer can it fly.

Touch the wings and it dies.

Porcelain-sharp on my skin, a single point that presses against each mark of black. Cutting them out. Ridding me of Elle's branding iron, of the reminder I have carried with me too long.

The sigh of blood as it escapes my veins, the whisper of wind from beyond the house, and out into the dawn I go.

Nature's colour has been stolen, bleached by the sun. Rain so long away that even here, where the rays don't quite reach, things are struggling to grow. It is all a sameness, the pixels of the world blended together, so hard is it to differentiate between earth, wood and other.

Who knew one slice could offer up so much blood?

My hands are clean, but the filth I still feel. The stain on my body because of what I did to my boy. Must I get it all so wrong? Must I be presented with one mistake after another, a veritable conveyor belt of how my intelligence was never enough? That I tried so hard, too hard, and ended up with nothing at all?

My feet lift from the ground; it is only now I realise I have come all this way with nothing but skin to protect them. The scar by my big toe peers at me from between dust and earth, a reminder of the family I have lost.

Legs take me to the river, remembering the way, although I do not look, afraid now to look. Peeling back the layers, my clothes in a pile for someone else to find. Chill from my soles up and around my knees, then over my belly, my belly where once he grew. My chest, my throat now wrapped in water, up and over my face, my eyes, my everything.

There is something transcendent about water. It is the only thing that calms me, cocoons me, protects me. When I was a child I would spend hours lying submerged in the bath, letting the water filter out the world. Breath would burn in my lungs as I held on to that moment, to the absence of being, because down there everything became diluted and shrouded and altogether different.

All is quiet. All is still as once it should be.

Is this what it was like for him, for my boy? Lifted, held, limbs liquid and loose, no noise in his mind, no pain in his innocent soul. My fingers reach onward, my spine curves and stretches with the will of the river. So under will I stay, allow it to take me.

A tightness. Small, but there, sat against my heart. It is nothing, I am nothing.

It grows. Persistent. My body cries out to breathe, but open my mouth I cannot. Not here. Be gone, be not what they think. Be not the one who has no reason more. Not daughter, not mother shall I be. For without he, down here is better. Down here I can let go, be free.

Fog filters through, weaving upward from toe, to grow and

filter out all else but what has been. Pictures of memories of sights once seen. Of people and places, faces and more. Of creatures and flowers and stories galore. Backwards and forwards and all around I fly, until suddenly nothing.

A drop, a plop, of sound that spears the water, sends ripples along my arm. Another that caresses the bone of my collar, making the water change, renewed.

Where am I?

Who am I?

What am I?

I am me. I am not her. I am who I choose to be.

Take it back, take back this life and do it once more. Do it better, do it greater than before.

Go back, go up, go all around again. He has not died for nothing. I still remain.

The first breath pulls and rips and hurts more than I prepared for, but it is what I need. This reminder that I can give myself another chance. Neck stretched full I suck in the air, let it rattle around inside of me, force oxygen into my blood. Fingers grab *typha latifolia*, using their lengths to pull me to the bank, to the earth.

Rain has come, great fat droplets of purification that stream along my spine, washing away the river. Washing away what it is I was about to do.

This river that ends in the ocean, that lifts into the sky then falls all over again. The cyclicality that simply is. No control, no pattern, everything and anything colliding together in random motions that ripple throughout the Universe. So much all at once that none of us can see, none of us can change.

Hands and knees dig into dirt as I retch up the river, belch it from my centre.

Is it luck that the river runs not fierce, that the absence of rain has kept it meek, or did I know when I entered that I could leave?

No matter more. What's done can never be undone.

CHAPTER TWENTY-SIX

Forget-Me-Not: True love, memories

People collect things for all sorts of reasons; they refuse to throw them away for a million more. Boxes are stacked up in the corner of the kitchen, labelled according to whether they will be going into storage, sent to charity or the dump. The therapeutic value of decluttering, of ridding my life of unnecessary objects, is undeniable, but even in my most rational, most pragmatic of moods, I am finding it difficult to part with certain items.

A porcelain dish in the shape of a mermaid, bought as a summer souvenir on my first trip abroad. A well-thumbed copy of *Matilda* that is missing the middle pages. A stone painted to resemble a mouse, complete with string tail and pine-cone ears.

A photograph of Elle and I in the south of France. I was as pale as she was tanned, standing with our backs to the sea, flushed cheeks and sand in our hair. We had spent the morning exploring rock pools, collecting shells and cartwheeling along the beach. As if we were children, as if there was nothing else in the world that needed our attention. It was the last time I can remember feeling truly happy.

'What are you doing?' Elle stands in the doorway, pointing at my waiting suitcase.

Despite myself, despite it all, I am happy to see her. She still has this effect on me, which is probably why I have been avoiding her, avoiding her presence, because it is always too much to be around her. It makes me behave irrationally.

'What does it look like I'm doing?'

She looks around the half-empty kitchen. 'Tell me you're having a clear-out rather than selling?' Her gaze lingers on the door through to my workshop. To the rows of now-empty shelves.

Behind the door is a box containing the crib I bought for him. The crib I intended to assemble myself and place under the window in my bedroom so he could watch the dancing leaves of the silver birch, sleep under the same stars as my father, wherever he might be.

'Sort of. Robin and I are going to South Africa and then I've decided to go travelling, so I've put the house up for rent.'

'When are you leaving?' She steps inside the kitchen and my body stands to attention, fearful of what is yet to come.

'Today, in a few hours.'

'Seems a bit, I don't know, sudden,' she says as she leans against the counter, drawing an invisible circle on it with her finger. 'And when are you coming home?'

'Whenever I decide where home actually is.'

'Meaning you don't know.' She puffs out her cheeks in an attempt not to cry, not to show me any emotion, which is strange, as usually this is her go-to, her way of taking control. 'I don't understand how you could do this again.'

'This isn't about you.' I will not do this. I cannot fight anymore. 'For once this isn't about you.'

'Says the person who runs away whenever things don't go according to plan.'

'I would say losing a baby qualifies as a good enough reason to have a bit of a breakdown.'

'That's not fair,' she says with stammering voice. 'You can't put a blanket of rationality over the world and assume everyone else deals with the bad stuff the same way as you.'

Neither of us speaks, we just sort of shuffle around one another, unsure as to what happens next. It makes the air taste strange.

'I was hoping we could talk.' Her words come out as a whisper, like a child afraid to ask for something it desires in case the answer is no.

'What's there to talk about?'

'I'm leaving Patrick.'

'I kind of figured as much.'

'So you're not upset?'

Of course I'm upset, but not about that, and I don't have any intention of picking apart my feelings one more time to discover why exactly this is. Maybe I predicted the untimely end to her and Patrick's marriage as soon as she admitted she intended to leave him. Maybe I just don't have the energy to care anymore.

'No, I'm completely fine with whatever it is you decide to do with your life, Elle, I just don't think it can include me any longer.'

'Don't say that. Don't ever say that.'

'Why not? Our entire friendship was built on lies.'

'I know. And I'm sorry,' she says as the tears betray her, falling into upturned palms.

The sight of her, head bent as she collects her grief, loosens something within, sends forth a thread of my own sorrow and allows it to show itself, allows me to feel.

'What for?'

'For all of it. For not telling you who I really was. For never admitting how I felt. For pretending to love Patrick simply so he couldn't take you away from me. For allowing you to be the surrogate.'

I am so surprised by this genuine apology that, without thinking, without questioning if it is the right thing to do, I find myself going over to her and giving her a hug. Rediscover the way our heads automatically make room for the other, the way

I know she isn't wearing heels because I would have had to bend that little bit further forward to reach her, the undeniable scent that belongs to her and her alone.

'You know, I often think about that day,' she says as we break apart and she leans against the wall, not yet ready to look at me straight.

'The day we met.'

'How different each of our lives would have been if we hadn't been seated next to each other in maths.'

'Oh, I think you would have turned out just fine. You hungry?'

She nods and I open the nearest cupboard, take out a half-eaten packet of Jaffa Cakes, take one, then offer the rest to her. As always, she nibbles around the edge, picking off the chocolate and eating the orange jelly centre last of all. I swallow mine in two bites then go back for another.

'You really think my life is so much easier, don't you?'

'I used to. But I'm beginning to see you struggled just as much as the next person, only in a very different way.' I fill the kettle then rummage around in one of the boxes for the tea caddy. 'Lady Grey or builder's?' I ask, holding up the options and trying not to think back to that morning when I added a little extra to her beverage, so simple an action, so inconceivable the consequences. Had I known in that moment where it all would lead, I like to think I would have chosen differently. But everything is other now, everything is inside out, wrong and right all together and at once.

She points at the caddy of Lady Grey she herself gifted, then goes to look in the fridge for some milk.

'So often I wished I could trade places with you, even if only for a day.' She passes over the bottle of milk, its surface slippery against my skin.

I used to lie awake at night thinking about the exact same thing. About how I would wake up one morning to find I had changed places with Elle, get to be the princess for once.

'You were so sure of what you wanted and I hated you for it.' She takes two cups out of the cupboard by the sink, places them onto a tray next to the bottle of milk and teapot, wrapped up warm in the pink-knitted cozy Nana knitted for me.

'You wouldn't have wanted to be me.'

Picking up the tray, I go out to the garden, sit at the table and pour us each a cup of tea. The light now falls at a different angle to the last time we were here; the air, too, is changed, hinting at the season to come. She sits next to me, edges her chair closer so we are both warmed by the sun.

'So much of life is blind luck,' she says, blowing into her tea.

She is so hauntingly accurate that I don't want to dwell on the underlying meaning of it all. That if I had been born to different parents or even at a different time, my life would have been altogether other. Not better, nor worse, but it is terrifying to think, to contemplate, how what we are born into is tantamount to how our lives will turn out.

'I don't believe in luck,' I say, sipping my own tea and thinking, as always, of my father. Of how much I miss him.

Elle places the cup back on the table, crosses her legs, picks at her cuticles.

'But how else can you explain everything that happens? How so much of what we do is decided for us even before we're born, and I don't just mean DNA.'

'DNA?' Not only does she put the letters in the correct order, but in the right context too, and I must laugh, or pull a face, for she thrusts her cup at me, sloshing some of its contents over the table.

'See, I remember at least some of what you tried to teach me. We have a duty to our children to be the best possible versions of ourselves before bringing them into this world.'

It takes a second for her words to filter through my subconscious, for their meaning to become clear.

'You're pregnant.'

She lowers her head to try and disguise the way her mouth turns up at one corner, the way her hand instinctively strays to her belly.

'Yes.'

The beauty of life, of love, of how the world keeps turning sometimes, strikes me like a lightning bolt through my core, but how it is all mixed up and mangled with death and hate. How can I separate the two?

'But not with Patrick.'

'How did you…?'

'You couldn't get pregnant with him. There was no medical reason but it's almost as if your bodies knew it wasn't going to work, that you shouldn't get pregnant together.'

I wait, expecting. But no voice, no pictures of violence show themselves. I look across at the pair of secateurs sat atop the garden wall, anticipating that I will pick them up, plough them into her neck, her chest, her throat, over and over until her life is no more. Instead I find I am not angered by her revelation. By the knowledge that, once more, she gets to have at least part of what she wants and I do not.

Is this because of a change that has occurred in me? Or is it because I now understand that she too has suffered?

'I'm going to raise the baby by myself.'

Still no anger, no surprise either. In a way it seems pre-emptive to imagine her living in a terraced house in London with a kitchen in the basement and within walking distance of the river. At the same time it seems to make so much more sense than the life she is living now, with Patrick, with me.

'It was never going to work. Even before what happened with Conall, even before all the pregnancy issues we were having, we just weren't right for one another. You know me better than anyone, but I was so blinded by his adoration, by the fact he was so… so much more. That he would choose someone like me was mind-blowing.'

255

'Someone like you?'

'Oh, come on. You and I both know that when people see me they never look beyond the superficial.'

I have to give her this one.

'See, you admit it. But at some point you have to stop relying on what's on the outside, to be true to who you are. I have no desire to end up like my mother, constantly battling to stay in the past, to be someone who bears no resemblance to the person they used to be.'

This is remarkably deep and philosophical for Elle and the realisation that I have been ignoring her, only seeing her in a way that benefited me, is like the moment when I was stood in my childhood bedroom, holding out both my arms and turning around then back again. My mother had asked me what I was doing and I said I didn't understand why left could be left, but then, when you turned around, it became right. She told me it was a question of perspective.

'You're laughing at me.'

'No, I'm not.' I'm not. I'm laughing at my own, self-inflicted ignorance.

'Yes, you are. You've got that look on your face. The one you would reserve for when I made some comment about how I thought pigeons only lived in England, or that time I saw a satellite and thought it was a shooting star.'

I can't help it, I chortle at the memory.

'You thought you were so good at hiding it, at pretending you didn't think I was a complete idiot, but I knew, and I loved you all the more because of it.'

'What do you mean?'

'You didn't question me, didn't try to make me into someone else. But you also saw the real me, the one who had no desire to end up exactly where I am today.'

'With Patrick?'

'No, a bored housewife whose only relevance in life is how

many children she can produce or if she supports her husband's goals.'

She's more like me than I ever really saw.

'That's why I was so jealous when you disappeared to Hong Kong.'

'Wait, you were jealous of me?'

'Of course I was. You didn't look back for a second. Just packed a bag and left. Started again, did what it was you wanted rather than the socially acceptable option.'

'I left because I wanted what you had.'

'Oh, Christ.' She takes hold of my hand and I don't let go. 'And now because of me you can't. I'm so sorry, I shouldn't have told you. I've been so insensitive and I never even stopped to consider how all of this has affected you, affected your future.'

'It's okay.' And it is. 'I mean, to have the possibility, the choice taken away, is both cruel and unfair, but that's not what hurts the most.'

'Then what?'

'The idea that I wasted an opportunity. That we could have brought this beautiful baby boy into the world and he would have been loved and protected by everyone around him. For that to be gone is so much worse than the idea of never being able to have children.'

In some small way I have come to terms with his death, with understanding that I never had a burning desire for children. I simply wanted what I thought would get me the end goal, the ultimate prize, the raison d'être. Now I see it would have been wrong for me to be his mother, even though I would have loved him with every tiny part of my being. It is what I am due for being so flippant about life, about giving life to another, about being responsible for someone other than myself. I need now to learn how to be kind, to think of someone else and not just my own desires and needs. I need to learn to be better, the person my father would have wanted me to be.

257

'There are other options,' she says, still cradling my hand in her own. The weight of it is different, but also familiar, and I know this is what I have missed more than anything. Her, with me, not him.

'I don't care about Patrick.'

'You don't?'

Love and hate are so closely linked, so powerful and co-dependent. That wealth of feeling which is impossible to control. I hated Elle because I loved her.

'It's not that simple.'

'Nothing ever is.' She sips her tea and stares into nothing.

'There's something I need to tell you.'

One quick shake of her head. 'Don't. How much of who did what to who actually matters?'

It matters to me. Or at least it used to. But when I lost my child I stopped believing in cause and effect, that anything I did made any difference.

'Sometimes I lie awake, blinded by the depravity that grows inside of me.' It is my turn now to cry. 'But if I only think bad things, does that mean they'll never happen?'

Elle doesn't answer, instead leans forward and rolls up her top to reveal the mark we share.

It's happening all over again, me being sucked back into her atmosphere, one that fills me with so much need. Yet this is altogether new and unfamiliar, because we seem to have finally become equals instead of rivals.

I may not be able to bear life, but I can certainly learn to adjust, to transform all over again.

Always a decision, always a moment to choose.

'Is it true?'

I look up to see Patrick marching around the house towards us, and Elle's head turns at the sound of her husband's voice, but not before I notice the distress in her eyes.

CHAPTER TWENTY-SEVEN

Poppy: Sleep, peace and death

'Is what true?' I take a sip of my tea, watch his movements over the cup's rim. Notice the way he is clenching and unclenching his fists, then hopping from foot to foot like a boxer before a fight.

'Don't pretend like you don't know.' He speaks to me, but all his energy, all his focus, is directed at her.

'Patrick, please.' Elle stands, hands raised.

'So you're not even denying it?'

'What are you talking about?' I ask, although it is abundantly clear we all know exactly what he's talking about.

'As if you weren't in on it as well.' He turns to me, presenting a face I have not seen on him before. One taken over by something altogether more dangerous and I cannot help but think of my mother, of how she once claimed I was only attracted to Patrick because of his similarities to my father. But now I fear there was something else I recognised in him too.

'Patrick, this has nothing to do with her,' Elle says, a catch to her voice.

'Of course it does.' He swings one arm out, catches the end of a chair and sends it toppling over. No one goes to right it. 'She can't help but meddle in our lives. Always has, from the very beginning, telling us we weren't right for each other.'

'I never…' I have never explicitly said so, but the implication has always been clear and, for the first time, I can't bring myself to utter the lie.

'Oh no, far too clever for that, aren't we?' He kicks at the upended chair, scraping iron on stone. 'You've been layering it on for years, with the culmination of offering up your womb, safe in the knowledge it would prove to be the very thing that destroyed us.'

'That's not what happened,' I say, looking between the two of them. 'You can't possibly believe I wanted for him to die.'

'No, but it made it so much easier to break us apart when he did.'

Before I know it, Elle has crossed the space between them and punched him in the face. He looks back at her, as if her reaction was exactly what he'd expected, what he wanted her to do.

I always thought he was the one who was trapped, living a life he didn't want, and it was my fault for putting him there. But he made the choices, just as we all do. No one forced him into anything.

'I should have chosen you.' He looks over at me. 'Would have been so much easier.'

To be offered the thing I thought I wanted, needed, for so long and discover it wasn't real after all? So much time wasted. I am such a fool.

'I'm leaving.'

'What a surprise.'

There's this thing that happens to his voice when he's annoyed or upset. The heritage comes through, changing the intonation of the words and making it seem as if he's pretending to be someone else altogether. But which version of him is the real one? I've never been able to figure it out. Perhaps none of us will ever know who we really are, which part of ourselves we are hiding, pretending not to recognise and why.

'And you wonder why I'm leaving you.' The disdain in Elle's voice is all too clear. The hidden truth that neither husband nor wife wanted to see now revealed in all its twisted glory.

'So you finally admit it. Plucked up the courage to tell me the truth? Shame I had to hear it from your lover first.' He storms across the lawn, stops in the middle of it and throws his head back, howling to the heavens.

'You spoke to Harry?' She steps onto the grass and I follow, two scared little mice approaching the cat, wondering whether or not it will strike.

He spins round, spittle collected at the corner of his mouth. 'I should've decked the bastard. But don't worry your pretty little head about him, he's fine.'

'He told you?' Elle stops. Glances at me, then back at Patrick.

How much did Harry tell? Does he know his instincts about Elle and I were right, just not the way he believed?

'Didn't have to. He turned up at the house looking all dandy like, but clearly not expecting me to answer the door. Asked me how I was, where you were and then all the pieces slipped neatly together.'

He still doesn't understand. Not completely. Thinks Elle is leaving him for another man when in fact she's leaving so she can finally be free.

Because we only see what we choose to. Only believe the information we want to be true. We find it so easy to conceal, to disguise, what is so blatantly obvious. If only we allowed ourselves to accept that we, too, are capable of being cast aside.

Elle wanders towards the greenhouse, picks up one of the shattered pots and looks at me, a thousand questions hidden behind those eyes, then puts it back down again. 'I didn't mean for it to happen.'

Patrick snorts in response. 'No, you just accidentally fell backwards and your knickers came off.'

I have to bite down on my lip to stop myself from laughing.

'Don't you feckin' laugh at me.' He is suddenly so close I can smell the cigarette he will have smoked after Elle left the house that morning, along with his distress, bitter and full. 'Wouldn't want all your secrets spilled, now would we?'

'Patrick, you need to calm down.' I see Elle step closer, but find myself unable to move, unable to flee.

'Don't tell me to calm down.' He hurls the words across to her. 'You invited him into our house, no doubt fucked him on our bed. The house I bought you because it was in the right area, with decent schools and close to your diabolical parents.'

'Leave my parents out of this.'

'Why? Because aren't they responsible for creating the stupid creature I was lucky enough to marry?'

'She's not stupid.' I speak the words without pause, without calculating whether they are the right ones to say. It is instinctual and tells me so much more about my relationship with Elle than the intervening years ever could.

'Well, then that makes me quite the idiot,' he says, wiping one hand over his face. 'For believing she loved me, for being so blinded by lust I actually thought I was lucky enough to have been given the life I never thought I could have.'

'What do you mean?' This makes no sense. He wanted to study, to learn, to do more than the requisite marriage and children society tells us we should all aspire to.

He shakes his head, sinks down onto his haunches and picks at the dry grass, ripping out the blades then tossing them down again. 'People like us are the builders of tomorrow, the pioneers, the developers, the ones who create and influence our future. But this means we don't get to have what everyone else does. We don't get to have normal.'

'There's nothing wrong with normal.' I want to be normal. I

want the 2.4 children that go along with the white picket fence. I want family rows, parents' evenings and sleepless nights. I want it all, so much more than I ever knew.

'For her, maybe, but you and I both know we would have been so much more content surrounded by like-minded souls, not these vacuous creatures who care more about money than anything else.'

'Stop talking about her like that.' The fury begins to swell inside of me. The monster I inherited from my mother gleeful at the prospect of being set free.

'I'll talk to her any way I want to. She's still my wife.'

'I don't want to be,' Elle says, bringing our attention back to her. 'I never really did, but I could see you loved me so very much. More than I ever thought someone could love me. More than I thought I deserved.'

She stands with arms wrapped around her already swollen bosom and I am overcome with a desire to protect her. To shelter her and her unborn child from any harm. To make good of the mess I have created. To give her the future I cannot have for myself.

'When did it all start?' Patrick is crying now, but the tears are laced with something other than sorrow and I am afraid he is so close to the edge, so close to letting go, that it will devour us all. 'When did you start lying to me? Sleeping with me and then running off to him? Tell me, where did you go the night he died?'

She doesn't say anything, cannot bring herself to look at either of us, to see the horror in our eyes.

His hand is around her neck in an instant, and he propels her against the fence. The tips of her toes scrabble at the ground as he spits out his wrath.

'You went to him, when my boy was ripped from this world. You had the audacity to sleep next to him when your best friend was being stitched back together and I was doing everything in my power to get back to you.'

My mind spins with this new level of comprehension. That while I was mourning his death, she was burying her guilt in the arms of another. I look, but don't see, as his fingers squeeze tighter, the skin below her eyes dotted with tiny maroon spider-webs as the capillaries struggle to allow her blood to flow. It would be so easy to do nothing. To allow him to finish the story. To do what I set in motion all that time ago. To let him take the blame for what was my intended outcome.

But I love her too much and it's not just her he is hurting.

'Patrick, please, let go of her. She's pregnant.'

His head whips round at my words; then his hand releases its grip and he takes a step away. I resist the urge to run to her as she rubs against the red of her throat.

'She's…?' There's a deep crease between his eyes. 'You're…?' he asks now of Elle, whose hands won't stop shaking.

I watch as he goes through a series of emotions, cataloguing each as they take hold then dissipate into his features. The place-ment of hands on hips, shoulders slumped as he battles his own understanding. The hope, the joy, the sudden despair.

'You're pregnant.' He looks across at her then, but whether or not he expects her to answer none of us will ever know, as he seizes both her arms, picks her up and half-throws, half-pushes her against the fence. The reverberations ripple outwards along the wood, leaves of the clematis covering it fluttering in furious symphony.

'So he gets to be a father and I don't?'

'Patrick, please, I never meant to hurt you.'

'Too busy thinking about yourself to worry about poor old me.'

'Patrick, you have to let her go.' I try to pull him off her, to stop him from creating a scenario from which he can never return. To stop the burden of any more pain.

'Stop telling me what to do, you loathsome, loathsome woman.'

He pushes me and I stumble over the broken pots, feel their

264

edges rough against my skin. Pots I first planted, then destroyed, and I look down to see that some of the seedlings have survived. That there is a gathering of poppies pushing out from in among the remnants of my greenhouse. That, despite it all, they have found a way to survive.

Something else. The spade. With a thick handle that has molded to fit my palm so neatly, its weight as familiar as the scent of grass after summer rain. So to pick it up is without doubt the most natural thing for me to do and I lift it high. Metal that catches the setting sun as it traverses the sky to strike him clean across his back, making him turn, seek out the one who dares to challenge.

In that moment I could change it all. Raise my arm once more, bring down the spade's edge over and over until his body is broken and his fury all bled out.

This is my choice. Now. This very second of my existence is the one that will define me.

'Are you insane?' He bears down on me, seizing hold of the spade, but I cannot let go. As he tries to wrench it from me I topple forward, landing against him, breathing him in, finding that his scent now turns over my mind in a way I no longer like, no longer want.

Choose the life you want to live.

'Let go,' he yells at me, and we perform some kind of ridiculous dance, two marionette dolls with a drunkard controlling the strings.

He half-lifts me off the ground, the very tips of my toes digging into the earth as he tries to shake me loose, like a spider caught in his shoe.

'Let go, Jane,' she begs and my fingers slip away.

It could have all been so different. It could have all been so perfect. If only Elle hadn't pretended to be someone else. If only one of us had dared to speak the truth.

'I wish I'd never met you,' he snarls down at me. 'I wish I'd never met either of you.' His turn now to lift the spade, its intended victim standing with fear etched all over her incredible face, and I leap forward once more, scratch at him, beat him, do everything I can to stop what he is about to do.

His arm swings back, collides with the side of my head, and I find myself falling once more.

* * *

'Don't move.'

Elle's face tipped forward, making her cheeks puff out, and I imagine this is how she will look when the baby has taken hold of her body. How she will be resplendent in pregnancy, all her curves filled out the way they are supposed to be.

'Stay still,' she says to me. 'Help is on its way.'

A tight, but not unpleasant, sensation has settled in my chest, the sort of feeling I would have on the morning of an exam. I look up to see a swarm of petals raining down on me and the colour of them is startling. My eye follows one to the flowerbed onto which I have fallen.

'It's just blood.' Elle's voice is shaky. 'Just a little blood.'

Now that's a fucking understatement if ever I heard one. Dark, viscous liquid oozes out from under me and I move my fingers through it, bring my hand up to the sky, see it run in ruby rivers down my palm. My hand moves a little more, finds a shard of glass protruding from my centre, the very point of it winking in the light.

Broken windowpanes that I, myself, shattered with a garden spade. Laughter collects at the back of my mouth and I feel it bubbling away at the irony.

The garden stirs, waiting, listening to me, and I look up at the great grey lid of sky as the afternoon stretches and sags. My taxi will be here soon. Robin will be waiting for me to call, to tell him I am en route to the airport.

'Hold on, you have to hold on. Don't worry, you're going to be fine.'

Her face. Her beautiful face is distorted by fear, but she is here, with me. Stroking away my hair and holding tight to my hand. He is over there. I can see the edge of his shoe if I turn my head a little.

She loves me.

He loves me not.

I am bleeding. I feel it seep from underneath and into the soil. My life feeding the plants that will continue to grow, long after I am gone. It would seem I do have a purpose after all.

I listen to the faltering beat of my heart. Hear the way it is singing in forgiveness of all I have done; but no more now, my time is up. The world curls around me, shadows edging close, and I think of my father, of how I would like to lie in the earth with him.

Something falls to the earth beside me and I stretch my eyes to see. A small, clear vial, empty now of liquid, with a label written by my own hand. A vial I once gave to my best friend, but now she gives it back to me.

'Belladonna,' I whisper as my heart flickers another dull beat. The side effects of this particular poison are numerous, but include headaches, paranoia and dizziness. Tiny particles that could be hidden in a caddy of tea. Clear droplets added to a bottle of gin. The false promise of a gift, but one meant to harm rather than absolve.

Her face once more, shutting out the sun as she comes close, leans down to place a gentle kiss on my cheek, to whisper against my ear.

'Did you really think I wouldn't figure it out?'

CHAPTER TWENTY-EIGHT

White Tulip: Forgiveness, serenity

One year later

A year ago today I lost my best friend, the love of my life, to a tragic accident. At least, that's the story I've allowed everyone to believe and it is, in part, true.

Although, if I hadn't interfered, perhaps Jane would still be here, alive and kicking. Or perhaps she would have discovered the truth about what was really in that bottle of gin I gave her. A token of my affection, much like the tincture she gave me all those months ago. Maybe the headaches, the delusions and all those forgotten moments would have made her see what it was I had done. Made her see that revenge is so much sweeter when least expected.

Or maybe the voices would have forced her into the bathtub, where she would have been found with her skin sliced open and the water stained ruby-red.

It would have never come to an end if she had survived, our sad excuse for a friendship. All those years fighting one another

268

over everything and nothing at all. Even if she had lived, we would still be no closer to a resolution, a peace of sorts. Because there's so little room between love and hate, the lines forever blurred by all the things we are too scared to admit.

I made her suffer, just as she did me. Neither of us capable of committing the final act. No, we needed Patrick to finally break us all apart. To make us see how another kind of poison was already there, seeping into our veins, causing chaos with no need for any help from a little plant.

Jane deserved to die, but that doesn't mean I don't still miss her.

I think I knew from the very first moment I saw her that she was the one. My soulmate. The person who would mean more to me than anyone else in the world. With those ridiculous glasses and shoes at least one size too small. The way she trotted along behind her mother, trying so hard to blend in, to not be noticed. But how could I not notice her? The way her eyes flicked over every tiny little thing. The way her lips were always slightly dry because she chewed at them whenever she was nervous. The long, slender fingers that scratched at scars she thought no one could see.

She was so vulnerable, a lost soul, just like me.

Because, for all the boys who longed to screw me, and all the girls who longed to be me, Jane just wanted to be my friend. And I loved her for it, in a way I never believed possible.

Then she met Patrick, and my entire world fell apart.

I know she thought it was the other way round. That I stole him from her. But he was the one to cause all the pain and heartache. He was the one who fell in love with me and I hated him because he couldn't see how amazing Jane was. But I also hated her for choosing him instead of me.

She didn't love me, couldn't love me, the way I longed for her to. Every time I tried to make her jealous, to make her see, she misunderstood. Thought I was revelling in all the glory bestowed on me by others. Misinterpreted everything I ever said or did, never saw how it was all for her.

The stolen moments, the memories that bound us close. Listening to the sound of her virginity being taken, holding tight to a cigarette as the smoke curled towards the sun, wishing upon wishing it could have been me that caressed her spine, that made her call out in release.

Black dots on our skin, a way of tethering me to her forever. To try and take away her pain because she was the only one who ever saw me, who ever got close enough to try. But even she didn't want to know, didn't want the spell to ever break.

Living a lie is exhausting, but she wouldn't let me go. Not when I fell pregnant the first time. Knew it would bind me to a life I wasn't ready for. Nor when I nearly fell from the top of the Ferris wheel and finally found the courage to show her how I felt, except I was so stoned it made no sense to either of us. Always looking for the right words, any words, to explain the confusion that sat, tangled in my soul. A confusion that bound me to her even when it hurt the most.

She saved me, over and over, which is why I didn't see what it was she intended to do.

I knew why she left. Why she never said goodbye, and even though every day felt like I was living someone else's life, in a way I thought I was saving it for her. Making the picture-perfect existence so she could come back and see I was happy. Except the only person I managed to fool was myself. She knew from the very beginning Patrick and I would never work, even if she didn't truly understand why.

Then she came back and I was fool enough to think it a second chance. Even thrust upon her the idea of running away together. Raising our children in a very modern kind of way. But she didn't see, didn't want to see, anything other than the betrayal she'd found me guilty of long, long ago.

Grief can do strange things to a person. Guilt even more so.

Because I blamed myself for that baby's death. Which is why I had to say goodbye, to tell him how sorry I was.

A perfect little nose. Ten fingers, ten toes. Midnight hair and skin as white as the driven snow. Features I told myself he inherited from his father, because I didn't want to see the truth screaming at me of what they had done.

Even at the funeral, when she confessed her sin in the presence of God. Even when Patrick went to her, even when she ran. I didn't want to know because then it would all be undone. Everything I had ever wanted and more was a lie.

Until I went to her house. Decided to offer up a flower of all things. Went around the back to see if she was hiding and found the back door ajar. Stood in the kitchen, a room that used to hum with the essence of her but stood silent and still, as if it, too, were mourning a loss I could not see.

A pale-blue notebook left open on the kitchen counter. One containing the lopsided words of a child, along with pictures of rainbows and butterflies. I don't know what made me pick it up, take it back to her workshop and place it on the shelf with all the others. I don't know if I meant to look at all the vials on which were written symbols in neat, black script. I don't know if I ever intended to go through each of those notebooks in turn, seeing all of Jane's inquisitiveness, her obsession, written out before me.

I don't know what might have been had I not seen the box propped up against the far wall containing an unmade crib.

My feet took me upstairs, to where a room sat painted in blue, with a mobile hanging from the ceiling and a chair waiting in the corner for a baby to come home. Then to each and every other room, where I opened the cupboards wide and found more than I should.

That was when I knew. That was when I saw, and still I couldn't bring myself to hate her. No, that came after Patrick and I returned from Ireland. When I came across a letter addressed to the father of Conall MacFarland. A letter containing the results of a test to determine his parentage. Just a simple little test all about DNA that ripped my soul in two.

Because he knew. Or at least suspected, and said nothing.

That is when my love flipped all the way over to hate. For them both. The two people I had convinced myself were all I ever needed. The two people who took away my tomorrow, along with the belief that I too deserved a family, one with memories still to come. Memories we would create together, carving out a future that contained us all.

So I sent Patrick to her with a gift, much like the one she first gave me. Knowing she would empty that bottle in a bid to drown out the voices that never leave her be. Knowing she would be rewarded with the same confusion, the same paranoia, the same sense that something with the world would never be right.

I don't think I could ever have brought myself to kill her, much as she never followed through with her own, twisted plan. So many times I wanted Jane to choose me. So many times I tried to make her see. If only one of us had been brave enough to tell the truth. Even at the end, perhaps I could have forgiven her. Because without the other we never made sense.

Until the promise of a child, another life, another chance, made me see I could never have found peace, resolution, if she were still alive. We always came back together, one way or another, but it was broken, misguided and raw. I see that now.

Which is why I called Harry. Asked him to come over. And then I told Patrick I was going to see my darling, darling Jane. It is better that I can miss her, because it's the only way I can find forgiveness for us all.

My daughter sleeps against my chest. The gentle to and fro as I walk to where Jane now lies, underneath a great oak tree. Crouched low, I offer up my blessing of white tulips, wrapped in brown paper and tied up with string.

Acknowledgements

Writing a book is a bit like riding a rollercoaster. The inevitable highs and lows. The bits when you feel sick and want to get off because it was all just a terrible idea and a waste of time. Then the incredible rush, the hands-in-the-air moment when it feels like the most glorious thing in the world. And then it all comes to an end and you want to do it all over again.

Of course, it's all the more fun when there's someone sitting beside you to witness all the gory details, and for this book I am lucky enough to have had a plethora of companions to hold my hand along the way.

Firstly, I need to give thanks to Marian Keyes, for inadvertently giving me the idea for this book. Her opening paragraph, written as part of a magazine competition many moons ago, brought Jane's voice into my head – a voice that wouldn't leave me alone until I finally began to write her story.

My early readers and forever champions of my work: Debs, Kate and Cathy. You have always been so wonderfully supportive, ever since that first Faber course, and I am so very grateful for your expert eyes. One day we will meet outside of cyber space in a pub somewhere and raise a glass to Mr Bromley in thanks for bringing us together. An extra little thank you to Tom, who helped me find the idea for using flowers at the beginning of each chapter, and his kind words of encouragement not to give up on Jane's story.

Thank you to my other fellow writing buddies who gave me the courage to create Jane in all her twisted splendour: Allan, Aviva, Caroline, Chloe, Greg, Hynam, James, Laura, Natasha, Noel, Oscar, Rachel, Sophie and (dare I say it) even Danny. We were like a gaggle of new mothers when we met, all supporting one another through the births of our literary offspring (albeit with rather more drinking sessions), and I am very glad to know you all. In addition, it is a privilege to be able to bounce ideas off such a menagerie of geniuses, both for this book and all the ones we have still to write.

To Noel Smaragdakis and Rachel Burton, who read and commented on what felt like the millionth draft, but was, in fact, more like number three or four. You kept me going when I was banging my head against the wall.

Nia Beynon, my brilliant and kind editor, who loved Jane from the outset, almost as much as I do. Who saw the potential hidden among too many words and told me to save the fox for another story (which is exactly what I've done). Thanks also to everyone at HQ Digital, for the beautiful cover, the painstaking copy edits, and all the magic that goes into creating a book.

Finally, as always, thank you to my family for allowing me the space to breathe, to write. For understanding that the voices in my head are there to be written down and for telling me to never stop aiming for the stars.

Read on for a sneak peak of
The Girl in the Shadows…

CHAPTER ONE

Mathilde

Paris, France. Before.

'Death isn't your only option.'

'You know what she's like.' Spidery lashes fell onto ashen skin, the suggestion of a bruise already beginning to show.

'Then go to the police.' His words were accompanied by a bulbous cloud of nicotine that she swatted away, the movement rippling up her arm in an accumulation of pain. He held on to her as they crossed the street, tighter than she would normally allow.

A woman ran past, lean precise movements that Mathilde recognised without needing to look. She knew the woman would turn at the corner and cross the river, would return to this café to sit in the corner as she ordered her staple of coffee and eggs.

'At least go to the hospital.' He held the door open for her and she sank into the café's enveloping warmth.

'*Non.* No hospitals. No records, nothing that can be used to find me.' She sat at an empty table as he went over to the bar, found herself scanning the road outside, seeking out the retreating runner.

She had wanted to speak to her from the very first time. To ask her the story behind her scar, to find out if she too had suffered at the hands of another. But there was never a moment in which she felt able to step into the open, to reveal the truth she had kept hidden for so long.

And now she had to bury the lies even deeper.

He placed a glass mug in front of her. Amber tendrils seeped out into the steaming water as fragrant leaves teased her senses and her stomach complained at its lack of sustenance. She remembered the abandoned supper, her mind taunting her with the image she knew she could never forget.

'She will look for you.' He sipped his own drink, lips puckering at the bitter heat.

'I know.'

'Then let me protect you.'

'You're sweet.' She dropped her head, tucked a curl behind one ear.

'But not sweet enough.'

It was too much. The effort of trying to exist was slowly wasting her away. She had to run, to free herself of the endless to and fro, of camouflaging her pain. Pain that had become as commonplace as the setting of the sun.

There was no other way.

'Take this.' She removed the locket from around her neck, rubbing it against the ruby clot on her forehead before handing it over.

'Where should I leave it?'

'Somewhere it will be found.'

'And then?'

She dared not answer. A conscience that had been her downfall, a softness she had battled against still preventing her from uttering any untruth.

'Then go.' He swiped at the air, polished cufflinks catching the light and dancing over her face.

She stood on legs dragged down by the inevitable. The chair clattered to the floor behind her, but no one turned to watch, the hour too early for any other customers.

'Be careful,' she whispered. All too aware of the risk he was going to take, for her.

'You showed me a kindness I had long since forgotten.' He cupped her hand between his own, eyes focused on the movement of thumb over her wrist as the solace in his voice offered up a farewell. 'God will not spare my soul. It is tainted with the cruelty of too many years. But you still have the chance of living, of sharing your gift with the world.'

She took back her hand. 'I won't forget you.'

'You should,' he said as she opened the door, allowing the morning back in.

One step over the threshold, two steps to the kerb, three steps towards the river, four steps more. The road stretched out ahead, shadows waking as dawn seeped into the sky.

Dear Reader,

Thank you so much for taking the time to read this book – we hope you enjoyed it! If you did, we'd be so appreciative if you left a review.

Here at HQ Digital we are dedicated to publishing fiction that will keep you turning the pages into the early hours. We publish a variety of genres, from heartwarming romance, to thrilling crime and sweeping historical fiction.

To find out more about our books, enter competitions and discover exclusive content, please join our community of readers by following us at:

🐦 @HQDigitalUK

📘 facebook.com/HQDigitalUK

Are you a budding writer? We're also looking for authors to join the HQ Digital family! Please submit your manuscript to:

HQDigital@harpercollins.co.uk.

Hope to hear from you soon!

ONE PLACE. MANY STORIES

ONE PLACE. MANY STORIES

If you enjoyed *Love Me, Love Me Not*, then why not try another thrilling read from HQ Digital?